T0365963

MERCY

J.C. Tolliver

authorHOUSE®

AuthorHouse™
1663 Liberty Drive
Bloomington, IN 47403
www.authorhouse.com
Phone: 1 (800) 839-8640

Published by AuthorHouse 03/14/2018

ISBN: 978-1-5462-3106-6 (sc)
ISBN: 978-1-5462-3105-9 (e)

Library of Congress Control Number: 2018902560

Print information available on the last page.

PREFACE

Benton put his arm around Mercy and was trying to take her top off, and she brushed his hand away. Next, he was working his way up her dress and she had to keep him at bay. It was hard to contemplate what his next move would be, but she kept up with him. She could feel that he was starting to get angry with her. She was starting to get angry with him, and finally told him. "Please, just take me back to my aunt's house." She wanted to get back to her aunts before Benton became too drunk to drive her. It was also 10:30 and she promised her mother that she would be home by midnight. Benton just kind of laughed at her and said, "I'm not leaving the party now, I'm having fun with my friends, you need to just let go a little bit." She tried to fit in by making conversation with the other kids while Benton just kept drinking and getting louder. Finally, she decided that she would just get back to her aunt's somehow, without Benton. When she got up to leave, Benton said, "Why are you leaving when we are just starting to have fun?" She replied, "Benton your drunk and I don't want you to drive me so I'm just going to get a ride back to my aunt's house. Benton looked at her funny and replied, "Go ahead then, you are not going to ruin my night. My friends were right, I shouldn't have brought you. I'll find another girl who would love to be with me and give me what I want." Benton went back into the house like he didn't have a care in the world.

DEDICATION

This novel is dedicated, inspired by, and written for my first granddaughter.

"My Angel"

Lilian Britin Macwilliams

"MY DREAM"

There is no one else for me.
You are my beautiful dream.
You are my shining star in this field of faces.
I would follow you through time and space.
I would rather die old and lonely,
if I can't have you as my one and only.
Please love me and cherish me or at least look my way.
Please don't pay attention to what others say.
Let us show our love and marry for all to see.
Only then you will have the honor of having all of me.
J.C. Tolliver

PART I

CHAPTER 1

(1970)

Mercy, her name is Mercy. Her mother named her that because she prayed for mercy when she delivered her, the last of seven children.

Mercy sat in the dark, in the late evening, in the old church bell tower down the street from her house. The old, cracked bell hasn't rung here in this old church for years. The officials, here in Cincinnati, Ohio have been discussing rehabbing this old church for years now.

Mercy was wearing her white, cotton sun dress that had been handed down to her from her four older sisters. She rarely got anything new to wear, even her bras were hand-me-downs. Mercy had to wear a slip with this dress because it had been washed on the board and hung in the attic to dry so many times, it was see-through. Her mother didn't like for her to wear it and threatened to throw it away all the time.

Mercy's slip was damp and sticking to her, even though it was cool and dark in here, she was still sweating. She was starring through a long crack in the concrete wall. Mercy turned sixteen today and she is in love! She is in love with a boy named Benton. Benton is two years older than she and is graduating high school this year. She didn't think he even knew she existed. Mercy knew that Benton would be walking to his car, a 65 Mustang, from his part-time job as a stock boy at the corner super market. He walked past the old church the same time every day, not knowing that Mercy was watching him.

Mercy came up to the bell tower every day, just to get a glimpse of him. He was SOOO handsome! He had almost black hair, medium complexion, and gorgeous blue eyes that she could stare into forever. He also had a nice build. He was one of the most popular boys in school and quarterback of their high school football team.

Benton's family had an old history and old money to go with it in this city of Cincinnati. They owned a lot of businesses here, even the super market where Benton worked every day after school. They lived in an area called Clifton, where there were many old mansions in a gas light district. They believed that their son should learn the value of a dollar and earn his own money for what he wanted. Of course, they had to keep up appearances, so they bought the Mustang for Benton for his sixteenth birthday. They would also pay for his college education when it was time. According to them, Benton would go to college whether he liked it or not. His mother pushed him, every day to study and she was always hinting he should go into politics. He really wanted to go anyway. He was smart, and he wanted to be a doctor. He would start next fall.

Benton never gave Mercy a second glance at school. She was, after all, way too young to be his girlfriend. Benton had dated several girls from school but had never really had a steady girlfriend that she knew about. He told his mother that he just hasn't found a girl that could hold his interest for very long. Once, Mercy overheard Benton's mother in the grocery store, talking about the poor, white, trash that lived in Northside and how that area was getting so bad with crime that they should move that store out of this neighborhood.

CHAPTER 2

Mercy's mother was raising four girls and three boys with very little help from Mercy's father. Mercy's mother, at forty-five, and after having seven children, was still quite beautiful. Mercy's father had little to do with his own children. Her father liked to drink just a little too much. At least he did work a night shift job at a car company. He had lost so many previous jobs due to his drinking. He always told Mercy's mother that, "They just fired me for no good reason!" When he landed this job three years ago, Mercy's mother told him that he had better not get fired from this one or she would throw him out on the street, and she meant it. Mercy's mother and father got along okay, they both just kind of went their own way, living in the same house. Mercy's mother doled out all the discipline and made all the rules. Mercy's mother believed in keeping her kids in line with a switch, a very thin piece of a branch that made a swooshing sound when you waved it through the air. Mercy knew her mother was very smart, and she could never see what her mother saw in her father as far as a husband and father.

With all the laundry, cooking and work to do around the house, mother made sure that all the children did their chores. Mercy's mother also worked outside the home when she could. Mercy being the baby of the family, got off with doing very little chores. Instead of doing chores, Mercy could read or do her homework. Mercy's mother always told her how smart she was and how she was going to grow up to be something special if she just kept up with her studies. Mercy believed her mother.

Mercy had never been allowed to date yet and has never had her first kiss. She dreamed about that first kiss with Benton. It would be soft, and sweet and lingering. These thoughts made her feel hot and tingly all over just thinking about it. Once, Mercy had asked her mother if she could date and her mother said she could date when she turned eighteen. Mercy told her Mother that most girls were dating at fifteen and Mercy was angry, but she also knew there was no arguing with her mother. One of Mercy's older sisters had become pregnant at sixteen and she dropped out of school and married the baby's father. Mercy guessed that was why her mother wouldn't let her date until she was eighteen, because she became afraid that would happen with her also. Mercy's mother told her that she needed to concentrate on school right now. One night a boy from school called her and her mother grounded her for it because she said it was inappropriate. Another time, Mercy was walking home from school with a girlfriend and her girlfriend's male cousin and her mother switched her legs for "Walking the street like some whore."

Even though she was perfectly innocent of any wrong doing and knew the boy was walking with her and her friend, just to be nice and make sure she made it home safely, her mother wasn't believing it. Her mother would switch her legs again if she could see her now, sitting in the bell tower, starring at some boy.

In two more years, she would be allowed to date. She had been asked out a couple of times already but was too embarrassed to tell the boys that her "Mother wouldn't let her date" so she made some lame excuses. At 18, she could date, and she also knew that Benton would be graduating and going off somewhere to college at the end of this school year. She was in love and she had to tell Benton before he left. One day soon, she would come down from the bell tower, and wait on the sidewalk to talk to Benton, one day when she was feeling brave. Right now, she would rather sit here and dream about him, because if he shunned her, it would literally break her heart. Maybe she would just wait a little longer before approaching him. She loved everything about him, his walk, his talk, his laughter, his clothes, his smile, his lips, his eyes, and the list goes on and on.

This afternoon, she is starring hard through the crack in the bell tower and it is starting to get dark and she hasn't seen him. Where is he?" She had to see him tonight, on her birthday! Her heart felt like it was pounding right out of her chest. Two hours later, and she still hadn't seen him, maybe he was sick and had someone else take him home. Finally, she had to go home. Her mother would switch her legs again for coming home after dark.

Mercy walked quickly back toward her house. The houses here were very close together with small front yards. This used to be a very nice neighborhood but now was run down and filled with, what others called, "poor white trash". A few houses down the street from hers, lived a boy named Travis.

He is also very handsome, with boyishly good looks. He's

tall at 6'2", with sandy blonde hair, and blue eyes. He has a certain toughness about him that you would imagine cowboys having. Mercy knew that Travis liked her from talking to the kids at school. She grew up playing with Travis until they reached their teen years, then they just kind of separated and made their own friends. Travis loved to play guitar. He was sitting on his front porch playing it as she walked by. Travis loved country music. He had his guitar with him wherever he went, it was like an extension of him. Mercy yelled, "Hey Travis, how are you?" He yelled, "Great, Happy Birthday! I see you walk past here almost every day. Do you have a job or after school activities or something?" She had to tread lightly here because she didn't want anyone to know what she was doing every day, that was just for her to know. She said, "No, I just like to take a walk every day, getting in shape, you know." He replied, "Well, maybe I could come with you one day." Mercy's mind was racing, "Maybe someday you can." She hurriedly walked past his house. Mercy could feel his eyes on her back as she walked towards home.

Travis remembered her birthday! Of course, it would be like him to remember something like that. Mercy knows that Travis has always liked her, but she had hoped, just as friends. She found out through the grapevine at school that Travis wanted to be more than "just friends", he wanted to be her boyfriend. Travis knew that Mercy knew how he felt about her, but she tried to pretend that she didn't, and they were still "just friends". Mercy knew a lot about Travis because his mother and hers were good friends, but also because they have known each other since first grade. When Mercy was near him, she could sense how much he cared about her.

CHAPTER 3

The end of the school year was coming up soon, prom night, graduation for Benton. Mercy knew that Benton was going off to college in the fall and she couldn't imagine not being able to see him every day. Mercy wanted to go to the prom this year and thought she could talk her Momma into letting her go. She still wasn't allowed to date but mothers knew prom night is special and she wouldn't want her to miss prom. Okay, she decided that she was going to "bite the bullet" as they say and ask Benton to the prom. She decided to wait until Friday after school. That way, the other girls at school could not make fun of her if they overheard her ask Benton. If he said "No" and the girls at school laughed at her, she would be so embarrassed.

It's finally Friday! She couldn't keep her mind on anything at school and she felt like everyone knew what she was about to do. In her mind, everyone was talking about her and how strange she was acting today. In class, she was called on by a teacher who saw her staring out the window daydreaming. She thought about what she was going to do this afternoon and she was so nervous. She started questioning her decision to ask Benton to the prom. She was so afraid that he would just dismiss her completely, breaking her heart. Finally, by the end of the school day, she decided she would go through with her plans. She knew if she didn't ask Benton today, she would never get another chance and her love would be lost.

She would go to the old church and wait for Benton to walk down the street to his car. First, she had to go home and see if she couldn't make herself look prettier. When she got home, she put her favorite sundress on, a little mascara that belonged to her sister and her sandals. She tied her long hair up with a ribbon. She was so glad that her mother wasn't home, she would ask her all kinds of questions and then she would make her stay home. She left her mother a note that she would be at the library. She got ready fast and left for the church.

She walked fast on the other side of the street, hoping that Travis wouldn't see her. She didn't think that he did. When she got to the church, she went in the side door that was always open and ran up to the bell tower to watch for Benton through the large crack. She waited and watched, he should be coming down the street in about fifteen minutes. She was sweating from running up here and her heart was pounding, and she was breathing hard. She tried to calm herself down and tried to make herself breathe more slowly. After only ten minutes, she saw him walking down the street towards his car. She thought, "It's now or never."

Mercy ran down the steps of the bell tower, she felt like her heart was pounding out of her chest. When she got to the bottom, she was out of breath. She stopped after the bottom step and took a couple of deep breaths to try to steady herself. She stepped out onto the sidewalk on the side of the church. She walked around the church like she was just out for an evening stroll. He was walking towards her. When he got within a few feet of her, she could see his puzzled expression. She stopped in front of him. At first, she couldn't make her mouth move, her tongue was so dry and then, she squeaked out, "Hi Benton."

She felt stupid, but then he came closer and said, "Hi Mercy." She wondered how he knew her name but didn't ask. She said, "Nice day out today, isn't it?" Boy, how lame can you get! He said, "Yes, it is." and started to walk past her to his car. The tiny voice in her head screamed, "Ask Him!" She looked Benton in the eyes and said, "There's something I'd like to ask you." He replied, "Sure, what is it?" Her mouth was so dry and so at first, she only got a squeak. Benton looked at her funny and she tried again, "I'd like to know if you'd like to go to the prom with me?" Waiting with what seemed like an eternity and holding her breath, he said, "Sure, why not?" She seemed to melt. She felt so good inside, like cotton candy and chocolate cookies. He said, "I've seen you around school, I don't know why we've never talked." Mercy knew why, because she was two years younger than him, and because she wasn't accepted into the circle of the "popular girls". He said, "Where do you live so I can pick you up?" Mercy knew that her mother would insist that he pick her up at the front door and she really didn't want him coming to her house because of its worn-down condition. Also, because her mother would give him the third degree, and possibly mention that this is Mercy's first date, embarrassing her. She told him where her house was, and he said, "I'll pick you up around 7:00". The prom starts at 9:00 and he said they were going to meet two other couples at a fancy restaurant called La

Petite, before the prom. She said, "That sounds great, I'll see you around 7:00 next Friday". He started walking to his car, looked back at her, and said, "Can I give you a ride home?" She would love nothing more, but she knew that she better not let her mother see her being dropped off in a car by a boy or her mother would switch her legs, and surely would not let her attend prom. She said, "No, that's okay, I have a couple of errands to do." He replied, "Okay, I'll see ya later." She walked up the street with purpose like she had so much to do and so many places to go. She was so excited inside, she was about to burst! "Could this really be true?" "OMG!" She didn't even think about what she would wear to the prom. She didn't have a prom dress and her sisters didn't have anything nearly nice enough or small enough for her to borrow. How she wished she could have a new dress. She would talk to her mother about it when she got home.

When Mercy arrived home, her mother was sitting at the kitchen table drinking a cup of coffee and smoking cigarettes. Everyone in her house smoked except her and her older sister. I guess it was just the cool thing to do at the time. Her mother asked her why she was so late getting home from the library. She said she had a lot of studying to do. She hated lying to her mother, but she just didn't see any other way. Anyway, she sat down and looked at her mother. The way that Mercy's eyes shined, her mother could tell that she was excited about something. Mercy said, "Guess what? A boy named Benton asked me to the prom today!" Mercy said that Benton ask her because if her mother knew that mercy had ask him, it wouldn't be proper in her mother's eyes. Her mother was raised very strict and being "proper" was very important to her. Her mother asked, "What kind of a boy is he, do I know him?" Mercy told her that he came from one of the rich families in Clifton, he was very nice and a good student. Mercy told her all the things that she thought her mother wanted to hear. Her mother seemed to like the idea that Benton came from a good family. Her mother said, "Okay, you can go to the prom because that's something special in high school and you make good grades, but, I want you to be home by midnight and I want to meet this boy before he takes you out." Mercy was thrilled that her mother was going to let her go. Mercy's mother said, "Believe it or not, I was young once to and remember how important prom is to a girl." Timidly, Mercy asked, "Mom, I know we don't have a lot of money, but is there any way I could get a new dress? Her mother replied, "Probably not, but I'll see what I can do about getting you something proper to wear." Mercy didn't need an expensive dress, but she didn't want to embarrass Benton in front of his friends by what she was wearing either. Mercy didn't know much about today's fashion, but she sure didn't want to look like what Benton's mother described as "poor white trash" either.

Mercy knew her best friend, Madison wasn't home tonight, and she couldn't wait for school tomorrow to tell her about her date. She probably wouldn't believe her. Mercy wondered if Benton would tell any of his popular friends at school who he was going to the prom with or what he would say if one of the more popular girls ask him to go with her. Would he say he was going with her? She didn't know, but she guessed it would be all over school if he did. That would give the girls at school a lot to talk about.

On Monday morning, Mercy walked down the halls of the high school with her head held high. She felt important now that she was going to the prom with Benton. She had heard through the grape vine that the more popular girls had ask Benton to the prom, but he told them that he was going with someone else. He didn't tell them he was going with her. Was he embarrassed by her?" She didn't want to think about all that. She just wanted to be happy that he was going with her.

Mercy met her best friend, Madison, for lunch. Madison has been her closest friend for the last three years. They did everything together. Mercy told Madison that she was going to the prom with Benton. At first Madison didn't believe her. When Madison finally realized that Mercy was serious, she was very happy for her, if not a little jealous. No one had asked Madison to the prom yet, and she didn't think it was going to happen. Oh well, Madison was used to being shunned by the popular people at school, so this was nothing new to her.

Only four more days until prom! Mercy still didn't have a clue as to what she was going to wear. Madison said she would check in her closet to see if she had anything appropriate that would fit her friend, but she never did check. Madison couldn't believe that someone as popular as Benton had asked Mercy to the prom. She didn't know how she pulled that one off, she never did say.

After school, Mercy walked in the back door and said, "Hello", to her mother. Mercy hadn't mentioned again what she was going to wear to the prom. She didn't want her mother to feel bad because she worked so hard just to keep food on the table for all of them. She didn't want her mother to change her mind about letting her go.

Mercy went up the steps to her bedroom that she shared with her three other sisters. There were three bedrooms in this house, one for her parents, one for her brothers and one for her and her sisters. Mercy slept on a twin-size roll-a-way bed in the corner. On her bed, she found a big, white box with a beautiful pink bow on it. She didn't know what it was, but when she got closer, she saw her name written on it! She very carefully took the bow off the box as not to destroy it. She gently took the lid off. Whatever was in the box, was covered by clean, white, tissue paper. On the top of the paper was a little card in a white envelope. She opened the card and it read, "For my sweet girl Mercy, Love, Momma". She laid the box on the bed and gently peeled back the tissue. She couldn't believe it! There was the most beautiful, pale pink dress she had ever seen! It was sleeveless and had about two-inch straps, it was a little low cut, which surprised her. She gently took the dress out of the box and when she did, she found another smaller wrapped package in the bottom. She opened the small package and it was a pair of pretty, pink sandals to match the dress. She hurriedly put the dress and sandals on. They were a perfect fit. She felt like a princess. She twirled around the room, watching herself in the dresser mirror. She imagined herself dancing with Benton. After a few minutes of admiring herself in the dress, she took it off and hung it in the closet. She couldn't believe what a lucky girl she was.

She had to go downstairs and thank her Momma! She hurried downstairs where her Momma was in the kitchen. She ran over to her and gave her the biggest hug and said,

"Thank you Momma for the dress. It's the most beautiful dress I've ever seen in my whole life, I love it!" Mercy asked, "How were you able to afford such a beautiful dress for me?" Her mother replied, "Don't worry about it, it's okay." Her mother said she was so glad that she liked it and wanted her to try in on again so that she could see that it fit her well.

While Mercy was upstairs, trying the dress on again, her mother reflected on the last few nights of staying up until two and three in the morning, sewing on that dress until her fingers were sore. She purchased the dress from the Goodwill store. She washed, ironed and starched it and then she went over the entire dress fixing tiny rips, replacing some of the sequins and bringing the dress back to its former brilliance. She then purchased the inexpensive sandals so that Mercy would have something new. Mercy would never have to know where it came from and she wouldn't tell her because she didn't want Mercy to feel "second best" on her big night.

When Mercy came down the steps with her new dress on, her mother just stared at her. She looked like an angel, the vision of loveliness. Her mother always was partial to Mercy and now she thinks she is the most beautiful young girl she has ever seen. She told Mercy how beautiful she was and to go and hang up her dress so that it didn't get soiled before the prom.

One of Mercy's sisters was going to cosmetology college and she said that she would fix Mercy's hair for her on her special night. She would corral Mercy's long, black locks into a beautiful up-sweep with a few tendrils hanging down. Her other sister would help her do her nails.

Mercy couldn't wait to call Madison and tell her about

her new dress. That evening, before bed, she finally got a chance to call her best friend. She told Madison all about her new dress and what a special night the prom was going to be. She did confess that she was very nervous about going out to dinner with Benton and his friends. She didn't know what to talk to them about or if they would even talk to her.

CHAPTER 4

The big day had finally arrived! Her plan was to primp all day and to make sure that she looked as beautiful as she could. Her sisters did her hair and nails as they promised, while teasing her all along about going on her first date and maybe having a first kiss. Sisters could be cruel. They were full of all kinds of advice. Mercy was just too nervous to listen to any of it and let it go in one ear and out the other.

Mercy's sister was going to take her over to her aunt's, where Benton was going to pick her up. She had passed Benton a note at school the day before of where he should pick her up. Her aunt lived near Clifton in a little nicer house than they had. Mercy didn't want her mother to know that she was ashamed for Benton to see where she lived, so she told her mother that Benton was picking her up at her aunt's because he lived closer to her, which was true. That was okay with her mother after all, because her mother wasn't feeling well and wanted to go to bed early. She knew that her sister would check this boy out. She asked her sister to take pictures of them. Her mother reminded her that she had to be back from her date by midnight. She kissed and hugged her and said, "Honey, I hope you have the time of your life tonight." Mercy replied, "Thank you again Momma for making this night so special for me. I love you so much!"

Benton was picking her up about six thirty. It was four thirty now and Mercy decided that she better get going. She wanted to take her time because she didn't want to get all sweaty and her hair to fall by getting ready too fast. Her oldest sister dropped her off at their aunt's house about five thirty. Mercy put her dress and new sandals on. She put a little bit of hair spray on her hair and a little dab of her aunt's perfume on her neck. She looked and felt like a princess.

At exactly six thirty, Benton knocked on the door and her aunt let him in the foyer. Mercy hurried to the foyer before her aunt could give him the third degree. Benton looked at her and told her how beautiful she looked. She told him he also looked very handsome in his black tuxedo. Then, from inside his tux jacket, he pulled out a wrist corsage. It was a gorgeous pink carnation with a little bit of baby's breath with long, pink and white ribbons hanging down. He opened it for her and put it on her wrist. Mercy's aunt insisted on taking a few pictures before she would let them leave. She said they made a very cute couple, which embarrassed Mercy and her cheeks turned red.

On their way out the door, her aunt told Benton that Mercy's mother wanted Mercy to be home by midnight. Benton assured her aunt that he would have her back on time. Benton had his Mustang all washed and waxed for the occasion. He opened her door for her just like a perfect gentleman. Mercy could see her aunt watching them from the side window of the door and she knew her aunt would approve.

They were going to meet Benton's friends at the

restaurant in downtown Cincinnati. Their conversation on the way to dinner seemed light and easy. Benton already knew that Mercy was beautiful, but she looked especially beautiful tonight. Benton's friends, the two other couples going to the prom, already had a table for them. Benton's friends had all bet on who he would bring to the prom. His friends were all shocked when they saw who he was walking through the door with. His friends weren't even sure who Mercy was. They had seen her at school but none of them knew what her name was. When Mercy and Benton got to the table, Benton introduced her. His friends just starred because they knew that Benton could have gone to the prom with anyone he wanted and didn't know why he came with this poor white trash. They thought that maybe it was a bet or something. They sat down, and the waiter took their drink order, which was all soft drinks since no one in the party were twenty-one. They ordered a couple of appetizers, one of which was escargot. Mercy didn't know what that was and didn't want to sound stupid asking, so she declined an offer to have any. Besides that, she thought it looked disgusting. They all ordered dinner. There were things on the main menu that Mercy didn't even know how to pronounce. She just ordered some soup and salad like her mother told her to do. She told Mercy that a lady did not go out and eat like someone starving to death.

The two other couples and Benton talked about school, college and sports. Mercy contributed very little to the conversation, sensing the other two couples didn't like her or approve of Benton's choice for the prom. All three of the guys split the bill, and finally it was time to go to the prom. The prom was being held at a very lavish hotel in downtown Cincinnati, called The Kingsley Manor. They pulled up in front and were met by valet parking. Benton jumped out the car and came around to Mercy's side to open the door before the valet guy could. They walked up the steps and he held the door for her again. Under the big, beautiful chandeliers, were photographers taking prom pictures. Benton asked her if she'd like one and she said, "Yes!", while the line wasn't too long. They had their picture taken on a make-believe swing with a garden background. Benton was smiling but Mercy had a big grin on her face. They walked into the large banquet room to look for the table where all of Benton's friends were sitting. None of Mercy's friends were there. Benton pulled the chair out for her and they sat down. The girls at the table started giggling behind their hands while looking at her. She heard one girl whisper loudly, "Why did he bring her here?" Another girl whispered, "I can't believe that he would bring someone like her". The way that Benton looked at them, they got the point that they had better be quiet about his prom date. They all sat and talked while the DJ played the music, no one talked to her, they just looked the other way when she caught their eye. After what seemed like forever, Benton asked Mercy to dance. The dance was a slow dance and she was thrilled that he would be holding her in his arms. He put one hand around her waist and held her other hand in his, then he pulled her closer. She could feel him slightly trembling, then she realized that he was nervous about bringing her here also. She could feel his warm, sweet breath on her neck as they danced. They didn't talk while they were dancing, but locked eyes a couple of times. The dance was over way too soon! Maybe he would ask her to dance again. They went back to the table and sat down. Benton asked her if she'd like a drink, she said, "Yes" and he replied, "I'll be right back". One of the more popular girls at the table, named Amy, looked Mercy straight in the eye and said, "Where did you get your dress? I gave one to the Goodwill just like that one last year." The girls at the table laughed out loud. Mercy's face turned red and no words would come out of her mouth. Her eyes started to fill up with tears at the meanness of the girls. When Benton returned with their drinks, he took one look at Mercy's face and he knew something was going on. Benton gave Amy a look of disgust and suggested to Mercy that they leave the prom and go to a party on his street, at a friend's house. She said okay but she needed to go to the restroom first.

While she was in the bathroom stall, she heard the bathroom door open and familiar voices of the mean girls came in. Mercy came out of the stall to wash her hands. While she was rinsing her hands, one of the girls said, "What are you doing here with Benton? You know you don't belong here." Another said, "You can wash your hands all you want but you will still be poor white trash when you are finished." Mercy ignored them and left the restroom as quickly as possible to find Benton.

She met him outside, where the valet had already retrieved his car, he opened the door for her and got in himself. He could tell she was upset and he apologized for the girl's behavior. He didn't know what was going on inside the restroom. Mercy tried to make light conversation with him, on the way to his friend's house.

Mercy found out that Benton would be leaving for college August 25th. He wouldn't be home until fall break, right around Thanksgiving time, and hopefully, she would see him then. She knew that when he went off to college, he would only be interested in sorority girls, not young, high school girls like her.

Benton and Mercy arrived at his friend's house and there was a big party going on inside. The adults of the house had gone out for the night. It looked like half of the school was there. They made their way back to the den, where there were other kids lying around on couches, drinking beer and eating snacks. Mercy was drinking coke, she knew her mother wouldn't approve of her drinking and she didn't want to go home drunk when her mother trusted her to go out this one time.

As they lay back on the couch together, Benton turned her way and gently kissed her lips. She had often dreamed about this first kiss with Benton and what it would feel like. What a thrill that was, just the way she imagined it would be! Soft and tender and sweet. Benton was drinking one beer after another. With each beer, he kissed her a little harder and a little more demanding. She really didn't care for how he was kissing her. She tried to tell him to let up on the beer a little bit and he told her she was acting like a prude. He said she should lighten up a little bit. This hurt her feelings and made her feel very uncomfortable.

Benton put his arm around her and tried to feel her breast and she brushed off his hand. Next, he was trying to go up her dress and she had to keep him at bay. It was hard to contemplate what his next move would be, but she kept up with him. She could feel that he was starting to get angry with her. She was starting to get angry with him, and finally told him. "Please, just take me back to my aunt's house." She wanted to get back to her aunts before Benton became too drunk to drive her. It was also 10:30 and she promised her mother that she would be home by midnight. Benton just kind of laughed at her and said, "I'm not leaving the party now, I'm having fun with my friends, you need to just let go a little bit." She tried to fit in by making conversation with the other kids while Benton just kept drinking and getting louder. Finally, she decided that she would just get back to her aunt's somehow, without Benton.

As she was walking down the steps of the house, Benton came unsteadily after her. He said, "Why are you leaving when we are just starting to have fun?" She replied, "Benton your drunk and I don't want you to drive me so I'm just going to get a ride back to my aunt's house. Benton looked at her funny and then replied, "Go ahead then, you are not going to ruin my night, my friends were right, I shouldn't have brought you. I'll find another girl who would love to be with me and give me what I want." Benton went back into the house like he didn't have a care in the world.

Mercy got herself under control, wiped her eyes with a tissue she had in her purse. She'd have to go back in and look for a phone. She found a phone in the kitchen of the huge house. She didn't know who to call. She couldn't call her house or her sisters or brothers because if her momma picked up the phone, she'd never let her go out again anytime soon. Her brothers and sisters all shared one car between them, which they purchased with their own money and they were always fighting over who was going to drive the car, where. The car was probably in use and it wouldn't be there anyway. She would call Travis. He may be a little angry with her because she didn't go to the prom with him when he'd asked, but she didn't have anyone else to call to make sure she got home before midnight and it was already 10:45. She called Travis's house and let the phone ring about a dozen times with no answer. She waited five minutes and tried again, still no answer. She told herself that she would try one more time. On the third ring, Travis himself picked up. He said, "Hello" in his wonderful, southern drawl. She said, "Travis, I'm in Clifton at a after prom party and it's not going so well, could you come and pick me up and take me home?" He told her he would borrow his dad's pick-up truck and be there within thirty minutes. Mercy crept back outside without anyone noticing her, to the front steps. She stood over to the side, kind of behind a bush, to watch for Travis.

It was almost thirty minutes on the dot when she saw Travis's red pick-up truck pull up the drive. She ran down the drive to meet him and hopped in the truck. Travis said, "What's wrong, are you okay?" Mercy said, "I'm okay and I don't want to talk about it, can you please just take me home?" Mercy had told her aunt that she may go on home after the prom instead of back to her house. The night came rushing back to her and she started crying these huge, uncontrollable tears. Travis pulled over to the curb and scooted over next to her and put his arms around her for comfort. His embrace was so warm, his arms were well muscled but soft at the same time. She felt comfort in his arms. He held her forever it seemed, letting Mercy cry on his shoulder for as long as she wanted. Travis told Mercy, "If Benton had done anything bad to her that he would just go right in there and kick his ass." Mercy said, "Please, no Travis, there's been enough drama for one night." She assured Travis that she was fine. Travis started driving her home and neither one of them spoke all the way to her house. The porch light was on and she knew that her momma would still be awake in bed, waiting for her or waiting to hear from her about her big night out.

Travis stopped in front of her house. It was exactly 11:55. Mercy thanked him for all that he'd done for her tonight and said one day she would return the favor. Travis kissed her on the cheek and told her not to worry about anything, everything would be okay.

Mercy walked on their little walk around to the back of the house and went to the back door, trying not to wake anyone up. Her momma was sitting at the kitchen table, reading a newspaper and eating a piece of cake. When Mercy walked in, her mother's eyes were beaming. Her mother looked at her face and asked, "What's wrong?", "Nothing", Mercy replied. Benton got a bad headache and Travis had to bring me home. Her mother said, "Well, it looks like you have been crying, if that boy harmed one hair on your head, I'll kill him." Her mother could be so dramatic sometimes. Mercy assured her mother that she was fine and told her mother what a wonderful time she had tonight and repeatedly thanked her for letting her go to the prom. Mercy told her mother that she was very tired, and she was going to bed.

Mercy crept up the back stairs to the girl's bedroom, so she didn't wake anyone up. She pulled off her beautiful dress and hung it in the closet and put on her pajamas. She climbed into bed. She laid there thinking about what had gone wrong tonight. She guessed it was the drinking. She had no way of knowing that Benton liked to drink since she never really talked to him before. She also thought about what the girls at the party said to her and the humiliation and shame covered her just like a blanket she was laying under. It seemed like it took forever to fall asleep.

The next day, she went over to Madison's house and she told Madison everything that had happened. Madison already knew from what her other friends had told her. Mercy thought that she was going to die. How could she go to school on Monday morning and face all those people that were at the party? She also found out that, after she left, Benton got together with Gloria, another popular girl at school, and took her home later that night.

Later that afternoon, Mercy went home and when she walked in the back door, her Momma and sisters were standing next to a big, long, white box. They said "Mercy, it's for you." The box held two dozen, long stemmed, red roses, along with a card. The card said, "Mercy, please forgive me, please let me take you out again." Mercy was angry and thrilled at the same time. Mercy's mother said, "That's an awfully expensive present for a date that went that well." What does that boy need to be forgiven for?" Mercy just said that he probably felt bad because he had such a bad headache, he couldn't drive her home and assured her mother that everything was fine. Mercy cut the end off the roses and arranged them in a big jar that they had in the kitchen.

Monday morning came too soon! When she walked down the hall at school, it seemed like everyone was staring at her. She spotted Benton coming out of the classroom as she was passing by. Benton caught up to her and said, "Did you get the roses?" Mercy answered, "yes". Benton asked if he could take her out again to make up for their disastrous date. Mercy said she would think about it, but she wasn't sure. One of Benton's friends was standing nearby, and Mercy heard him say, "Poor, white trash, she should feel lucky if anyone asked her out." Benton gave him a look that said, "You better shut up." Mercy told Benton to call her in a couple of days and she would tell him her answer then.

Days turned into weeks, then school was out for the summer and Benton was graduating. He never did call Mercy for a second date. She waited, thinking that every day was the day that he would call but the phone never rang for her. She just figured that he listened to all the bad things his friends had to say and changed his mind. Oh, how she still loved him, even after all of this. She wished a million times that her prom night would have turned out differently. She wished that Benton could have been more of a gentleman, like Travis.

By lunch time, news had gotten around school about the girl named Gloria. Gloria is a girl that you don't take home to mother. Benton spent the rest of the night with her after the prom, Gloria was pregnant! Mercy didn't know how far along she was, but she almost started crying when she heard the news because she thought that it was Benton's baby. It felt like someone had punched her in the stomach, she couldn't breathe. Madison pulled a small brown bag out of her school bag, which held her lunch and told Mercy to breathe in it. After a few minutes, she was better. No one seemed to know who the father was, since Gloria didn't really have a boyfriend, at least none that anyone knew of. For the rest of the day, even in the restroom, Mercy listened to all the other girl's conversations to see if they knew who the father of Gloria's baby was.

When the bell rang at the end of the day Mercy walked out the door and as she was walking, she heard one of the more popular girls say, "I know the baby belongs to Benton." Mercy started crying and cried as she walked all the way home. Oh, how she hoped it wasn't so. She still loved Benton and she wanted more than anything, to be the one to have his baby, not some stranger she didn't even know. She still hoped for a life with Benton. She was sure that he would ask her out again before he went off to college and then they could have settled their differences about prom night. Mercy knew he still had feelings for her by the way he looked at her when they had passed each other in the hall.

CHAPTER 5

Her summer was uneventful. She hung out with Madison and Travis and did the usual summer things. She got a part-time job at a local fabric and craft store. Mercy was trying to save money for a car to use when she went off to college.

The first Monday morning after Labor Day, it was back to school again. The summer flew by. The air had a fine mist in it and was dark and gray, just how Mercy felt today. She would miss seeing Benton at school. Benton left for college last month. Mercy overheard Benton's mother talking in the super market and she said he was going to one of those fancy colleges up north and wouldn't be home until November, his fall break. Benton was taking pre-med. He certainly was smart enough to be a doctor. Mercy thought, he was head of Student Council and a million other things when he was in high school. Mercy also made better than average grades and was a lot smarter than most of the people in her family. She knew she wanted to go to college, but she didn't know what she wanted to be yet. She would be the first person in her family that she knew of, to go to college. Her older sister dropped out of her cosmetology classes after only four months.

(1972)

Mercy was a senior this year and couldn't wait for school to be over. Her mother talked to her about going to college. Even though her parents couldn't afford college, they knew that they lived below the poverty level and Mercy could get enough grants and free money to go to college. Her mother told her she should go to "secretary" school. There wasn't really anything special Mercy wanted to do so she let her mother talk her into going to school to be a secretary, to wait on someone else, to be at someone else's beck and call. Her mother said her other choice, she could find a rich man to marry and have babies. Somehow, the latter didn't seem too appealing to Mercy. The only man she wanted to have babies for is Benton. She told her mother that she would think about it. Benton was due to come home for fall break and she didn't want to think about anything else right now. She didn't know what, but she knew she had to devise a plan to see Benton while he was home, otherwise, he wouldn't be home again until Christmas.

Thanksgiving weekend was fast approaching. The Friday after Thanksgiving, she went to the mall with Madison. Madison's father let her use his car. Mercy couldn't afford to buy anything, they were just hanging out. She was walking along, kind of looking down and not really paying much attention and BAM! She ran right smack dab into Benton. She said, "excuse me." When she looked up into those beautiful, blue eyes, she was in shock. She couldn't believe it was him! They made small talk, as Madison kept pulling on Mercy's arm. Madison didn't like what Benton did to her friend on prom night. Finally, Benton quickly said, "There is going to be a bar-b-q down on the Ohio river at a friend's house tonight and he wanted to know if she could meet him there. She said she would see what she could do and then she let Madison pull her towards the door. When they were outside, Mercy's face lit up and she was so excited to see him, much less to be asked out by him! Madison wasn't excited in the least and told Mercy that Benton had hurt her once and that she should stay away from him, of course, Madison was also jealous. Mercy knew where his friend, Todd, lived on the river. She would have to find a way to get down there. She wouldn't tell her mother because she knew that her mother wouldn't allow her to go. Her mother was still curious about what had happened on prom night and didn't believe Mercy's whole story. Mercy knew that she would have to lie to her mother one more time, to see Benton again. After this weekend, he wouldn't be home again until Christmas. She decided to tell her mother that she was spending the night with Madison. Madison would tell Mercy's mother the same story if asked, although Madison still wasn't too excited about Mercy going, especially lying to Mercy's mother. Again, Travis was the only one she knew with a car. She stopped at his house on the way home. She knocked on the front door. An old, tired-looking woman opened the front door just a crack, just enough to see who it was. Mercy knew this was Travis's Grandma. She said, "What do you want?" Mercy replied, "Is Travis home?" The elderly woman said that he was home, he was upstairs playing his guitar, as usual. The old woman was never overly friendly towards Mercy. Once, she told Mercy that if she ever broke Travis's heart, there would be hell to pay from her. Mercy was afraid of Travis's Grandma. She let Mercy in and told her to go on upstairs, where Travis was sitting on his bed, playing guitar. Mercy went up and lightly knocked on Travis's bedroom door. "Come in!" she heard him shout. When she opened his door and he saw that it was her, he jumped up, smoothed his hands down his shirt and combed his fingers through his hair. He was standing there looking a little self-conscious, which Mercy thought was odd for him. He said, "Hey Mercy, what's up?" "Not much" she replied. I have a really big favor to ask of you Cowboy." She had been calling him cowboy for a few years now. Travis said, "Of course, you know I'd do anything for you." "Can you take me somewhere tonight?" He said, "Sure, is this a date, I knew you would go out with me sooner or later. Where do you want to go?" For a fleeting minute, he thought she wanted to go somewhere with him, but that good feeling it gave him, soon vanished. She said, "Would you take me down to the river tonight, to one of Benton's friend's house? I know where it is." He looked puzzled for a moment and then he tried to hide the disappointment on his face as he said, "Sure, I guess so, what time would you like to go?" She answered, "Oh about nine o'clock, can you pick me up from Madison's house?" He said, "Is Madison going?" She said, "No, just me." Travis said, "I thought you were over that Benton guy?" He could see clearly on her face that she wasn't. Mercy said that she was going to see other people she knew there also, but Travis wasn't buying what she was selling. Mercy asked him how he was doing and what he had been up to lately. He said, "I've been working at the garage with my dad a lot, but I still have to keep my part time job as a stock boy down at the supermarket. Mercy said, "Oh, Cowboy, that's wonderful that you are working at your dad's shop." Travis replied, "That's what I'm going to do after graduation, work with my dad. He eventually wants it to be a father/son business." Mercy said, "I'm glad you know what you want to do with your life. I still don't know what I'm going to do. My mother says I could be a secretary or find a rich husband. Neither one appeals to me. I'm kind of kicking around the idea of going to nursing school up at Christ Hospital in Cincinnati. It will take me two years but if I can make it, I will be pretty much set for life. People will always need nurses." Travis replied, "It looks like you are pretty well set on what you want to do with your life also." They both laughed and gave each other a light hug. Travis loved Mercy more than anything and would do anything just to be with her for a few minutes, even if it meant taking her to see another guy. To hug her was like heaven. She was so warm and soft and felt like a newborn bird in his arms, light and fragile. He thought, "Well, here goes nothing, I'm going to ask Mercy out yet again. All that can happen is that she will say no." He's used to it, she has said "no" to him several times before. "Mercy, would you like to go out with me next weekend, to the movies or something? Of course, she said, "no" again. She says she loves him as a friend but rather leave dating out of it. He said, "You can't blame a cowboy for trying. I'll never give up on you Mercy." Mercy told Travis" Bye" and that she would see him tonight at Madison's house. He said, "Okay, do you want me to go ahead and take you over to Madison's house?" Mercy said, "No thanks, I'll just walk over to Madison's house." Mercy would have liked the ride, but she didn't want to take a chance of anyone in her family seeing her in Travis's truck. Besides, Madison only lived one street over. She started walking over to Madison's house. She had a few moments to herself to think. She still really loved Benton, but she would have to find out tonight if Gloria's baby was his or not. She just didn't think she could be in a relationship with someone who already had a baby. She thought about Travis. He was such a good guy, and so handsome. She just never thought of him as boyfriend material since she grew up with him. She thought about if he could ever be her boyfriend in the future, and she just didn't think so.

She got to Madison's about 7:30 that evening. Madison's parents were home and sitting in front of the television. Madison's mom yelled, "Hey Mercy!" when she started up the stairs to Madison's room.

Madison's family was as poor as hers but at least Madison was an only child and therefore, she had her own room. They listened to music while they painted their fingernails. About 8:30, Madison went down to tell her parents goodnight. She said that she and Mercy were tired and would probably go to bed early. Madison went back upstairs. Madison had twin beds in her room and they made up one of the beds to look like Mercy was sleeping in it. It looked perfect. Mercy then climbed out the second story window onto the trellis and down. She walked a couple of houses down to meet Travis. Travis picked her up at exactly 9:00. Travis really didn't like helping her to sneak out of the house and he told Mercy that. Mercy didn't say anything, just thanked him for the ride."

Twenty minutes later, they were at Benton's friend's house on the river. Mercy hopped out of the truck and thanked Travis again, He said, "Do you want me to pick you up later?" Mercy said, "No, I'll find a ride, thank you so much Cowboy for bringing me down here. You could tell what house it was by all the cars out front and the balloons on the mailbox. They called it a bar-b-q party. There were so many people there, some Mercy had seen before at school and some she hadn't. She walked around the house to the back. The back walk was full of teenagers walking on the walk from the house to the river and back. There was a huge bon-fire down by the river and you could see some people with sticks in their hands roasting marshmallows. She casually walked down the walk and she saw Benton sitting on one of the hay bales sitting around the fire, talking to some of his friends. She walked right up to him and said, "Hi, how ya doing?" He jumped up when he saw her. She looked like an angel in her white dress and long, black hair. She seemed to have a glow about her. He couldn't believe how excited he felt to see her. He knew he could have almost any girl here, but he wasn't interested in any of them. He had one girl sitting by him that had her arm through his like she was holding him tightly and giving Mercy a look that could kill. He said, "Hey Mercy, I'm doing fine, how bout you?"

She said, "fine thanks." He asked her to sit down beside him. She noticed as she sat down that everyone was staring at her. Of course, the mean girls were there, and she knew they all hated her. They were all so jealous of her, and Mercy didn't know if she liked that feeling or not. She and Benton made small talk for a while, and the girl next to him didn't let go of his arm the whole time and it was obvious that Benton was trying to let go. Mercy noticed that Benton was drinking coke also, instead of beer like the rest of the guys here. Benton got her a drink and then he asks her if she'd like to take a walk down to the boat dock on the river. The girl that had been hanging onto him said, "Benton, remember, you were going to tell me about your college?" Benton, barely looking at her said, "I'll tell you about it later." The girl was so angry, her face was turning red. Mercy said, "I'd love to take a walk with you Benton." As they were slowly strolling down the walk, Benton casually took Mercy's hand in his. This sent a thrill through Mercy and she was struck by the feeling of its casualness. They made small talk and Mercy ask Benton how he liked college. He said he liked it very much. He didn't tell her how being a freshman at college made him feel like the lowest of the low. He didn't tell her how the other guys bullied him. He didn't tell Mercy that the other guys made fun of him because he studied so much. He only told her the good things about college. Mercy told him of her plans to go to nursing school and he thought that was great. Finally, he said, "Mercy, I'm really sorry about our first date. I should have stood up for you. I was a jerk and I hope you can forgive me for that." Mercy said, "Don't worry, I've already forgotten about it. He told her how beautiful she looks in the moon light. He gently brushed her hair back off her cheek with the back of his hand. Her skin was as soft as velvet. He leaned down and gently kissed her full, soft lips. He looked up and saw that her eyes were closed, he pulled her closer to him and kissed her again, being very gentle with how he held her. His kiss made her knees feel weak, it felt like he was holding her up. She was dizzy with the pleasure of his kiss. She considered this her first real kiss, the first one they had while they were alone. She wanted her first kiss to be special and it was everything that she had ever dreamed it would be.

He finally turned her lose and stepped back to look at her. He said, "You are a very special girl, Mercy and I'd really like to see you again when I come back into town on Christmas and maybe we could write or call until I come back. She said that she would write or call him and that she would miss him while he was gone, but she was glad he was doing well in college. They spent the rest of the evening talking, laughing, kissing, just like they had been doing it forever. Benton ask her if she would be his girlfriend and if she would come up to his college sometime and see him and see where he lived. She said she would like that very much. The very envious looks that she got from the other girls there made her very uncomfortable, but she tried to ignore them. Benton whispered in her ear, "They can't hold a candle to you, just ignore them." They roasted marshmallows, made smores laughed and had a great time. It was getting late and Mercy regretfully had to go. Benton asked her if he could take her home and she said that would be very nice. She told him she was staying at her friend Madison's tonight and he could just drop her off there. They got in his Mustang and he took her back to Madison's. It didn't go unnoticed by the other girls there that they had left together. The mean girls decided that Mercy would pay for coming to the party and taking Benton away. Mercy asked him not to pull right up to the house because she didn't want to wake anyone. He went around to the other side of the car and opened the door for her. He took her hand to help her out. He gently pulled her to him and kissed her goodnight. She said, "Sweet dreams" and walked on to Madison's a couple doors down. He watched her walk down and disappear to the side of the house to make sure she was safe and then he got in his car and went back to the party. Neither he or Mercy saw the red pick-up truck parked across the street on a side street.

Benton wasn't the only one who wanted to make sure Mercy was safe tonight.

Mercy quietly climbed the trellis up to Madison's room and in through the window. She heard a truck go by the house, but all was quiet in the house. Madison was half awake and groggily, she asked Mercy if she had a good time. She said she had a wonderful time and that she would tell her all about it tomorrow. Mercy couldn't sleep. She wondered if this night could have been any more perfect. She was in love with Benton. She lay there remembering every second of being with him tonight. His smile, his touch, his warm kiss, his thoughtfulness. She wished she could have stayed at the party forever. The night just went too quickly.

The next day, she told Madison everything that had happened on her date with Benton. After what seemed like the hundredth time of telling it, Madison wished she'd never even heard the name Benton.

Mercy spent most of the afternoon at Madison's and then she walked home. Her mother asked her if she had a good time and she said that she had a great time. Mercy went up to her room to do her homework for Monday, but all the pages seem to blur together. She was so tired, she closed her eyes for just a second and she fell into a deep sleep, with her head on top of her pile of books. Before she knew it, it was 6:00 and her mother was calling her to come down for dinner.

Mercy's mother said that one of the financial advisers from Christ Hospital had called and wanted to talk to her about coming to nursing school next year. It was really, at that moment, that Mercy decided she wanted to go.

CHAPTER 6

Christmas vacation was finally here! She and Benton had talked on the phone a few times and had written each other. They did more writing than calling because of their parents. It was going to be a very uncomfortable Christmas dinner at Benton's house and at hers and she wasn't looking forward to it, but she was so looking forward to seeing Benton. Couldn't she and Benton just go to a nice restaurant? She knew that would never go over well with her parents and they would just be more suspicious of them.

Benton came home on December twenty third. She hadn't gone out with anyone else since Benton left, even though her mother had finally relented about her dating. Her mother decided that Mercy was mature enough to date now and she wanted Mercy to get Benton off her mind, even if for a little while. Mercy's mother was afraid that Mercy would run off and marry Benton and never go to college. Benton called the day of the 23rd and ask Mercy if she'd like to go to dinner with him. Of course, Mercy said, "yes". Benton still didn't know exactly where Mercy lived. She would have to give in now and tell him. She gave him her address, Mercy started cleaning up the house. Her mother didn't know what had come over her, but she liked the new

Mercy. Mercy's Mother always said, "We might be poor, but we can be clean." Mercy was still nervous about Benton coming to her house. She knew deep down that it really wouldn't matter to him, but it did to her.

Benton pulled up out front around 6:00 and came to the front door. Mercy let him in and then introduced him to her mother and her sisters and one of her brothers. Mercy's dad was down the street at the bar. After introductions, Mercy quickly hurried Benton out the door before any inquisitions could start.

Benton took Mercy to Friday's in the mall for dinner. She just ordered an appetizer and drinks. After dinner, they strolled through the mall hand in hand. Benton loves to shop, and he would love to buy nice things for Mercy. She felt awkward about letting him buy her anything nice because she felt her mother wouldn't approve and she'd just have to hide whatever it was. At the end of the evening, they sat on Mercy's front porch talking. Mercy said, "You know, I'm really nervous about going to your house for dinner tomorrow night." Benton told her not to worry that everything would be fine, besides, who wouldn't love her? He kissed her good night and said, "I'll pick you up tomorrow night around 7:00. She just nodded okay.

Christmas eve came so quickly! This would be the first time Mercy had ever been to Benton's house. She was nervous to meet his family and have dinner with them. She found something nice but simple to wear. A dark green skirt and a red sweater. She looked very festive and she was also in the Christmas spirit tonight.

When she arrived at Benton's and walked into the dining room, every head turned to look at her. She was the first girl that Benton had ever brought home to meet his family. They were all very cordial but not overly friendly towards her. They were all dressed to impress. She made Benton promise before-hand, not to leave her alone and just sitting there by herself. He was at her side all evening. They had a huge dining room and tonight it sat twenty people. Mercy was very nervous when she sat down. There were three forks, two knives, two spoons, two glasses, one of which was full of ice water. She wasn't quite sure which to use at what time. She just watched Benton and followed his lead. Dinner was seven courses and it was delicious.

During the middle of dinner, Benton's mother looked at her and ask, "So dear, where do you live?" She told them, and Benton's mother almost fell off her chair. She also asked about her family and where she was going to school next year. Benton saved her by changing the subject.

Benton's family had three maids and two chefs that cooked everything. They started cooking days before Christmas eve celebration. Benton's mother was very picky about what and how dinner would be served. After dinner, they all gathered around the piano in the front room while Benton played Christmas carols for them. Benton was quite an accomplished piano player. Of course, his mother raved about him the whole time he was playing. After about an hour of playing, Benton got up and said he thought it was time to get Mercy home for her own Christmas eve celebration. Mercy's family didn't celebrate on Christmas eve, just Christmas day but she didn't tell them that. After they were in Benton's car, he said, "Well, how did you like my family?" "Oh, they were all wonderful" she said. He knew she was saying that to be nice to him and that was okay. Mercy asked him "So, why didn't you tell me you played the piano so well?" He replied, "I am classically trained. I don't advertise that at school or everyone would think I was a real nerd."

He got Mercy home and walked her up to her front door and kissed her good night, several times. The front door flew open and Mercy's mother said, "Mercy, get in here, this ain't the Drive-Inn Theater." Benton said, "Yes Mam!" and sort of skipped down the driveway to his car.

When Benton returned home, his mother was sitting at the little kitchen table having coffee with her sister. She asked, "Benton, is that your new girlfriend?" He said, "No, she is just a friend of mine, that's all." His mother said, "Good, because Mercy comes from the wrong part of town and you could do so much better." Benton asked her what was wrong with where Mercy lived, and she said, "There's a big difference in social, economic, education and pride in one's self and she didn't think that Mercy qualified. She wanted Benton to date one of her friend's daughters who was going to Harvard at the time. Benton wasn't surprised that his mother was so closed minded and critical of others, he had heard it before. Benton said he might see someone else sometime. He was secretly disappointed in his mother and her way of thinking about people in the world. He would go to bed and have "sweet dreams" just like Mercy told him to. Tomorrow was Christmas day and Benton couldn't wait to give Mercy the gift he had purchased for her and hoped that she really loved it. He had a feeling that she would. He didn't sleep well that night. He couldn't get Mercy off his mind. He thought about how sweet and gentle she was and how good she felt when he held her in his arms.

The next day, Christmas, there was a very light snow falling, which gave everyone the Christmas spirit. Benton was going to church with his parents and then he was going over to Mercy's house, which of course, his mother complained about.

He knocked on Mercy's door and she answered it right away. After he stepped in, she gave him a big kiss, right in front of everyone and his face turned a bright red. He followed her eyes upward and saw that they were standing under the mistletoe and they both laughed. There were a lot of people here in this small house, sister's, brother's and their boyfriends and girlfriends. Mercy's older sister had a four-year-old little boy. Mercy didn't tell him she was an aunt. On Christmas day, Mercy's family ate about two in the afternoon. Because of such a small kitchen, food was served buffet style, and everyone found a seat where they could to eat. Mercy's parents were from the south and they served a lot of southern dishes. Benton had to ask Mercy what some of the dishes were, like milk gravy, cornbread, fried corn and chess pie. He thought that everything was delicious. Mercy's mother seems to like that he went back for second's. He was totally stuffed. After dinner, the women cleaned up the kitchen and put the food away while the men watched television. Benton tried to talk to Mercy's father who was sitting in his favorite recliner, but her father fell asleep. Mercy's brothers talked to him and seemed very nice, but he couldn't wait for Mercy to get finished in the kitchen. It wasn't too long before the women finished up the kitchen and then it seemed like everyone was leaving to go somewhere else. That was okay with Benton and Mercy. They wanted to have some time together.

Later that day, they were sitting alone in the small living room. Mercy's mother went to lay down for a while and Mercy's dad went to see a couple of his buddies. Mercy could tell that Benton was excited about something the way his eyes were sparkling. Benton told Mercy he had a gift for her. He pulled out a little black box from his coat pocket. Mercy looked at him excitedly and said, "I'm sorry, I didn't know that we were buying each other gifts. I don't have anything for you." He replied, "That's okay, it's just a surprise, that's all." He handed Mercy the box and she opened it. It was a beautiful, silver necklace with a pendant of two hearts intertwined, hanging from the bottom. There were two tiny tanzanite stones in the top of each heart, surrounded with tiny diamond chips. Mercy said, "Oh Benton, I've never owned anything as beautiful as this! Will you put in on for me?" He did, and it looked beautiful with her black hair. Suddenly, her face fell, and she lost all excitement. Benton asked her what was wrong, and she said that her mother probably wouldn't approve of her accepting such an expensive gift from a boyfriend. They both thought about it and decided she should just wear it under her shirts where no one else could see it but it would be close to her heart. He gently kissed her and told her how much he loved being with her, how beautiful she was and how much he would miss her when he returned to college. He told her he would write to her as often as he could. Mercy loved hearing how much he cared for her and she told him the same. They spent a few hours talking and too soon it was time for Benton to leave. They kissed several times on the front porch and hugged each other like it was the last time they would see each other.

The next day while Benton was walking down his walk

and getting into his car, his mother was waving goodbye out the front window. Benton's mother was not happy because she knew that Benton was leaving a little early so that he could stop and see that poor white trash.

Mercy didn't know he was coming by to tell her goodbye again and was she was excited that he did. They talked for a few minutes and Benton again told her how much he would miss her. They kissed goodbye and she walked him to his car. She had to know the answer to the burning question about Gloria's baby. She guessed that there would be no good time to ask about it, so she would ask him now as he was walking to his car to drive back to school. Suddenly, she turned and looked Benton in the eye and said, "Benton, is it okay if I ask you a question?" "Of course," he said. She hesitated slightly, not sure if she wanted to hear the answer herself. "Benton, Gloria at school is going to have a baby and some of the rumors floating around is that the baby is yours, and well." He looked very surprised at her question. "Of course, the baby isn't mine, I haven't been with any girls like that." Mercy said, "I thought you spent time with Gloria after I left the party on our first date." Benton replied, "We hung out at the party, that's all it was." Mercy had a hard time believing him after he couldn't keep his hands off her that same night. "Sorry, Benton, I just had to ask, I hope you forgive me." Benton told Mercy not to believe everything she heard from the people at school, they just love to gossip.

When Benton left, Mercy received a strange phone call from Benton's mother. She asked her if she had time to come over and chat with her for a while. Mercy didn't see any harm in talking to her, so she agreed. Benton's mother was going to send her driver over to get her.

About forty-five minutes later, a black limo pulled up in front of her house. Mercy was glad that everyone in her house was either gone or asleep. She ran out of her house as the driver was opening the door for her. Mercy knew that a lot of neighbors would be watching out their windows. Mercy had never ridden in anything as nice as this. She felt like a queen. She also wondered what Benton's mother had to talk to her about.

When she arrived at Benton's front door, it opened before she could even knock. Benton's mother said, "Usually, my butler answers the door, but I did because I was excited that you were coming. Please, let's go inside and sit down where we can have a little private chat. This won't take long." Mercy thought this was kind of strange and couldn't imagine what on earth Benton's mother would have to talk to her about, so she was a little nervous, not to mention, a little scared of her. After some small talk, Benton's mother said, "Mercy, let's get straight to the point.

I know that you said you are planning on going to nursing school and you and your family could use some financial help. This was her way of saying, "You live in a poor neighborhood." Mercy's face turned red and she felt the embarrassment of her words, so she didn't say anything. Benton's mother went on, "Well, I have an offer for you. You know that Benton is my only child, and I have great plans for Benton's future. I don't want him tied down with feelings for a girl right now, emphasizing "girl." You and I both know that you aren't right for my son." At this, Mercy became angry and stood up. She continued, "Please sit down. I'm not trying to make you angry, you are a very sweet girl, just not right for my son is all. I am prepared to offer you fifty thousand dollars to further your education and to help your family. It would insure your education at nursing school. I just want you to stay away from my son and forget about him." Mercy thought, fifty thousand dollars is a lifetime of money for my family and would insure her education. Mercy thought about it for a few minutes and then said, "I'm sorry, I can't do that. I can't take money from you because there is no way I could ever stay away from Benton. I love him, and I will be with him for as long as he wants me. There is no amount of money that would make me leave him." Benton's mother replied, "You are a foolish girl, and selfish. That amount of money could really ease some burdens for your family. I won't ever be making this offer again." Mercy's face was red with anger. How dare she think she could just buy her off. Mercy knew that she was used to getting her own way. Mercy stood up and answered in a very cold tone of voice, "I understand and would like it if this conversation never happened. I would hope that you would keep this conversation just between us. Benton would be very angry with you, not to mention, disappointed in you. Benton told me you are always trying to manipulate him into doing what you want." She turned on her heel and left the house. She climbed into the limo that was still sitting out front and ask the driver to take her home.

CHAPTER 7

(1972)

It was getting near the end of the year and almost time for Mercy's senior prom. She didn't date anyone but Benton and so far, no one had asked her to go on a date but him. She would like to go because it marks the end of high school and Madison and her new boyfriend were going. She would also be graduating in a couple of weeks and turning eighteen in May, two days after prom. She so wished Benton could be here for her prom and her birthday.

It was the Monday before prom and Travis caught up to her after school one day. Mercy noticed how Cowboy had really filled out, especially this last year. He had gotten a few inches taller and his shoulders had gotten a lot wider. Mercy didn't know how she hadn't noticed this until now. They made small talk and then he asked, "Mercy, I would really like it if you would go to the prom with me." We could double date with Madison and her new boyfriend, if you'd like." This is our last year of high school together and I think it would be really nice if we spent that night together." Mercy said, "Yes, it would be nice, I'll go with you. I was hoping you would ask. Since we are all great friends, it would be nice to spend one last night together partying before graduation." Travis replied, "Great, I'll pick you up at 7:00. We can all go to dinner first. I'll talk to ya later." He headed off in the other direction from her. When she got home, she would call Madison and tell her that she had a prom date and see if they wanted to double with her and Cowboy.

Mercy called Madison and they agreed that they would love to double. Mercy would stay with Madison the night before and they could get ready together. Benton was supposed to call her Wednesday, two days before prom, and she would tell him then of her prom plans to go to the prom with Travis. Benton knows that she wants to go, and he also knows that Mercy considers Travis as just a friend. Wednesday evening, Benton did call, and they told each other how much they missed each other. Mercy asked Benton, "You know I would really love to go to my senior prom. Would you care if I went with Cowboy? You know he is just a friend and we are going with Madison and a few other friends." Benton didn't really like her going anywhere with another man, but he replied, "Sure, Mercy, I'm happy that you get to go to your senior prom, no problem."

That evening, Mercy found the old prom dress that belonged to one of her sisters. The dress was pale blue with thin straps, floor length, and matched the beautiful necklace Benton had given her. The dress was a satin type of fabric and very form fitting. She couldn't believe that her mother had approved of this dress. She also found the shoes her sister wore with it and even though the dress and shoes were a little big, they would do for one night. Mercy would ask her mother to clean the dress for her.

Benton sent Mercy flowers for every occasion that he could not be with her. He especially overdid it on Valentine's Day, sending her five dozen red roses. The day of the prom, while sitting in the kitchen, having coffee with her mother, there was a delivery person at the door. The man had a package with Mercy's name on it, which she had to sign for. Mercy took the package back to the kitchen and opened the attached card. The card read, "Happy Birthday Sweetheart". She opened the package and there was another black box. It contained a beautiful bracelet that matched the necklace he had given her for Christmas. Mercy loved the bracelet and thought it was beautiful. Mercy did show the bracelet to her Mother and her mother said that she thought it was alright if Mercy kept it. Mercy still had not shown anyone the necklace Benton bought her, except Madison. Best friends share everything.

When Mercy arrived at Madison's that evening, they both went right up to Madison's room as usual. She and Madison had been friends for a long time and loved each other like sisters. Mercy showed Madison the bracelet that Benton had sent her for her birthday. For the first time, even though it had been there before, Mercy saw jealousy in Madison's eyes, and she didn't like having the feeling of knowing that. They told each other everything. They stayed up late that night talking. Madison asked, "Mercy, have you and Benton done it yet?" Mercy answered, "Well, that's none of your business, but no, we haven't. You know how I feel about doing that before marriage." Madison said, "Oh, you are as old fashioned as your mother. Everybody does it in high school. Mercy replied, "It might be old fashioned, but I decided a long time ago that I am saving myself for my wedding night. Have you done it with anybody?" Madison replied, "Of course silly, almost everyone has." Mercy knew that Madison has had a lot of boyfriends. Madison is gorgeous, and guys just automatically gravitate towards her but now Mercy thinks she knows why she had so many boyfriends. But of course, not the popular guys at school. They stayed up late, talking about everything from school to past loves, or at least Madison's past loves.

The next night, Travis and Madison's boyfriend were there to pick them up at 7:00. They both complimented the girls on how beautiful they looked. The necklace and bracelet did not go unnoticed by Travis, but he did not mention them because he was pretty sure he knew where they came from. He seemed to have a weird nervousness about him tonight. They gave the girls corsages while Madison's parents took pictures, saying they would save a couple of photos for her to show to her Mother. Mercy's mother still was not feeling very well, and she was probably in bed now. She had been going to bed early. All four said their good-byes to Madison's parents and of course they told the four of them to be careful. They left for dinner.

They arrived at the prom at 9:00 and had their prom pictures taken, like everyone else, and then went on inside. The music was loud, and the couples were all dancing, laughing and having a great time. Travis did not ask Mercy to dance until the band played a slow song. Of course, Mercy said she would like to dance. Travis seemed to hold her a little too close and a little too stiff. She wondered why he was so nervous when they both grew up together. She could feel his body trembling a little bit. When they had finished dancing, and were walking back to the table, one of the mean girls said, "That's it Mercy, stick with your own kind." Mercy looked right through her like she wasn't even there. All four of them had a great time and it was over too soon, at midnight. Mercy stopped in the restroom on the way out. The mean girls were in there and the one that sat next to Benton the night of the bon-fire said, "That's good that you are dating one of your own kind, stay away from Benton." Mercy ignored them.

Travis dropped Madison and her boyfriend off at after prom party they wanted to go to. They invited Mercy and Travis along, but Mercy said she wanted to get home because she was tired, and she would pick up her things at Madison's tomorrow. Madison called her a party pooper. Mercy was just going back to her house. She didn't feel like going to an after party where everyone was loud and drunk. Travis pulled his truck up to Mercy's house. On the way home, conversation seemed to be strained between Mercy and him. When he parked, he turned to Mercy and said, "Mercy, this is the last night we might see each other, so there is something I'd like to tell you." Mercy said, "Okay, but don't look so serious, you're going to give yourself a heart attack." He said, "I am serious, I've never been more serious in my life." Mercy noticed that he was visibly shaking, and she could almost swear that his teeth were chattering. Sweat broke out on Travis's forehead, his beautiful blue eyes seem to be penetrating hers as he stared into the depths of her soul. He scooted as close as he could to her in this truck. "Mercy", her name sounded so sweet and sensual on his lips. "Please listen, I have something to tell you and then I won't ever talk about it again, but you have to know." "Know what?" "I love y..."

Mercy interrupted with "Please, Cowboy, let's not have this conversation now. Travis replied, "It's now or never and would you please, please, just listen to me?" Mercy looked miserable but said, "Okay" but she felt uncomfortable. Travis started over, "Mercy, I love you. I've loved you since we were little kids, grew up together and went to school together. I have always loved you and I always will." He looked deep into her eyes for any sign of hope that she might love him back. "I wanted you to know this and to know that if anything ever happens between you and Benton that you will know I am here waiting for you." "Travis" Mercy answered in a tender voice, as she gently touched his handsome cheek, you know I'm in love with Benton and you know that I have always loved you as one of my very best friends. I've never thought of you as a boyfriend, you've always been like a brother to me and I love you dearly in that way. She knew, of course, that these words were not exactly what every man wanted to hear but they are true. Travis said, "I know that now, but one day, you may change your mind. You know that I would love and cherish you forever." Mercy thought that was too close to a proposal and she had to find a way to gently let Travis down and get out of this truck. "Travis, please don't think I don't care about you because I care about you a great deal, just not in the same way that you care for me." Travis bent over and kissed her lightly on the forehead and said, "I'll never stop loving you and I'll never stop trying to win your heart. I am here for you always." At that, he squeezed her hands and kissed her cheek. He said, "I better get you inside." He climbed out of the truck and went around to open her door. Since Mercy had a long dress on. Travis picked her up out of the truck and gently sat her on the ground. They were standing very close and could feel each other's breath in the cool night air. Travis said, "Come on, I'll walk you to the door." Mercy hurried and told Travis goodnight as she quickly reached for the door. Travis just stood there and watched her go.

Once inside, Mercy leaned against the door, trying to catch her breath. Wow, she didn't see that one coming. She knew that Travis liked her, but she didn't know how much he loved her. Mercy wondered what it would be like to be Travis's girlfriend, if she had never met Benton, she and Travis might have had a chance. Maybe it's just a crush, she didn't know but she was pretty sure that this would affect their lifelong friendship. She went straight upstairs to her bedroom with tears in her eyes, realizing that she did love Travis, she just knew that she loved Benton more. She loved Benton with that all-consuming love and passion and she loved Travis more like an old boyfriend. She felt sad for Travis tonight, she felt sad for herself, she felt sad for Benton. This was one night that she would never forget. It's not often that a man tells you he loves you and will love you forever.

Two days later, she woke about 10:00am and went down to the kitchen. Her mother was already up, making bacon and eggs. Her mother turned to look at her and said happily, "Happy eighteenth birthday! Mercy was so happy to see her mother up and looking well. She said, "Thank you Mother," and gave her a big smile. Mercy saw the big white flower box on the table and said to her mother, "Aw, Benton remembered my birthday!" Mercy opened the box of a dozen pink roses and found the card. The card read, "For the most beautiful woman in the world, thank you for one of the best nights of my life. I will remember it always.

Happy Birthday! Love, Travis. Her face must have slightly fallen, and her mother noticed. Her mother asked, "Who are those from?". Mercy smiled and answered, "They are from Travis, thanking me for such a wonderful prom night." Her mother answered, "Isn't that nice?" Her mother knew that Mercy had thought that they were from Benton. Her mother said quietly, "Travis is a really good boy, you should get together with him more often." When Benton called that evening, Mercy told him all about her senior prom night, except of course, the last part about Travis. Benton just didn't need to know about that. Benton was genuinely happy that she had a good time. Mercy couldn't see how Travis looked at her with love in his eyes, but Benton had seen it, on more than one occasion, but he wasn't worried. He trusted Mercy and believed she loved him. Benton told her that he knew she only thought of Travis as a friend and nothing more. They talked a while and Benton said, "I'll talk to you soon. It won't be long, and I will be on summer break. I can't wait to see you. A short while later they hung up. Mercy did not tell him about the roses Travis had sent her or that he confessed his feelings for her.

The next Friday was Graduation night at the local community college! All of Mercy's friends and family were there. She couldn't believe that thirteen years of school was finally over! Her family was going to have a graduation party for her at her aunt's house in Clifton because her house was bigger and could hold more guests.

Mercy's mother was there but she had not been feeling well lately and not been able to work as much. Her mother never complained or said what was wrong, just that she didn't feel well, she was tired all the time. Mercy's father also showed up at the party but was really drunk after only an hour into the party. He walked around the party insulting anyone that he could and being his obnoxious, drunk self. Mercy gave up being embarrassed by him a long time ago. Travis got her father into his truck and he took him home, then he returned to the party.

Benton couldn't be here this weekend, but he would be home in a couple of weeks for summer break. Mercy was standing there daydreaming about Benton when Madison touched her arm and told her to, "Wake up!" they were having a party. Madison was leaving this party soon, to go to other graduation parties where there were no parents present, just beer and lots of guys. Madison tried to talk Mercy into going with her, but Mercy thought it would be too rude to leave her own party. When Mercy arrived home that evening, she found a small package on the front porch. The package was addressed to her, but she guessed it wasn't necessary to sign for this one. She took it back to the kitchen and opened it. It was a beautiful ring that matched the bracelet and necklace Benton had given her for Christmas and Birthday. She tried on the ring and it was a perfect fit! She wondered how Benton could possibly know her ring size. Benton had given her so much, she was starting to feel a little bit overwhelmed. She had never showed the necklace to anyone except for Madison. She had just received the bracelet a week ago from Benton for her Birthday and wasn't expecting another present from him. She loved it, it was so beautiful! The card inside simply read, "For my Sweetheart's Graduation, love Benton." Mercy's mother walked into the kitchen while Mercy was admiring how the ring looked on her hand. She wasn't to happy to see Mercy receive another expensive gift, since she had just received a bracelet from Benton, but she didn't say anything. Her mother knew how sad that Mercy had been lately and how much she missed Benton. She would let her keep the gifts. Mercy just sat there giggling for the next half hour.

CHAPTER 8

Benton came home on July fourth weekend. He would be home until early September when he went back to college. He said his college classes were hard but that he was doing well and making the grades. Mercy was so proud of him! Mercy wasn't sure exactly what day Benton would be home, he never said. Benton showed up at Mercy's house on the evening of June 3rd. His mother was so happy to see him. Benton gave her a light kiss on the cheek and had a quick cup of coffee with her. He told his mother, "I have to empty my car of the things I brought back from college and then I am going out." His mother replied, "you don't have to leave right away. Will you be here for dinner?" He answered, "Probably not." His mother never asked where he was going, she already knew.

Benton knocked on Mercy's door about five that evening. Mercy answered the door herself. She was yelling and jumping up and down while she was kissing and hugging Benton. She was so happy that he was home! He was equally as happy to see Her again. Benton took Mercy out to dinner and then they came back to Mercy's house. They spent a few hours talking on the front porch and catching up. Of course, there were a lot of kisses and hugs involved.

Mercy and Benton had a good time at Benton's house at their Fourth of July bar-b-q. They ate, and Benton got to see everyone in his family. His family teased him good naturedly about when he and Mercy were going to get married. Every time this was mentioned, Mercy could feel cold daggers from Benton's mother's eyes. Mercy wore her ring that Benton had bought her, and the ring did not go unnoticed by Benton's mother. She knew that Mercy could not afford a ring like that and knew that Benton had given it to her. She hated Mercy and Mercy knew this, but she tried to be cordial for Benton's sake. She didn't want him to have to worry about her feelings. After doing their own fireworks that night, Benton took Mercy home.

When Benton returned home, his parents were waiting for him in the library. He father said, "Benton, it's good to have you home son and we are so happy that you are doing so well in college." Benton's mother mimicked his feelings. Benton's dad looked at him seriously and said, "Son, I know you want to be a doctor, but I was hoping that we could maybe get you into the family business somewhere. Maybe you could take some business courses. You could be running our grocery chain one day." Benton's mother jumped in and said, "Benton, this is your legacy. You could travel the world and have anything or anyone that you wanted." Benton caught that last remark. Benton replied, "Mother, father, I think I have found the one person that I want to spend the rest of my life with." His mother rolled her eyes to the ceiling and his father just made a hump sound that he makes when he is displeased. His mother said, "Oh Benton, this girl is not right for you, you know that. She comes from the wrong side of the tracks, she lives a completely different lifestyle than you do, and you know that it will never work out between the two of you." His mother could see the anger rising on Benton's red face. He said, "Please don't ever talk badly about Mercy again. I'm sorry but if you want to be in my life, you will have to accept Mercy. As I've said, I love her. I am going to ask her to be my wife on Christmas Eve." Benton's mother became angry, then said, "If you marry that girl, we will take away your generous trust fund that you have been living off this past year and we will not leave you anything in our will." Benton said, "Then I will just have to live with that and make my own way, many people do. As I've said, "I love Mercy and I'm not letting her go for you or anyone else." The conversation turned back to whether Mercy was invited to their huge Chalet in the Smokey Mountains. Benton said that he would ask Mercy to come that night. Then, Benton said, "It's getting late, I'm going upstairs to my room" When he left the library, he could hear his parents quietly arguing. His mother ran the house and his father ran the businesses, and they both just left each other alone to do their own thing most of the time, but about Mercy, they both agreed that Benton was setting his sights too low.

Benton laid down on his bed and picked up his phone and dialed Mercy. "I hope it wasn't too late to call, hope I didn't wake anyone up." "No, it's okay, what's up? Benton told her that he would like for her to go on a vacation with him and his family to their chalet in the Smokey's. Mercy said, she would love to. She had never been on a vacation in her whole life! She told Benton that she would have to get an okay from her mother or she wouldn't go. She said that even though she is eighteen, she still lived with her parents and so therefore, respects their wishes. She already knew what her mother would say, "absolutely not". She didn't believe in guys and girls spending the whole night together before marriage, even if Benton's parents would be there to chaperone. Her mother would say, "It just, ain't right."

The next day, Mercy phoned Benton and told him she couldn't go and how sorry she was but that she still respected her mother. Besides, her mother was still feeling "under the weather" as she put it and Mercy just felt that she needed to stick around the house, just in case her mother needed something.

Benton said he would really miss her but that he had to go. If a least for one week, you know, it's a family thing they do every year. Mercy said, "Of course, I understand, I will just miss you that's all." Benton said they would be leaving the next day and that he would be back in one week. He said that he would see her in just a few days. Mercy told him to go and have a good time with his family and not to worry about her.

The next afternoon, Benton drove himself down to the chalet in the Smokey's. It took him five hours to get there. It was so beautiful, he really wished Mercy was here with him, she would so enjoy the beautiful scenery, but he respected the fact that Mercy still obeyed her mother's wishes. The chalet sat on the side of the mountain and had a long, winding driveway up to it. It had ten bedrooms, huge foyer with fireplace and large kitchen. The chalet had a wraparound deck on the first and second floors. It really was a beautiful place.

Benton was walking up the steps and there were a lot of people sitting on the deck. One was Bailey, a long-time friend of the family and his ex-girlfriend. Maybe not girlfriend, but Benton had dated her a few times. The fact that she was here, Benton knew, was all his mother's doing. His mother liked Bailey and he was sure she invited her here this week. Bailey's family had money also and Bailey was well educated. She also knew how to sit and talk to anyone. Benton's mother always thought that she and Benton would make a great couple. When Benton walked up the steps, with a surprise on his face, he looked at Bailey and said, "Hey Bales, how are you, it's nice to see you again." Bailey said, "What? No hug?" Benton hugged her lightly. He knew that Bailey still had feelings for him, but he didn't want to get anything started with her again. He went on inside to see the rest of his family, aunts, uncles, cousins. Bailey followed him in, chatting all the way. He fixed himself a drink and pretended to be busy talking to others. Bailey was always just outside of his peripheral vision the whole night. Finally, she announced that she was leaving and ask Benton if he would walk her to her car, you know, bears around and all. He agreed and seemed to be rushing her along to her car. Bailey turned and said, "Nice seeing you again Benton, do you mind if I stop over again tomorrow?" He didn't want to be rude to her, he knew that she like spending time with his family, so he said, "Of course, that would be fine. Bye Bales" He turned and went back into the chalet.

The next day after Benton left, Mercy was just kind of moping around the house. Mercy's mother knew how sad she was because she didn't get to go to the Smokies and she felt bad because she could never afford to take her kids on any king of vacation. She knew Travis was a nice boy and she had known him and his family since he was a little boy, she trusted him. She told Mercy that she could drive down and spend the day with Benton if she could get Travis to drive her but that she couldn't spend the night, she'd have to be home by midnight. Mercy's mother told her she had to work the next day and that she wouldn't sleep a wink until Mercy walked through the door. Mercy was elated but she didn't want to get too excited until she called Travis and ask him if he could take her. She phoned him, even though it was only seven in the morning. Surprisingly, Travis answered the phone. He was happily surprised that it was Mercy. She said, "Travis, how would you like to go on a road trip?" He sounded suspicious as he said, "Where do you want to go?" Mercy told him her plan to go down to the Smokies to see Benton for the day and that she knew that it would be a lot of driving and she would understand if he had a prior commitment or just didn't want to." Travis wasn't doing anything else today and he thought it would be a nice ride back to nature. "Sure, sounds like fun." Are you sure Benton wouldn't mind you riding down there with me?" She said, "No, he wouldn't mind, he would just be glad to see me." Mercy told Travis that she would give him some money to help with gas and that she would pack them a lunch. They planned for Travis to pick her up around eight in the morning, which would put them down there about one in the afternoon and then they would leave there around seven in the evening to get Mercy home by midnight. Mercy was so excited to be going to see Benton and even more excited just to be getting out of the house and going someplace different. She also had to admit to herself, she would enjoy spending time with Travis.

It was a long ride but seemed to be going fast. She and

Travis talked easily about the past summer, going off to college and, of course, Travis has always held to the dream of making it big in the music world one day. They talked about old times and growing up together. About eleven, they were both getting hungry and started looking for a place to pull over and eat. Mercy's mother had put together a nice lunch for them of left over fried chicken and potato salad. They found a beautiful spot on one of the mountain overlooks where they stopped to eat and enjoy the view. Travis just enjoyed the view looking at Mercy. He would never get tired of looking at her, she was so beautiful. He loved how her beautiful, blue eyes, framed by her long, dark eyelashes, sparkled when she talked. He could stare her eyes forever. He loved her beautiful, full lips and dreamed of kissing them. He dreamed of running his hands through her long, soft, dark hair. He was caught up in looking at her sitting on this beautiful mountain and her beauty put the mountains to shame. Travis thought she looked like an angel. He came out of the wonderful trance when Mercy said, "Travis, why are you looking at me like that?"

He said, "Well, to be honest, I was just thinking about how beautiful you are." Mercy felt slightly embarrassed with the way this conversation was going and she said, "Thank you Travis, we better get going now if we want to keep to our time schedule. She picked up the blanket and leftovers and off they went.

Mercy sat quietly in the truck while Travis played with the buttons on his radio, trying to find a station they could listen to without static. Mercy was thinking about the way that Travis was just looking at her when they stopped to eat. There was no doubt in her mind that she thought Travis truly loved and cared about her. She cared about him a great deal, and if she were honest with herself, she would admit that she was very attracted to him. When he told her he loved her, she started thinking how she felt about him. Did she love him like a brother or was there something more there? Now that she was thinking about him as "boyfriend" material instead of a big brother, she found that she was more and more attracted to him every time she saw him. Maybe she did love him, she didn't know but what she did know was that she did love Benton. She loved Benton so much and she missed him so much when they weren't together.

They should arrive at Benton's family's chalet in about fifteen minutes. They still were traveling up higher into the mountains. They hadn't seen any bears on the way so far. Mercy had never seen bears before in the wild and she thought they were wonderful creatures.

Mercy started to ask herself if it was such a good idea to surprise Benton or should she have tried to call him and let him know they were coming. She thought he would be happy about it since he loved her so much. She knew his mother wouldn't be happy to see her, she all but said she hated her dating her son. It had been a couple of days since she'd seen Benton and she thought that he was just going down to the chalet to meet his relatives and then come right back to be with her. She just missed him, and she knew that after this week, she wouldn't see him again until Christmas. Ordinarily, he would be home for a fall break around Thanksgiving, but he was working near his college as an intern.

Travis found a post with the correct address and drove

back the driveway which was pretty much up hill. There were a lot of cars parked on each side of the driveway. Travis found a spot not too far away. There were a few people standing out on the front porch and they introduced themselves as friends of Benton's. They told Mercy and Travis to go on in and have a drink. When they walked in, there was a large great room full of people and Benton's mother was standing in the middle, talking to a girl about their age. She kind of rolled her eyes at Mercy and excused herself to Bailey, saying, "I'll be right back." She walked over to Mercy and Travis and looked right at Mercy as she said, "What are you doing here, my dear? Is Benton expecting you?" Mercy said, "I thought I would surprise him." At the mention of his name, Benton came out of the kitchen to see who had just come in. "Mercy!", he rushed over and picked her up and swung her around. "How did you get here?" He noticed Travis a few feet away. "Oh, he brought you." They both hugged, and you would have thought that they had not seen each other in a month instead of only a few days. Bailey gave Mercy a shrewd look. Bailey stepped up to Mercy and said, "SOOO, who do we have here?" Benton remembered his manners and said, "Bailey, I'd like for you to meet my girlfriend, Mercy." Bailey said, "Nice to meet you Mercy." Mercy answered, "Nice to meet you Bailey." All the while, Mercy is trying to figure out what relationship Bailey was to Benton. Bailey said, "Benton's mother was so nice to invite me for the week. It's been a long time since I've seen Benton and it will be nice to catch up for a few days." Mercy was very curious to find out exactly what roll Bailey did play in Benton's life. Mercy wouldn't ask him now in front of everyone.

Benton and Mercy walked around the Chalet, drinking their soft drink and mostly stealing kisses and staring into each other eyes, which bored Travis to tears, not to mention he was jealous of their easy repour. Benton asked Mercy if she happened to bring her swim suit so that they could go hot tubbing in the huge hot tab. Mercy answered, "No I wouldn't be caught dead in a swim suit in front of these people." Benton said, "I don't know why not, you are the most beautiful woman here." Mercy blushed, then changed the subject and tried to include Travis into their conversations. Travis was eating from the huge dinner buffet put out to guest, so entertaining him right now was not a problem. Benton and Mercy decided that it would be a good time for them to go for a short walk in the woods. They stayed close to the Chalet but walked down a trail where there was a small garden and a beautiful, white gazebo. They sat and talked. Benton asked, "How did you get Travis to bring you all the way down here for just one day?" Mercy said that Travis wasn't doing anything else today and was more than happy to bring her.

Benton knew how Travis felt about Mercy, he could see it on his face every time he looked at her. A couple of years ago, in high school, Travis went as far as to tell him that he better take care of her or he would have to answer to him. Benton never forgot that. Travis is a big guy and would make a formidable opponent. Mercy finally got around to asking about Bailey, "Who is Bailey?" It seems like she likes you a lot, is she related to you?" "No", Benton said, as he took a deep breath, "She is an old girlfriend of mine. My mother invited her. She and my mother have always gotten along." Benton didn't tell her that Baileys family was rich also, but Mercy already figured that out by the way Bailey dressed and acted. Mercy said, "Bailey is really a beautiful woman". Benton replied, "Yeah she is alright." Don't get any ideas Mercy, she and I have been over for a long time. She doesn't mean anything to me anymore."

On the way upstairs where the other guest was, Benton grabbed a beer from one of the caterer's trays. Mercy tried not to notice, she didn't want to make a big deal out of Benton having a beer. Of course, he offered her and Travis one, but they both declined. Neither one of them drank, they weren't judgmental, they just never got into drinking with friends and Travis had a long drive home later.

Mercy's time with Benton was up before she knew it, it was almost 7:00 and time for her and Travis to get going. Mercy told Benton it was time for them to leave. Benton said, "Mercy, it is getting late, why don't you and Travis just stay for the night and leave tomorrow?" Mercy replied, "I can't, I promised my mother that I would be home by midnight." Benton said, "Do you turn into a pumpkin at midnight? For God's sake Mercy, you are 18 now." Benton doesn't normally speak to Mercy that way and Mercy knew it was because of the beer he was having. He's had about eight or nine by now and his speech is starting to slur. Mercy didn't begrudge him a good time tonight, celebrating with his family.

Bailey interrupted their conversation whenever she got the chance and flirted mercilessly with Travis. She was drinking quite a bit also, Mercy noticed. Bailey said, "Yes, it's a shame that you have to leave so soon but I will look after Benton when you leave." Mercy said, "That's okay Bailey, Benton is a big boy and I don't think he really needs looking after. Bailey sent daggers through her eyes at Mercy. Benton walked Mercy and Travis out to his truck and gave Mercy a long kiss and hug goodbye. Benton said, "Travis, drive careful with my girl." He told Mercy, "I'll be home in a couple of days and I'll call you when I get in." Mercy whispered, "I love you." Benton has never told Mercy he loves her, and he still didn't today, however, Travis took a quick look at Mercy and quietly whispered to himself, "I love you to." Mercy never could understand that if Benton loved her, why couldn't he ever say I love you back. Some guys were just like that she guessed.

When Travis and Mercy got on the road, it seemed to be darker out here than usual. Mercy was quiet, contemplating how the day went and already missing Benton. She wondered about Benton's and Bailey's relationship, she just couldn't see them as boyfriend/girlfriend material.

Mercy ask Travis if he met any girlfriend material at the party. Travis said, "You are the only woman I love." Again, Mercy wondered why it was so easy for Travis to say but not Benton. Mercy asked Travis to turn the heat on in the truck, it was getting a little chilly. About thirty miles away from the Chalet, Travis's truck started lurching and making a funny noise and then it quit running all-together. Travis told Mercy not to worry, that he knew this truck inside and out and he would fix it and they would be on their way again. When Travis went to the back of his truck to get his tools, he realized that he had left them at the Dad's shop. It wasn't like him to go anywhere without his tools or even his large flashlight. He told Mercy, he was so sorry about his truck quitting on them and that he had AAA, but he was sure that they wouldn't come up here on the mountain this time of night. Mercy would have to call Benton's chalet and get someone to come and get them. They would go back to the chalet and get some tools, then Travis could fix his truck and they could also call Mercy's mother and tell her that they would be late getting back home so she wouldn't worry.

Cell phones had been on the market for just a few years and they were very large, not unlike a home phone. Travis had one in his truck that his dad had given him, so he could call him while Travis was out working on someone's vehicle. Mercy called the chalet and a man answered. Mercy asked to speak to Benton. The man apparently handed the phone to Benton's mother. Benton's mother said she didn't know where Benton was now but, of course, she would have someone come and get them. She offered for them to spend the night and they could go and fix the truck tomorrow. Mercy said, "Thanks you, I am so grateful for your help." Benton's mother hung up the phone and went to find her own personal driver to go down the mountain to pick up Mercy and Travis.

Benton's mother saw that Bailey was out enjoying the hot spa by herself and she saw an opportunity to cause trouble between Mercy and Benton. She walked over to where Benton was standing at the bar and said to him. "You have practically ignored Bailey all night, what with Mercy here. Bailey is out having a drink and enjoying the spa all by herself. Why don't you go out there and get in the spa with her?" Benton felt a little guilty for ignoring her while Mercy was there, so he agreed to go out and visit with her. Benton's mother just smiled and said, "That's a good son. I'll bring both of you a fresh drink."

It was kind of spooky on the mountain in the dark.

Mercy sat in the truck, huddled against Travis and Travis couldn't think of anything else but that this trip could not have turned out any better, even though he apologized to Mercy a dozen times for his truck. He put his jacket over the them both. Mercy was warm, and she was so beautiful with the moonlight shining through the truck's windshield. Travis rested his head on top of hers and drank in the sweet smell of lavender. Mercy could feel his warm breath on her forehead. She thought, for the moment anyway, that all was right with the world. Travis thought how nice it would be to have her sit like this for the rest of his life. They both were quite warm.

With what seemed like forever, the driver of Benton's mom showed up. Travis locked up the truck and left his cell number on a piece of paper on the windshield just in case a policeman showed up. It was only about a forty-five-minute ride back to the Chalet but at night, because of animals, it was about a seventy-minute drive. At least, Mercy thought, she would get to see Benton again. Mercy couldn't afford one of those new cell phones and Travis's phone was dead. Mercy would call her mother from a land line at the Chalet and let her know what was going on.

Benton went to the back of the chalet where the spa was. His mother was right, Bailey was in the spa all by her lonesome. Benton walked up to the spa and Bailey said, "It's kind of lonesome in here all by myself, would you like to join me? Benton said he'd like that and went to the changing room next to the spa where he always kept an extra pair of swim trunks and put them on. He thought there wasn't any harm in joining her and talking about old times. When he got in the spa, Bailey came over and sat right next to him.

He asked her if she was enjoying herself and she said that she was. They talked some about what they had been doing for the last year and before Benton knew it, Bailey had her long, slim fingers resting on Benton's thigh. Benton's mother came out to the spa with a drink for them both, as promised, still not mentioning that Mercy and Travis were on their way back. Benton started drinking the drink that his mother brought them and thought it tasted strong. He thinks it was a Long Island Iced Tea. After only a few sips of his drink and the heat from the hot tub, he started to feel a little light headed. He knew that Bailey was coming on to him. She leaned over close to him and kissed him with a long kiss that seemed to last forever. Benton knew that he shouldn't let her do that, but he was pretty sure that he had made it clear from the beginning of the night that Mercy was his girlfriend now. He knew that he needed to get out of the spa before Bailey's kisses sent him over the edge. He didn't try to stop her in any way because her kisses were soft and sweet and brought back memories of good times.

Bailey didn't really love Benton anymore, she just wanted to take him away from Mercy for no other reason than she could. She loved the power she had over men. She took pride in the fact that she could get any man she wanted, even if he did belong to someone else. Besides, Benton was a great kisser. Suddenly, in a drunken blur, Benton opened his eyes and there stood Mercy and Travis. Mercy with a shocked look on her face. Mercy had tears in her eyes and she said, "Ooh, that's why you wanted to stay here a couple more days! She turned around and walked away, pulling Travis's in tow. Even though he wants Mercy to be happy, Travis was secretly smiling on the inside.

Benton's mother was looking out the back window. She didn't like to see her only son hurt but she knew that Bailey could help him get over Mercy. Mercy was not the type of girl for Benton.

Benton stumbled over his own feet, trying to get out of the spa and stand up, while Bailey just let out a little giggle. He looked back at Bailey in a haze and wondered why she was happy about his unfortunate situation. His mind was so groggy, and his head was spinning. He didn't know how drunk he was until he climbed out of the spa, stumbling over his own feet while trying to walk. Mercy and Travis were getting into the drivers back seat with flashlights and tools and were leaving. Benton couldn't seem to make his feet move fast enough to catch them before they left.

Mercy's heart was broken. She never thought in a million years that she would see Benton kissing someone else. She had tears in her eyes, but she could not cry because she was so angry with Benton and Bailey. Bailey struck her as the sneaky kind, but she trusted Benton. How could he do this to her? Didn't he love her?

Mercy and Benton had plenty of times when they were making out and could have had sex, Benton really pushed hard sometimes but Mercy always told him she wasn't ready. She wanted to save herself for the right time and place. Boy, is she glad now that she didn't give into Benton's pleadings and her own desire. Is this why he betrayed her? Were his basic needs greater than his love for her? Would he blame his betrayal on his drinking? These are the questions she asks herself all the way back to Travis's truck. She felt like her whole world was crashing down on her right now. Travis was there to comfort her, as always. Travis was solid, she could depend on him when she couldn't depend on anyone else.

Travis quickly fixed his truck and they were on their way home again. This whole night seemed like a nightmare. They didn't talk much on the way home. Mercy sat and cried quietly. Travis held her hand all the way home. He didn't know what to say to her to comfort her, so he just gently held her hand. Travis pulled up in front of Mercy's house around two in the morning. Mercy quietly went up the back stairs, even knowing that her Mother would be listening for her before she herself could go to sleep.

CHAPTER 9

Vacation was over, and Mercy was starting nursing school at Christ Hospital tomorrow. Benton had called her house at least a dozen times a day and came to her house at least once a day, trying to talk to her before he had to go back to college. Mercy didn't want to talk to him, she was that hurt. She thought a lot about what happened, and she wasn't even sure she ever wanted to see Benton again.

Travis stopped over frequently to see how she was and she did see him for a short while. They would sit on the front porch and talk. She wanted to talk about anything but Benton and Bailey. She also took a walk at least once a day, it helped clear her head. She would walk up to the old church where she used to sit and watch for Benton to come by. She missed him so much and wanted to see him and she loved him, but her heart still hurt too much. Mercy finally told her Mother what happened because she told her Mother a lot of things that went on in her life and she thought that maybe her Mother could give her some insight. Her mother basically told her that if Benton cheated once on her, he would probably do it again but that she had to follow her own heart and figure things out because in the end, it was her decision. By the time fall break was over, she still didn't know what she wanted to do about Benton. She would go back to nursing school and put all her energy into studying.

Two weeks later, Benton was still calling her and trying to see her. She decided that she was ready to see him and told him to pick her up on Saturday and they would go somewhere and talk.

Benton was right on time to pick her up on Saturday, even after driving in all the way from college. He held the car door open for Mercy and she climbed in. She hadn't said anything to him yet, not even a greeting. They drove to a small coffee shop in town. They went in silently, sat down and ordered their coffee. Benton looked like he was scared to death. Mercy looked at him with tears in her eyes and started, "Benton, how could you have cheated on me with Bailey? I thought you loved me, do you? Suddenly, she wanted to talk and was full of questions. She was also feeling angry still. Benton looked her in the eye and tried to hold her hand, but she pulled it back. She didn't want him to touch her or she might fall apart completely again for the hundredth time. Benton looked at her with sad eyes and replied, "Mercy, I am so sorry for what happened, you don't even know how sorry I am. I didn't mean for it to happen and kissing was as far as it went. I'll do anything to make it up to you, to convince you that you are the only woman I want in my life." Mercy asked, "Well, what happened after I left the Chalet? "Benton replied, "Well, I'd just drank a few beers, nothing strong, then my mother fixed me a drink and told me I should go out to the spa and visit with Bailey because she was out there alone. I didn't see any harm in that. I just thought that we would talk about old times and what was going on in our lives now. The next thing I knew was that Bailey was kissing me. I don't want to sound like I wasn't responsible for what I did, because it was my fault that I let myself get in to that situation. Please forgive me Mercy, I would do anything to make you believe that I care for you a great deal and want you back." Mercy asked, "Care for me, I thought you loved me?" Benton said, "I do, I do". He still didn't say it. Benton went on, "Bailey knows that we could never get along, that is why we broke up in the first place, believe me when I say that I don't have any feelings for her other than as a friend." He looked miserable and at the same time, he did sound repentant. Mercy also realized that Benton's mother played a big part in his deceit. After a long, uncomfortable silence, she said, "I love you Benton, but you have to promise me that anything like that will never happen again. I can't go through something like this again." He said, "I promise Mercy, if you will just take me back, I won't even ever touch another drink." Mercy was surprised by this statement and was feeling a little selfish and she told him, "Alright Benton, I'll give you another chance but if I ever see another drink in your hand or if you do anything that even makes me the slightest bit suspicious, I will leave you and I will never see or talk to you again." Benton got up and came over to her side of the booth. He hugged her gently for a long while and then said, "Let's get out of here." He pulled up outside of her house and they kissed and hugged for a long time. Mercy felt like she was back where she belonged when he held her. They wouldn't see each other again until Christmas break.

Christmas break was here already! Mercy was on her way home from nursing school and Christmas break started tomorrow. She was glad to have the time off, she felt exhausted. She went to school Monday through Friday and still worked two nights a week in town at the fabric store for extra money. She also tried to help her mother out at home whenever she could.

Her mother was also still working but she had cut back to three days a week because she was still feeling sick most of the time. She had lost forty pounds in the last six months. She was stubborn about going to the doctor. Her mother always said that when you go to the doctor, you end up sicker because you always ended up with something wrong with you. Besides, her mother thought she could stand to lose a little weight. Mercy tried and tried to get her to go the doctor, telling her that she lost too much weight in too short a time and reminded her of how many days a week she could hardly get out of bed. Her mother was getting weaker by the day. Her father had insurance for the both through his work at the car company, but her mother said the deductible was too expensive. Her mother always had an excuse not to go see a doctor. On the days that her mother felt too bad to get out of bed, Mercy would take care of her in the mornings before she left for school and after she got home. Mercy would fix her meals and wait on her hand and foot. Mercy's mother really did not get any extra help from her brothers and sisters. They had all gone their separate ways with their own lives and were too busy to even visit occasionally. Of course, they all showed up on holidays for "Mom's" home cooking and then they would leave before the mess was cleaned up, leaving it all for Mercy to deal with.

The next year of school went pretty much like the first one only it was much harder. Mercy felt like all she did was study. She was keeping her grades up and decided that she loved nursing, loved taking care of other people. There was such a shortage of nurses right now that the pay for them was very competitive.

Benton was in his last year of pre-med. He would be finished with that when Mercy graduated in May. Mercy hoped that her mother would be feel up to coming to her graduation. Mercy's father would probably be home, sitting in his chair, staring at the television and drunk on her graduation night.

Graduation night was here! Mercy would be taking her state boards in a month to get her RN license, but they gave her a paper to use until then so that she could start work. Mercy's mother felt well enough to go to the graduation and Mercy could not be happier. Mercy had saved a little money from her part time job and so she decided to go shopping. She had intended to buy herself a new dress for graduation, but instead, she decided to buy her mother a dress. She had never bought anything nice for her mother her whole life. She bought her the most beautiful, blue dress she had ever seen. She hoped her mother would like it. She also bought her a pair of comfortable, black shoes to wear with it. Her mother was always complaining about how much her feet hurt. Mercy had to take a guess at the sizes.

When Mercy got home, her mother was laying down. She said she felt okay, just wanted to have enough energy to make it through the graduation and then out with Mercy for a while. When she got up and had a cup of coffee, Mercy said to her, "I have a gift for you. I hope you like it!" Mercy had wrapped the dress and shoes up in a big, white box, not unlike the one that her mother wrapped for her for her prom dress and shoes. Her mother opened it and took the dress out. Her mother looked at it and said it was the most beautiful dress she had ever owned. She asked Merch how she could afford such a nice dress on her part-time job and Mercy replied, "Don't worry about it, it's okay". The same words her mother had used on her. Mercy pleaded, "Please go and try it on Momma, I want to see if it fits". Her mother went to her bedroom and put the dress and shoes on. It fit perfectly, and Mercy thought that her mother had never looked more beautiful. Mercy's mother twirled around and said, "I feel like a princess". Mercy's exact words four years before. Mercy told her Momma that she had to be ready by six o'clock. Benton would be picking them up then. At that moment, Mercy's father walked in the bedroom and asked, "Where are you going at six o'clock?" Mercy's mother replied, "Remember I told you, Mercy is graduation from nursing school tonight?" He replied, "Well, I ain't going to go and sit and sweat in some auditorium with five hundred other people just to try to get a glimpse of Mercy getting a piece of paper. You can go without me." Then he looked at her mother and said, "I hope you are not gonna wear that damn dress. You look like a cow in it." Mercy's heart hurt but she didn't say anything. She knew that her father wouldn't go anyway, and it was just like him to make her mother feel bad, so he wouldn't feel guilty about not going himself. Mercy just kept her mouth shut and told her mother again what time Benton was picking them up. Mercy whispered in her ear, "Don't listen to him, you look beautiful." Her father went back to his chair and his beer.

Graduation was great and not nearly as lengthy as she had anticipated. The graduates were all congratulating each other and then one of Mercy's friends from school ask her if she was coming to the graduation party they were having at one of her friend's house. Mercy said she and Benton would love to come later but first they were taking her mother out to dinner and then back home. Mercy's mother was beaming with pride. It's not every day that you have a child that graduates from college.

Mercy and Benton took her mother to "La Pierre's", the fancy restaurant where Mercy and Benton had their first date. Mercy's mother had never been or even seen a restaurant as nice as this one. Even though it was Mercy's graduation, she felt like a queen. With Benton's help, they all ordered dinner and had easy conversation. Benton made a toast to Mercy and all her hard work. When Mercy and Benton were finished with their dinner, Mercy looked over at her mother's plate and said, "Momma, you hardly ate a thing would you like to take your dinner home? "Her mother replied, "No, I think I have eaten all I want, it was delicious." Her mother was starting to look tired, so Mercy suggested that they take her mother home, and her mother seemed glad about that. When they arrived at Mercy's house, she and Benton walked her mother to the door and then they left to go to the after-graduation parties. Benton did not seem too excited about going to any party of Mercy's friends but at least most of them were girls."

When Mercy's mother walked in the kitchen and started to make herself some tea, her father walked in and asked, "So, how was the spoiled, little brat's graduation?" Her mother looked at him like she just couldn't believe he could be so mean, but in truth, she knew that he could be.

The summer was great. Benton had borrowed his father's boat and they had gone boating on the Ohio River with Travis and Madison a few times. Toward the end of the summer, Benton started getting very moody. Mercy never knew what kind of mood he was going to be in when he picked her up to go out. He has been quiet lately and that is not normally his style. He'd been grumpy and short with Mercy. She didn't like these big mood changes at all. She wanted her old Benton back. When she would ask him, "What's wrong? he gave his standard answer, "nothing". Mercy thought the closer it got to him going back to college, the grumpier he got. She ask, "Are you in a bad mood because you don't want to go back to school" He replied, "No, I really like all of my classes and I'm not in a bad mood. I wish you would quit saying that and leave me alone about it." The Saturday night before Benton had to return to college, he thought that it would be nice for him and Mercy to go out to dinner alone.

CHAPTER 10

Mercy arrived home one night, after a long shift in the emergency room at the hospital, she was so tired. She got home about twelve thirty in the morning. Her mother was still awake and sitting in the kitchen sipping hot tea. Mercy came in the house and gave her Momma a kiss on the cheek and ask, "How are you feeling Momma?" Her mother replied, "Mercy, sit down, I have something I want to talk to you about." This kind of scared Mercy but she did as she was told and sat down next to her mother. Her mother started, "Mercy, I finally took your advice and went to the doctor a few weeks ago and the doctor had me get some test done." Mercy had that "deer in the headlight look on her face." Mercy started to shake, and it felt like it started in her toe's and moved up her body. She sensed that this was not going to be good. Her mother said, "The doctor says I have stomach cancer and that I need an operation to remove it." Mercy didn't hear anything after "stomach cancer". Mercy started crying uncontrollably. Her mother held her and whispered, "Don't worry, the doctor said he would take out part of my stomach and then I would get some chemo and radiation, which should cure me." Mercy was still crying but there was a little glimmer of hope in her eyes. Mercy replied, "Momma, I'm sorry I'm crying. I don't want to upset you more. I'm just scared for you. Of course, I will go with you to the hospital and make sure you get to all of your treatments."

Mercy sat and talked with her mother a while longer and then she told her, "I have a date with Benton tonight before he goes back to college, so I am going upstairs to see what I have to wear." Her mother hugged her and said, "Okay Mercy, I think I'll go and lay down for a little while." Mercy replied, "Momma, is there anything I can do for you? Do you want me to fix you something to eat?" Her mother replied, "No, I'm fine."

Mercy went up to her room, passing her father in the living room where he was sound asleep in his recliner snoring loudly. When she got up to her room, she lay on her bed and cried for her Mother until she thought she had no more tears left. "Maybe", she told herself, "It will work out alright and Momma will get well again." She put some cold water on her face and eyes, so they wouldn't look swollen for her date with Benton. She didn't really feel like going out but she knew he was going back to college and she needed him tonight. She wanted to be held in his strong arms and for him to tell her that everything would be alright.

Benton wanted to go to the Holliday Inn where there was a good band playing in the bar and they could order some appetizers. Also, he thought, he would have Mercy at a hotel. He and Mercy still hadn't had sex. They had come close a couple of times, but Mercy always stopped him, saying, "I'm just not ready". Benton thought that maybe tonight would be the night, after all, they had been dating for two years now, it was time. If she really loved him, she would.

Mercy took her time getting ready. She felt like she was in slow motion. Benton picked her up at eight thirty. He could tell that she was upset by the time they arrived at the hotel. They had not gotten out of the car yet, when he asked her, "Is there anything wrong?" The flood gates opened, and Mercy thought, "Not again, how could I have any more tears left?" Benton impatiently put his arm around Mercy and waited for her to stop crying and to be able to tell him what was wrong. Mercy finally told him, "My Mother just told me this tonight that she has stomach cancer and she needed an operation, then chemo and radiation." As a nurse, Mercy knew how hard this was going to be on her Mother. Benton was quiet for a minute and then said, "well, they can cure it can't they?" Mercy replied, "maybe, I don't know. We will see after her operation." Mercy thought that Benton would put his arm around her and give her some comfort or encouraging words, he didn't, he moved to his side of the car, looking annoyed. Finally, he said, "well, let's go inside and then you can go to the restroom and freshen up or do whatever it is that you girls do in there for so long. We can have some dinner and listen to the band." Mercy thought, "How callous of him, doesn't he know that I am in pain?" She thought for a minute and guessed since this was her last night with Benton until Thanksgiving, she would try to have a good time with him before he left.

They went into the hotel and Mercy went to the restroom and put some cold water on her face, again. She left the restroom and went to the large bar area they had, right inside the front door. The music sounded good but very loud like each instrument was trying to play "king of the hill." Benton found them a table near the front of the stage. Mercy asked Benton if they could sit in the back of the bar because she had a headache and the loud music would make her headache worse. Benton thought, "Oh, brother, this is going to be a good night. She is already complaining." Benton followed Mercy to a table in the back of the bar. Mercy had told Benton a while back that she didn't mind if he drank a couple of beers, she just didn't want him to get drunk on his ass and do something he would regret later, like the Bailey incident. Mercy never was a big drinker, but she did like an occasional glass of wine.

She thought she could use a whole bottle tonight. Mercy asked Benton if he would go to the bar and get them a drink. He said, "What would you like, a coke?" She looked him in the eye and she said, "No, I'll have a glass of white wine. No, never mind, please bring me a whole bottle." Benton looked surprised and thought, "This might turn out to be a good night after all." He returned with their drinks and sat down, just as the waitress was asking Mercy if they would like anything. They ordered a couple of appetizers and ate and drank while watching the band play and people dancing on the dance floor. The band finally played a slow song and Benton ask her if she would like to dance and she said, "yes". Benton held her tight on the dance floor and she could feel his hot breath on her neck. She was glad that she decided to come in here and try to have a good time with Benton before he leaves. She was enjoying herself. She could feel the effect of the wine she drank and was feeling very relaxed.

It was two in the morning before they knew it and just about everyone in the bar had gone home or up to their rooms. Benton and Mercy had danced almost every slow song the band had played. The bar was getting ready to close and the band was wrapping it up. Benton put his arm around the back of Mercy's chair and whispered in her ear how beautiful she was. The breath on her ear was hot and her head was spinning. Benton said, "Mercy, it's so late, why don't we spend the night?" At first, Mercy said, "no" but Benton was very convincing and so she thought since they had both been drinking, it really wasn't a good idea for either one of them to drive. Mercy finally said, "Okay, but only because we have both been drinking and I know I am a little drunk, but don't think that anything is going to happen just because we spend the night together." Benton knew that Mercy was drunk. This is the first time he had ever seen her this way and he knew he would change her mind once they got to the room, he was elated! He and Mercy were finally going to seal their relationship by making love. He hurriedly paid the bill at the bar and checked out a room before Mercy could change her mind. Mercy stood up and found it funny that she was a little bit shaky and her balance wasn't very good. She had never been drunk before. Benton gently held onto her and lead her up to the room. When they got in the room, Benton closed the door behind them, sticking the "Do Not Disturb" sign on the door handle.

Mercy went and lay down on the bed. She told Benton, "Wow, my head is really spinning." Benton lay down next to her on the bed and started kissing her. Her response made him feel like he could keep going. She kissed him back like she would never see him again. Benton pulled off his shirt and Mercy already knew that he was well built. She loved his hard muscles and the little patch of hair on his chest.

She ran her fingers over him and she could hear his sharp intake of breath and then him breathing hard. Benton had removed all his clothes and her blouse, bra and pants before she knew it. He did it very fast and she hardly noticed because she was busy kissing him. Next, he removed her panties. They were laying on top of the bed spread. Benton was running his hands over her body and relishing every minute of it. Maybe he did love her, he wasn't quite sure sometimes. She was so beautiful, and her skin just seemed to glow. Suddenly, Mercy sat up with a horrible look on her face. Benton already knew what was coming because of his experience with drinking. Mercy hopped off the bed and ran for the bathroom. She started vomiting and it seemed like it would never end. Her stomach hurt from the constant heaving. Benton lay on the bed naked and watched television, waiting for her to finish. Mercy rinsed her mouth out with the mouth wash the hotel provided and washed her face. Finally, Mercy came out of the bathroom, wrapped in a towel. She walked over to where her clothes lay on the floor, snatched them up and was heading back to the bathroom to put them back on. She was so embarrassed that Benton had seen her naked. She had never been naked in front of a guy before and she was suddenly very self-conscious about her body. Benton asked in surprise, "What are you doing?" She didn't answer him. Her mind was racing. "Why would Benton do such a thing?" She had told him countless times that she wanted to wait until she was married to give herself to her husband. Benton's response was always the same. "You know that we will be together forever." Mercy, all at once was furious with Benton. He tried to take advantage of her drunken state. As a matter of face, he kept encouraging her to drink more and more, even though she was getting a terrible headache again. She came out of the bathroom with her clothes on. Benton looked at her and asked, "Why did you get dressed?" She told him, "You took advantage of me, now I am leaving." He said, "You can't leave yet, I thought we were going to make love for the first time?" She said that she had never agreed to that and that wasn't going to happen, not tonight. Benton became angry. He jumped up off the bed, grabbed his clothes and got dressed. She could see him getting angrier by the minute. He didn't know why he wanted Mercy so badly when he could get any girl he wanted. He guessed it was the old thing, you want what you can't have. He walked over and punched a hole in the wall right next to Mercy's head and it scared her to death. He yelled, "son of a bitch!" Your nothing but a little tease, that's what you are. You never wanted to make love with me in the first place. I doubt that you would even like sex. Your just one big prude Mercy. It's apparent you don't really love me, and I'm out of here. I'll find someone else who wants to love me, someone who cares. I'll pay the bill on my way out, just leave whenever you want to. Mercy was stunned into silence as he left the room. She knew he had drank too much but she had never seen him like this and he had never talked to her like this before. When she felt like she could finally move, she walked over to the phone to call Travis. Travis would come and get her, just like he always had. She hated to call him this late, but she didn't have anyone else to call and she didn't have any money on her for a cab. When she felt like she could finally move, she walked over to the phone to call Travis. The phone rang about five times when Travis picked up. "Travis, it's Mercy, I'm at Holliday Inn. Do you think you could come and get me and take me home? I know it's late and I hate to ask, but please?" Travis answered, "Mercy you sound funny, have you been drinking?" He had never known of Mercy drinking alcohol of any kind. She replied, "Yes, I have, and I am a little drunk, so is it possible that you could come and get me? I don't have any money on me for a cab." Travis was a little worried and said,

"Of course, I will come and get you. Your where, a Holliday Inn? Are you okay?" She said, "Travis I'm fine, I just need to get out of here. Travis didn't put it and replied, "I'll be there in thirty minutes."

Mercy said on the side of the bed while waiting for Travis. She thought of her mother again and started crying again with the new wave of emotions. This has been the worst day and night of her life. She assured herself that her mother was going to be okay. Then she thought about Benton. She couldn't believe what came out of his mouth. She couldn't believe how he had talked to her, like she was a dog." Oh my God, she loved him so much, how could he do this to her?" He couldn't possibly love her.

True to his word, Travis picked her up within thirty minutes. She was waiting outside in the parking lot for him, it was about four in the morning. She climbed in his truck and it was obvious that she had been crying. Travis hated seeing the woman he loved in so much pain. He asked, "Do you want to talk about it? What happened? did Benton hurt you in any way? If he did, I'll kill that asshole."

Mercy answered, "Travis, Travis, please calm down, I'm okay." She started crying all over again. Great big sobs of grief for her mother and the loss of Benton, the man she loved." Travis pulled over to the side of the parking lot and just put his arms around her and held her there. Finally, Mercy told him what was going on with her mother. He felt so bad for Mercy because he knew that she and her mother were very close. He said, "I'm sure with treatment that your mother will be okay." He tried to assure her that her mother would be fine. Mercy noted the big difference in how Travis responded to the news about her mother and how much he tried to comfort her, as opposed to Benton barely caring. Finally, Travis said, "Mercy what are you doing here anyway, fearing the worst. She told him that they had come here for appetizers and to hear the band play. She said she felt like she needed a drink after hearing the news about her mother. She told him that she was having a couple of glasses of wine and she got drunk before she even knew what was happening. Mercy told him that since she and Benton were both drunk, that they shouldn't drive, and they decided to spend the night at the hotel. Mercy told him she was laying on bed, kissing Benton. Travis really didn't want to hear that but he didn't want to interrupt her while she was telling him what went on. She told him while they were kissing, she suddenly jumped up and went to the bathroom and vomited her guts out. Travis flew angry, "Did he hurt you? You better tell me if he did." "No, Mercy replied, he didn't hurt me physically, just emotionally. He wanted sex and I denied him. I've told him since almost the beginning of our relationship that I would not have sex with anyone until I was married. Maybe it's my fault. What girl my age hasn't had sex yet? From the way they talk at school, I'd guess not very many. What it boils down to is that I didn't give it up and Benton got angry and stomped out of the room. He paid the bill for the room and left me stranded with no way to get home." Mercy saw the hate in Travis's eyes. She knew that if Benton were here right now, Travis would hurt him. Travis already had told her, "If he hurts you, I will kill him!" After talking for a couple of hours, Travis said, "Well, I guess it's time to get you home, your Momma will be worried.

Mercy was heartbroken. She didn't want to lose Benton, but she didn't love him as much as she did this morning. He had turned into this monster that she didn't recognize. Maybe that's what happens when he has had too much to drink. Travis got her home and helped her out of the truck. He walked her up to the door and asked, "Do you want me to go in with you?" She said, "No, but thank you so much for coming to get me. You have rescued me twice now and maybe someday I can return the favor." She gave Travis a big hug and a kiss on the cheek and went inside. Mercy was walking up the back steps to bed and she could hear her mother moaning in her sleep, she did that a lot lately. When she got to her room, she lay down on her little bed and cried some more. She started thinking that maybe what happened was her fault, maybe she was a tease, she shouldn't have drunk so much and on and on until she fell asleep.

The next morning, Benton's mother was sitting at the kitchen counter when Benton walked in. She said, "Benton, you look like crap, what have you been up to?" He replied, "nothing mother." She noticed that his eyes were all puffy with dark circles under them, his lips were dry and cracked and his color looked very pale. She said, "Well, you look terrible, is there anything I can do?" He replied, "Well, if you must know mother, Mercy and I broke up last night over something stupid. That should make your day." His mother didn't ask what they argued about. She was so happy about it, she didn't think before she spoke, and she blurt out, "That saves me a lot of money." He looked at her strangely and asked, "What do you mean? What did you do Mother?" She told him, "Well, now that you are broken up, I'll tell you. I offered Mercy a whole lot of money to break up with you when you brought her home that first Christmas. That poor white trash of a girl had the nerve to turn down money that could have helped her and her whole family. I guess she was really in love with you then since she didn't accept my offer." Benton sadly said, "Yes, but I don't think so any longer, we had the worst argument ever. We had both been drinking and I said a lot of mean things to her and I don't know if it can be fixed. I love her for not taking the money and running when she could have, that means she's loved me from the start." His mother replied, "That doesn't mean she loved you, that just means that she's too proud to take help, that's all. Forget about her Benton, like I've told you, she doesn't fit in here in our world." Benton came very close to his mother's face and looked her in the eyes and said, "I don't ever, ever, want to hear you talk about Mercy like she was a piece of trash ever again, do you hear me Mother." Benton had never talked to his mother that way before. His mother was taken aback and shocked by his sudden abruptness. She said softly, "Okay Benton." Benton took his coffee out to the garden to think about how he could fix this whole mess with Mercy. If he had been Mercy, he would have taken the money rather than count on someone like him. She probably wouldn't take him back now after he said the things to her that he did, and he wouldn't blame her. He thought that once he had gotten her up to the hotel room that she would give it up to him, with his charming ways, like any other girl he had ever dated had done. He should have known that she wouldn't because she had already told him "no" so many times. He knew she had moral standards. He just thought that since she had been drinking, he could change her mind. He knew she loved him because she told him so all the time. He wondered why he had never said, "I love you" back. He wondered if he really loved Mercy or if she was just a challenge to him, or he dated her because he knew his mother would not approve and he was tired of her trying to run his life. He didn't know but he did know that he cared for her very deeply.

Benton spent the next whole day on the phone, trying to talk to Mercy. He thought that since they had both been drinking that she just might forgive him for what he had done. After about the fiftieth call, late in the afternoon, Mercy's father answered the phone and said, "Mercy is busy taking care of her mother, she has the flu or something." Mercy was right, Benton thought, her father is clueless. Her father had been told about his wife's stomach cancer of course, but he wasn't really listening.

Mercy was in her mother's room, holding a bucket for her wile her mother vomited for what seemed like forever. Mercy then wiped her forehead with a cold cloth and helped her change her nightgown. She was resting now. She looked very pale to Mercy and for the first time, she noticed that her mother looked old. It was hard to believe that the one person who took care of her and her family all her life, was full of life and vibrant, was so weak and pale. It was eight o'clock now and Mercy was bone weary herself. Her mother seemed to be resting well now. She kissed her on the forehead and lay down beside her on the bed in case her mother woke up and needed something. They both slept straight through until the morning.

Mercy's Mother got up the next morning, got dressed and was having a pretty good day. She has her good days and bad. Mercy had to go work the three to eleven shifts in the emergency room, where she normally worked nights.

Benton had called all day and Mercy had not answered the phone. Her mother said, "Why has Benton been calling all morning, and why aren't you talking to him?" Mercy said, "We had a big argument last night. I should talk to him, it was really both our faults." Mercy's mother asks, "Do you love him?" and Mercy replied, "I think I have loved him for a long time." Mercy's mother saw the pain and sadness in Mercy's eyes when she spoke of him. Her mother told her, "If you love the boy, then talk to him the next time he calls and try to work it out." Mercy thought about this and decided her mother was right, as usual, she would talk to him the next time he called, as she was sure that he would. He called right before Mercy was getting ready to leave for work and he was so happy that Mercy answered the phone. Benton said, "Mercy, I don't expect you to forgive me for what happened last night, but could we talk about it?" Mercy answered, "I don't want to put you off Benton, but I have to go to work now. It takes me forty-five minutes on the bus to get there." He said, "Could I come and get you and take you to work?" She said, "No, but you can pick me up around eleven thirty tonight after my shift. I usually get out of there on time. Meet me at the front of the hospital then. She told him good-bye and hung up.

Benton was elated that Mercy would talk to him! Maybe he could get her back after all. He would lay on the charm like he had with all his previous girlfriends. That's one thing he knew he could do best.

Benton picked Mercy up right on time, in front of the hospital. When she got in the car, he kind of looked at her from the side and he thought that she really didn't look too angry, just tired. He pulled over into the visitor parking lot, found a secluded space and turned the car off. They were both quiet for a moment. Benton said, "Mercy, you don't know how sorry I am about what happened, can you ever find it in your heart to forgive me?" She looked at him, she loved that face and he did look repentant. She said, "Yes, Benton, I forgive you. Can you forgive me?" He replied, "What for?" She answered, "I know the night was partly my fault. I don't ever drink, and it went right to my head. I guess deep down, I am a tease." Benton replied, "No, Mercy, you aren't. You were just standing up for what you believe is best for you. Mercy, I thought you loved me and wanted to be with me. Don't you trust me?" She said, "I do love you Benton and I do trust you but my body is a gift. It is a gift that I will give to my husband one day. I know that sounds so old fashioned, but I want the fairy tale. I want it to be the right thing to do so that if feels right." She kissed him and said, "I love you Benton." He said, "me to." She had wondered if he really loved her, so she ask, "Benton do you really love me? You have never said that you love me, just "me to." He looked deeply into her eyes and said, "Of course I love you, you know that." He kissed her gently and then followed with, "You know I would never do anything to hurt you." They talked and kissed for another hour and the Benton said, "I'll take you home Mercy, you look tired." She answered, "Yes, I was up really late taking care of my mother, she was very sick." Benton was racking his brain to remember what she had told him about her mother but couldn't remember what she was sick from, so all he said was, "I hope she's feeling better soon."

When they arrived back to Mercy's house, they saw Travis's truck sitting by the curve in front of the house. Mercy was scared for a moment. She didn't know why he was at her house this late hour. When Benton pulled up in front of Travis's truck, he got out to open Mercy's door. At that moment, Travis jumped out of his truck and ran over to where Benton was. Travis grabbed the front of Benton's shirt and pushed him hard up against his car. Benton was a little scared of Travis because Travis was a big guy, much taller, with broad shoulders, and stronger than himself. It happened so fast that Mercy didn't have time to react to what was going on. Travis was very close to Benton's face when he said, in a menacing whisper. "If you ever, ever, hurt Mercy again, you will have to answer to me and I promise you, it won't be pretty." At that, Travis let Benton go and started walking back to his truck. When Travis grabbed the door handle of his car, Benton very bravely said, "Oooh, I am afraid of you Travis." Travis gave him a look that could kill and Benton knew that he shouldn't push him. Benton was afraid of Travis and rather stay out of his way. Mercy jumped out of Benton's Mustang and ran over to where Travis was standing next to his truck. She yelled, "Travis, what is the matter with you, why are you so angry with Benton? It's not like you to threaten someone. I've never seen you this upset." Travis told her, "I'm sorry Mercy, I just couldn't help myself. This is the second time Benton has hurt you and caused you pain and it will be the last, I will see to that. I love you so much, and you know that. I would do anything for you and I would never hurt you like he has. You don't hurt someone that you love." She hugged him and seeing what state of mind he was in right now, she knew him well enough not to say anything about his actions. Travis loves her, and she knew that he was just looking out for her best interest. Finally, she said, "Thank you Travis for looking out for me, but I am a big girl now and I can handle Benton. I do love that you were willing to fight for me." He said, "Mercy, I'll fight for you until the day I die." Travis was being so dramatic. He continued, "Why don't you leave that jerk and let me show you how a real man should treat the person he loves." Gently, she said, "Travis, we have had this conversation before, I love Benton and what happened the other night was partly my fault. Please try to get along with him, I love you both." That was the first time that Travis could remember that Mercy said she loved him back. Travis got in his car and drove away. Benton walked over to where Mercy was standing and said, "That was fun. Can't he see that you love me and not him? He really needs to just get over it. You don't make it easy for him to stay away from you when you call him to pick you up all the time." This made Mercy angry, she said, "I've known Travis almost all of my life, we grew up together and he is like a brother to me. I don't love him in the way that I love you. He is just looking out for me. Can we please just forget about it?" Benton said, "Alright, but he better stay away from the both of us. Mercy kissed Benton goodbye and went inside the house.

Mercy's father was in the kitchen drinking coffee and eating a cheese sandwich. When she walked in, her father said, "Where have you been? Your lazy mother is in bed pretendin to be sick again, and I don't have no one to fix me any dinner. This made Mercy so angry, but she knew better than to start an argument with her father because she knew it would only turn out badly. Although he had never hit her, she didn't want him to get to the point where he might, besides, there was no point in talking to him. She answered, "I'll go in and see about Momma." He said, "Well, I guess I'll just finish this cheese sandwich and go on in to work. It's already one in the morning and I'm already two hours late. If I get fired, it will be your and your mother's fault. It's a bad day when a man can't even get a decent meal in his own house." At that, Mercy left the room to go and see about her Mother.

Mercy went into her mother's room and it was very dark. Usually she has a little night light on. Mercy felt her way over to a little lamp in the corner that wasn't very bright and turned it on. She went to her Mother's bed and her Mother didn't even move. Mercy felt her skin and it was very hot. She put a cool cloth on her forehead. At that, her mother kind of woke up and looked at her. She started talking gibberish, not making any sense and starting to get more agitated every minute. She didn't even know who Mercy was. Mercy assumed that her Momma had a bad infection and knew that she needed to go to the hospital. Mercy called an emergency ambulance. When the ambulance arrived, Mercy told them to take her mother to Christ Hospital, where she worked. She told them that her mother would get faster treatment there and because she knew everyone who worked in the emergency room.

When they arrived in the emergency room, there was no change in her mother's fever or mental status. They treated her right away. After running some test, they discovered that she had sepsis, a blood infection brought on by a kidney infection. They treated her with IV antibiotics and told Mercy they would have to admit her to the hospital. She would have to stay for three to four days, receiving antibiotics and until her fever and mental status returned to normal. Mercy stayed with her until she was taken to her own room. She made sure that her mother was settled in and then she whispered in her ear, "I love you so much Momma. I will be back in a few hours, please just sleep and get better." Mercy knew that she would have to go home and get a few hours' sleep. Mercy called a cab from the nurse's station and talked with a few other nurses she knew until it was time for the cab to arrive. It would be about a thirty-minute ride home to Northside. When she got home, she listened to her messages. There was a message from Benton and one from Madison. She hadn't talked to Madison in a couple of weeks, she had been so busy, and she felt bad about that. She would call her soon. She went up to her room and fell into bed exhausted.

Mercy woke early the next morning and was angry with herself for sleeping so long. She had set her clock but slept right through the ringing. She had wanted to call and check on her mother a couple of hours ago. She jumped up, put coffee on and then jumped in the shower. She heard someone come in the downstairs back door while she was drying off and then she remembered, it was time for her father to get home from work. She ran downstairs and said, "Hi Dad. I had to take Momma to the hospital last night and they admitted her. She has a bad blood infection from her kidneys." Her Father replied, "Oh yeah? Well that's too bad. When is she coming home?" Mercy told him that It could be a few days and that her mother had to have IV antibiotics. Mercy was in a hurry but didn't want to rush her Father's understanding of what was going on. Still, she asked him if she could use his car. He said, "Sure kid, just fill it up with gas before you bring it home and have it home by ten tonight, so I can get to work on time. They almost fired me last night for being two hours late. I told them there was a family emergency, which isn't a lie because having no body here to fix my dinner is an emergency. Look at how skinny I am Mercy." Truth be told, he had several rolls around his middle, overflowing his belt. She grabbed the keys off the table and said, "See you later Dad." Driving on her way to the hospital, she contemplated the fact that her father showed no concern over her mother in the least and never said anything about going to see his wife in the hospital. Mercy was finding it hard to concentrate on the road and she just got her license recently. She was saving money for a car and she almost had enough. No more busses!

When Mercy arrived at the hospital, she went straight to her mother's room on the third floor and the door was closed. She opened the door slowly and the room was dark except for the glow of the television hanging on the wall. She walked over to her mother and looked at her face. She seemed to be resting well. Mercy pulled a chair over to her mother's bedside, reached in and held her hand very gently. She had IV's in both arms. She looked at her mother's hands. Her hands were long and lean and wrinkled with brown age spots on the tops of them. Mercy loved her mother's hands. Her hands had been through a lot of life, like holding babies, working for other people, playing piano. These hands also dealt out punishment to her children. Her mother wanted so much for her children to grow up and do something with their life. She didn't want them to take after their Father, a drunk and a womanizer. Now that her father was older, he can't find another woman that wants him or would put up with his shit, except Mother. Mercy's mind kept wondering on like this until she heard, "Mercy, why do you have tears in your eyes?" Mercy looked at her and said, "Momma, you are yourself again!" Her mother replied, "Well, who else would I be?" Mercy told her how sick she had been and what was going on. Mercy was just so thrilled that her mother was better. Her mother said, "I've taken care of you all of your life, now it's you, taking care of me. Well, you know Mercy, nothing can keep me down for long. I've always told you, Heaven don't want me and the devil is afraid of me, so I'm not going anywhere soon."

Mercy stayed with her for a few more hours and then she had to go home and grab a couple hours sleep before work tonight and she had to manage to eat something during that time. She stopped on the way home and got a fast food cheeseburger. It tasted extra good because she was so hungry. She also prepared a meal for her father so that he wouldn't get upset about not having his dinner waiting for him when he woke up. Mercy really didn't care about her Dad's dinner, but she wanted everything to be calm when her mother came home tomorrow.

When Mercy pulled up to the curb of her house and shut the car off, she saw Benton in the rearview mirror, walking towards her car. Mercy rolled down the window and said, "Hi Benton." He replied, "Hi Mercy, can we talk? "She said "Sure, let's just go over and sit on my front porch, this car is hot. Benton ask her why she hadn't returned any of his calls and she told him about what happened with her mother and she just didn't have time to call. He said, "Mercy, someone always has a minute to call. I think you are ignoring me." Mercy didn't like where this conversation was going. She said, "Benton, I'm really tired, can we talk later? I've only had a couple hours of sleep in the last twenty-four hours." He answered, "Well don't you think our relationship is just as important as you and your Mother's? Besides, you know she is in good hands." This infuriated Mercy and her face turned a bright red. Mercy looked him in the eye and said, "Benton, I'm going into the house, and I'll see you in a couple of days." At that, she went inside, leaving Benton with a dumbfounded look on his face. He couldn't believe that she would just get up and walk away from him when he was trying to have a serious conversation with her. Maybe that is why he could never get the "I love you's" out.

One of the nurses had called Mercy a little earlier and told her that her mother had taken a turn for the worse. Her mother still had a fever, but she was confused again and combative. When Mercy walked down the halls of the hospital, towards her mother's room, she didn't see one person. It was eerily quiet. This annoyed Mercy because she knew that if her mother had wanted to, she could have gotten up and just walked out of the hospital without anyone knowing right away. Mercy walked into her mother's room and up to her bed and said, "Momma, how are you feeling?" Her mother replied, "I'm just fine and dandy,' and I'm not your Momma." Mercy got her attention again and said, "It's me, Mercy, Momma, you know, I'm your youngest daughter." Her mother went still and concentrated on Mercy's face, and replied, "You're not my daughter, my daughter is in school right now, it's only ten in the morning and you're not nearly as beautiful as my Mercy." Her mother was starting to get agitated now and said, "Well, where the hell am I? If I don't get someone here to take me home, I'll call a cab. This is a damn prison, that's what it is, they can't keep me, I'll kick all their asses! Those rat bastards better let me out of this God forsaken place!" At that, Mercy started to laugh. In all her twenty years, she had never heard her Mother curse. It turned into one of those belly laughs that hurt your stomach and you can't seem to stop. Her other looked at Mercy and started laughing also, even though she had no idea of what she was laughing at. Laughing that hard seemed to make her mother tired and she settled back down in the bed. Mercy just sat by her bed or doing any little thing that she could think of to make her mother more comfortable. When she finally slept, Mercy left the room quietly and went around the corner to the nurse's station. There were three nurses sitting behind the desk; snacking and talking to each other. She didn't know any of these nurses because she worked in the ER on the night shift. Mercy said, "UH, EXCUSE ME!" That got their attention and even scared them a little. Mercy continued, "I'd like to know which one of you is my mother's nurse, room 302?" One nurse spoke up and said, "I am, my name is Diane. Can I help you with something?" Mercy found her demeaner to be condescending and replied, "Yes, yes you can do something for me, or rather, for my mother." Diane quickly replied, "We are taking excellent care of your mother." To that, Mercy replied, "No, you are not. I have been in that room with my mother for the last two hours and not one person came in to check on her. Especially as combative as she was, she could have tried to get up alone and fallen, or who knows what else. I am a nurse also at this hospital and I know this is not how you were trained to take care of the patients here. My mother needs a lot of care right now and if I ever see her alone for more than ten minutes, I'm going to report you and I'm gonna kick someone's ass!" Mercy thought, yes Momma, that felt good." She turned to leave and said, "Please have the common courtesy to let me know if there are in changes in my mother's health."

When Mercy returned home, there was a message from Benton. She was so exhausted, she had to get a couple hours sleep, she would call Benton later. She went into the living room and her father was sitting in front of the television in his recliner, watching CSI. She said, "Hi Dad" and he returned her "Hi". He didn't even bother to ask how his wife was, just, "Is your mother coming home tonight?" Mercy answered, "No, maybe she will get to come home tomorrow. I must go upstairs and get some sleep before work tonight. I'll see you later Dad." On her way up Dad mumble, "lazy kids."

Mercy had set her clock for nine p.m., so she could shower and get ready for work. All her siblings had stopped by the hospital the last two days, except her one brother who lived in Florida. He did call her once while she was in the hospital. No one else wanted to help her take care of their Mother, but they were all there now like their one visit would be enough for her, like their visit was something special. She loved her brothers and sisters, but she didn't feel like they would desert her when she needed them most. Mercy just thought that they were jealous of her growing up because she was the baby and got more attention. Her older sister use to say, "Mercy, we all know that Momma loves you most." Maybe she did, Mercy didn't know, all she knew is that she and her mother were very close. Her mother never tried to be her friend, she was always in the role of her mother and she played it very well. She took care of all of them without complaint. She doled out the punishments, but there was never a day that Mercy didn't feel loved by her mother. She loved her father, just because he was her father, but for no other reason. How could he be so callous about his own wife's health? He was so selfish and only ever thought of himself and his needs.

CHAPTER 11

Mercy had only been asleep for half an hour when the phone rang. It rang several times and then she heard her father get up and get it. "Mercy, come down here, you have a phone call" he yelled. He laid the phone down and went back to his chair. Mercy rushed downstairs as fast as she could while half asleep. She grabbed the receiver, "Hello?", "Hello, may I speak to Mercy please?" Mercy replied nervously. "This is she, who's calling please?" Then she heard what she was hoping wasn't true. "This is Diane at the hospital, calling about your mother. She has taken a turn for the worse. She is no longer combative, and her mental status has improved but she has a high fever again and her pulse is thready, her breathing labored and her BP is high. Just wanted to let you know." Mercy said she would be there as soon as possible. Mercy went into the living room and ask her dad for the car keys since he was off tonight. She told him she had to go into work early and check on Momma. He said, "Okay, remember to fill it up with gas." Ten minutes later, she was in her uniform and out the door.

When Mercy got to her Mother's room, there was a nurse in there taking her vitals and another nurse hanging more IV antibiotics. Mercy could hear her mother's labored breathing from the door. Mercy walked to her bed, held her hand and said, "Momma, how are you feeling?" Her mother replied in a whisper, "I'm doing just fine child, they take good care of me here. How is your father doing?" Mercy was surprised and said, "He's doing fine, he just misses you." Mercy thought, "misses your cooking more likely." Her mother shut her eyes and she barely moved. She was breathing slow and very shallow. Mercy could barely see her chest move. Her mother whispered, "I'm so tired Mercy." Mercy replied, "That's okay Momma, just rest now. Mercy walked the nurse out and Diane told Mercy that there was no change in her mother since she had called her earlier. Mercy wanted to know if someone had called her doctor. Diane told her that she did, and the doctor ordered more antibiotics, a chest x-ray and lab test, which all of them had already been done, just waiting for the results.

Mercy went back to her mother's bedside and she appeared to be asleep, resting well. Mercy started to cry quietly. Her mother wasn't asleep and barely opened her eyes and said, "Mercy, I think my time is coming to an end." Mercy looked panic stricken and replied, "Oh Momma, don't say such things, you're doing fine." Her mother kept talking. "Mercy, out of all of my children, you are the one that I trust most. Please tell me that you will look after your father when I am gone." Mercy said, "Yes, Momma, I'll take care of him, just like you do." Mercy felt very uncomfortable talking to her mother like this. Mercy drew in a sharp breath. Mercy knew from working in the hospital that if someone thought they were getting ready to die, they were usually right. It was like they knew somehow. Mercy hoped that her mother was wrong. Her mother said, "Mercy, I'm not blind. I know what you think of your father, but you are wrong about some things. When you father doesn't seem concerned about me, doesn't come and see me here and acts totally selfish, it is just a wall he puts up to feel secure. He's just afraid that something will happen to me. He has always loved me, he just can't handle seeing me in the hospital." Mercy thought for a few moments and it was like a light that went on in Mercy's head. Her father really did love them all but put up a good defensive mechanism. Right now, Mercy was more interested in her mother than talking about her father. Her mother seems to be fading. She had quit talking and close her eyes. With tears running down her cheeks, Mercy said, "Momma, please don't go, not yet, I need for you to be here. I need you here to take care of me, teach me more things about life and love, please, you can't go yet. I love you so much, you are the best Mother in the whole world. I will let you rest and I will be back in a little while." That night, while working down in the ER, Diane paged Mercy to come to her mother's room. Mercy ran up the three flights of stairs, she didn't even wait for an elevator. When she was almost to her mother's room, an arm stopped her in the hallway. It was her mother's doctor. He said, "I'm so sorry, we did everything that we could, but your mother is without signs of life." Mercy had heard this speech from Drs. Many, many times in the hospital and until now, never new how much it hurt to hear them. Mercy fell to her knees right there in the hall of the hospital. She covered her face with her hands and just started screaming and crying at the same time. Mercy didn't know how she got there but she was in the visitor's lounge and someone was putting a cold washcloth on her face. Mercy knew that she had been screaming, she must have passed out, but now it was all coming back to her. The doctor telling her that her mother was dead. She couldn't believe it because her mother seemed to be resting well and talking in-between. Mercy found the doctor behind the nurse's station writing in her mother's chart. Mercy said, "What happened?" He 6told Mercy that they would do an autopsy, but he thought that she had died from a stroke.

Mercy decided to go in and see her mother before calling any of her brothers and sisters. She reverently walked up to her mother's bed. Mercy had seen plenty of dead people, but this was her Mother! Mercy didn't think she could stand it. She didn't think her life would ever be the same without her. Mercy was crying and decided to sit alone with her mother for a little while. She deserved it.

For the next half hour Mercy sat next to her mother. She whispered, "Momma, you have taken care of everyone else and now it's time for the angels to take care of you. I wanted so much for you to be able to see me walk down the aisle, to be there if I have children, but I know you will be watching from another place. I just want you to know that you were the best Mother that anyone could ask for. You taught me many good lessons about life and how to love, act like a lady and how to look for the best in someone. You sacrificed everything you had for us. I know that, and I love you for it. I hope I can be half the woman you are someday. I just can't believe that your heart won't beat any more, but I know a part of it beats inside of me. I'll see you again, Momma, I love you."

Mercy walked out of her Mother's room and called her siblings and her father. Her father sounded indifferent, but his voice was shaking. Mercy told him that she was on her way home. When Mercy got home, her father was sitting at the kitchen table, holding his head in his hands and crying. She went to him and just held him while he cried. She had never, in all her twenty years, seen her father shed a tear. At that moment, she knew what her mother had tried to tell her, her father loved her mother so much that the reason he acted the way he did was because he got so scared when her mother was sick, he was scared to death of losing her. Mercy said she and him would go down to the funeral home tomorrow and make the burial arrangements.

Mercy finally went to her room and cried some more. She needed Benton right now, but for some reason, she called Travis. Travis has always been there to pick her up. Travis knew her mother better than Benton and him and his mother would want to know of her death. She dialed Travis and he answered the phone. Mercy told him about her mother and he expressed his condolences and ask her if she needed anything or if she would like for him to come and sit with her. She said, "No thanks Travis, not tonight. I have a lot of people to call and arrangements to think about but thank you so much for offering."

Next, Mercy called Benton. He answered the phone on the second ring and said, "Hey Mercy, thanks a lot for calling me back. I've been waiting for two days for you to call me. What are you up to now?" Mercy replied, "Woah, slow down Benton and take a breath. My mother passed away today." Benton replied, "Oh Mercy, I am so sorry. Is there anything I can do for you?" Mercy said, "No, there isn't and thought he sounded very cold. Mercy hung up and then called her siblings that she didn't get a hold of the first time she called and gave them the news. They said, "Let us know when the funeral is, and we will be there." About ten minutes later, Travis showed up anyway. He sat with her on the front porch, with his arm around her. She thought to herself, "Benton should be here instead of Travis. He should have come anyway, just like Travis." Travis was young and strong and most of all compassionate. She took compassionate and comfort from him just being there. They sat like that, not talking, until two in the morning.

The day of her mother's wake and funeral was three days after her death. So many people brought all kinds of food. Almost anything you could imagine. Her mother had a lot of friends from church and work and they all loved her.

By midafternoon, the funeral was over and everyone she knew had been there, even Travis and his mother. Madison was also there but seemed to act a little cold towards Mercy. Mercy thought that is was because she hadn't called her in so long. Her father had kept a small life insurance policy on her mother to cover her burial expenses. Mercy was surprised at her father's foresight. She was glad that everything went so quickly. The one person that Mercy wanted to see the most was Benton. Although he sent flowers, he never showed up at the wake or the funeral to be with her.

Mercy had spent a couple of days with her siblings, until they had to return to their own lives. Her brother and sisters said that their mother didn't own much but whatever she and dad had, Mercy could have it. They weren't really being generous, they just knew that their Mother didn't have anything valuable except for her 14K gold wedding band that she never took off her finger for any reason. She was buried with it, as she requested so many years ago.

Late in the evening, on the fourth day after her Mother's death, Benton called. He said, "Mercy would you like to go out for dinner?" She said she'd love to, anything to get away from talking and thinking about her mother's death.

Benton and Mercy had gone out several times after that, but Benton seemed changed somehow. She couldn't quite put her finger on what had changed but he wasn't acting like himself. He didn't even kiss her as passionately anymore, like he was distracted. When she asked him about it, he replied, "Well, you know, kissing leads to other things, and we don't want a repeat of what happened last time we kissed too long and passionately. Mercy thought this was an odd statement coming from him. Usually, the more worked up he got, the more he liked it, even though he knew he wouldn't get the prize.

CHAPTER 12

Things continued pretty much the same in Mercy's life. Her father retired and has practically become a recluse, not talking to anyone. She hears him crying in the night because he misses his wife. Her father is looking very old and he has a broken heart. She doesn't know if he can take it.

Benton's family had a big party planned at Christmas time in their big house and of course, Benton asked Mercy to come, even though he knew his mother didn't approve. Mercy went to the party and met a lot of Benton's relatives that she hadn't yet met. Benton's mother was cordial to her, that's all. Mercy felt out of place and she was missing Christmas with her mother. She guessed she was standing their daydreaming when Benton tapped her on the shoulder and handed her a glass of fruit punch. Benton had a funny look on his face, like the cat who at the mouse. Benton and Mercy walked out onto the second-floor terrace. It was professionally decorated, beautiful greenery and the smell of snow in the air. There wasn't anyone else out her now, even though it was sixty-eight degrees, unseasonably warm for Christmas time. She looked at Benton and said, "Benton, are you ready? I didn't see you at my mother's funeral and you have been acting strange ever since." He said, "I'm so sorry Mercy, that I didn't make it, but I have been having issues with my mother. Nothing that concerns you. I'm sorry I haven't been myself lately." Benton gazed into Mercy's eyes and said with a shaky voice, "Mercy, I have something to ask you." She replied, "Benton, you know you can ask me anything." He took both of her tiny hands in his big, rough hands and got down on one knee. Mercy thought, "Oh my God, this was the last thing she thought would happen for a while." She started shaking also. Benton began, "Mercy we have been together since you were sixteen. We have been through many good and bad times together. I love your heart, soul and mind. Please, make me the luckiest man in the world and marry me. Will you marry me Mercy?" Mercy thought for a minute and then she said, "Well, I don't know Benton, you have never come right out and said that you love me. Do you love me Benton?" He gazed into her eyes and replied, "I love you Mercy. I love you more than even I can imagine. Since I met you by that church so many years ago, there has never been anyone else for me. I love you, I love you, I love you." Mercy looked at Benton and said, "I love you to Benton, I always have. Yes, I will marry you." She had tears in her eyes as he slipped the beautiful ring on her tiny finger. It was the biggest, most beautiful diamond she had ever seen, and it fit perfectly. She couldn't believe it, she was engaged! They stood and hugged each other for a long time and then Benton said, "It's chilly, let's go inside." They went in and went to where their name cards were at the main table in the middle of the room and sat down. Benton stood and started hitting his spoon on his glass to get everyone's attention. When he had everyone's attention, he asked Mercy to stand up beside him. He announced, "I would like to announce that Mercy and I are now engaged. I am the luckiest man in the world to have a woman like Mercy. I can hardly believe she said "Yes!" He turned to Mercy and said, "I love you Mercy" and she said it back. They sat down and there was a big round of applause and many, many well wishes. When his mother heard the announcement from the head of the table, she was livid. Her face was so red, Benton thought it looked like a tomato about to pop. Benton knew that she wouldn't approve but also knew that she would be angry because she didn't get to help him pick out a ring. His mother would have picked out a cheap, boring ring. When Mercy held out her hand to show everyone the ring, Benton's mother got up and left the table and went upstairs. Everyone else at the table wondered at her rudeness.

After dinner and some conversation with Benton's family, Benton said, "C'mon Mercy, let's leave this party. Let's go down to my Dad's boat on the river, it will be cold, but we can turn on the heaters. Mercy replied, "That sounds perfect Benton. A place for the two of us to be alone. It seems like the only time we get to be alone is in the car.

They said their good-byes to everyone, still not seeing Benton's mother, and scooted out the door. Benton still had his black Mustang that he got in high school. He kept it very nice. He asked Mercy, "Want to put the top down?" She laughed, "It's not quite warm enough for that." It was about a forty-five-minute ride to the marina where the boat was. Benton's father's boat was more of a yacht. It had three bedrooms, a kitchen, bathroom, living room and a large enough space to walk around the outside. It was a beautiful boat. Benton's dad hired a Captain to be on call always, in case someone wanted to go out on it. He hired another person to make sure it was clean every day and well stocked with food and drinks. Benton called ahead, before they left his house, to make sure the maintenance man, Rob, knew all his instructions. He would have a few cold bottles of champagne, chocolate covered strawberries, cheese and a whole spread just for them. He also had him put silk sheets on the king size bed with rose petals on the top.

Mercy and Benton pulled up to the boat in the marina and Mercy noticed that there were lights on inside the cabin. Mercy said, "I think you have surprised me enough already for one night." She was still excited to see what it was. When they got inside the cabin, it was warm and decorated for Christmas also. Benton showed her the Champagne and told her they had to have a toast to celebrate their engagement. Mercy said, "You know what happens to me when I drink, but okay we do need to celebrate one of the most important moments of our lives." He popped the cork on the champagne and poured each of them a glass. Mercy's just a little bit fuller. He also got out the chocolate covered strawberries that were on a tray with the other treats. Mercy said, "Oh Benton, you are so romantic." Then he gave her a long, passionate kiss and she kissed him back with just as much enthusiasm. He said, "Why don't we go into the bedroom. I have another surprise." Mercy looked suspicious. When he opened the door to the master bedroom, it was all aglow with candle light. There were fresh flowers around the room and the white, satin comforter was covered in red rose petals. Mercy said, "Oh Benton, it's just beautiful, how did you arrange all of this?" She was almost brought to tears because she loved Benton so much. She loved him as much as the first day she got up the nerve to talk to him the first time. They lay down on the bed in the rose petals and started kissing. At first, they kissed very gently, and then the kisses turned more ardent and Benton was trying to stick his tongue in her mouth and it was too rough, like he was smashing her lips. She pulled away from him and looked him in the eyes and he said, "I love you so much Mercy, you are all I have ever wanted." They went back to kissing, more gently now. Benton knew he had to go slow here. They drank more champagne. Mercy wanted him so badly also. Quickly she thought. "Well, we are engaged now, and we are going to be husband and wife, and he did finally say he loved me, maybe it's time for her to give herself fully to him." Benton could tell that Mercy was responding to his kisses in a good way. They made out for another half an hour and Mercy made Benton crazy with desire. He decided he would go for it. He thought that Mercy was ready. His kisses got rougher and he practically tore her shirt off. Mercy got scared and she raised up in bed and told him, "Please Benton, we have to take our time, we have all night." Benton replied, "Sorry, I couldn't help myself, you are so beautiful." He still couldn't seem to slow down. He got Mercy's clothes off except her bra and panties and then he started to undress himself. Mercy looked at him for the first time. He was such a handsome man, broad chest with just enough hair on it, strong, muscular arms, thin waist and long, strong legs. She knew he would look as good as he did with his clothes on. He lay down beside her on the bed and started kissing her all over, her neck, shoulders, up and down her arms, down her flat stomach to her panties. He was getting rougher by the minute. He turned Mercy over and started kissing her neck and back very hard, then he grabbed the back of her hair and started pulling it while he ripped off her panties. Mercy screamed, "Benton, STOP! It's not supposed to be like this, especially my first time. What's gotten into you? You're like some animal and now I am out of the mood to do it with you." "Oh God, not again." He said. "C'mon Mercy, I'm sorry, I got a little carried away. I've been waiting for four years now. (which he really hadn't) You can't expect a man to wait forever." Mercy's head was spinning from the champagne she had drank. Benton said, "Oh no, not again Mercy, are you going to be sick?" She said, "I don't think so, I don't know." She got up off the bed and started to put her clothes back on. Benton said, "What are you doing? Come back to bed." Mercy replied, "No, the timing of this just isn't right. I know we just got engaged, but I'm not ready to do this yet." Benton, trying to be tender replied, "Mercy, your just scared. Don't be afraid of me. I wouldn't hurt you for the world." She said, "I know that Benton, at least you wouldn't on purpose." Mercy thought about it for a second and maybe she was scared, maybe she still wasn't ready to give up the one thing that was hers to give. She didn't know why, she guessed that it was because the whole plan all along was to wait until her wedding night. She knew by today's standards, that was very old-fashioned thinking, but she didn't care, that's the way her momma raised her. She could hear her mother in the back of her mind saying, "Don't do it Mercy." Mercy had tears in her eyes because she just didn't think she could make Benton understand how she felt. He thought she was just being a tease or that worse, she didn't love him. Mercy said, "Benton, I'm sorry" and that's as far as she got. Benton jumped up and put his clothes on and said, "C'mon Mercy, I'll take you home. She said, "Benton, we just got engaged and it's supposed to be a happy day, please don't be angry with me." He replied, "I'm not angry, just frustrated. I don't understand, I thought you loved me." Mercy answered a little too shortly, "This had nothing to do with whether I love you or not, and by the way, you know I do." Benton replied, "Well, there is no sense in talking about this all night. The night is ruined now. I'll take you home." Mercy said, "Okay Benton, maybe that would be best. I do appreciate all of the trouble you've gone through to make this night so special."

CHAPTER 13

Benton wanted to drop Mercy off because he had other plans. If Mercy was not going to take care of his needs, then he would go to the one person who he knew would. He had been seeing another woman on the side. He didn't love this other woman, he loved Mercy. This was just to satisfy his needs. He didn't see anything wrong with it, it wasn't love, just sex. He thought that this other girl may be falling in love with him, but he had made it clear from the beginning that he didn't want a relationship with her. He knew he would feel better tomorrow after seeing his mistress. Besides, didn't most rich men have a mistress on the side? Wasn't that a sign that you were doing well for yourself?

Benton pulled up in front of Mercy's house and went around and opened the door for her. He walked her to the door and kissed her very gently on the lips. He told her, "Don't worry Mercy, everything is okay, I'm not upset with you. I love you Mercy. I'll talk to you tomorrow. Mercy felt relief after these words. She loves hearing Benton say, "I love you." Mercy realized how tired she was and told Benton she would see him tomorrow.

Mercy couldn't wait to show Madison her ring and tell her the news. She would call her tomorrow. When Benton pulled away from the curb, he was already on his phone trying to get a hold of his mistress. She answered on the fourth ring. Benton said, "Can I come over?" She replied, "Sure, I'll be waiting." Benton drove to her house, which wasn't very far from here. He got out of his car and knocked on the door. The woman answered and told him, "Come in Benton, you are out late tonight." He didn't say anything, he grabbed her and kissed her roughly, then pulled her towards the bedroom. Benton liked rough sex and he liked to talk dirty during sex. The first thing he did was tie the bitch up.

When Mercy got inside, her father was sitting in his recliner in front of the television, as usual, watching sports. Mercy told him the news and then showed him her ring. He didn't look excited about it. He just said, "When?" Mercy told him that they hadn't set a date yet. He responded, "Well, at least you are marrying someone with some money." He thought this could be very beneficial to him. Finally, he said, "Congratulations Mercy." Mercy knew that was a lot coming from her father.

Mercy went to bed that night dreaming of her wedding day. She would ask Madison to be her Maid of Honor. Mercy thought she would be thrilled. Mercy thought of what style of dress she would wear, something very simple, like a mermaid style and off the shoulders. Then it hit her, she couldn't afford a wedding. She knew that Benton and hopefully his mother would help with the planning. Mercy wanted lots of flowers, especially gardenia's, they were her favorite. She didn't know where Benton wanted to get married at, but she would love to get married in the little church down the street, where she first saw Benton from the bell tower. The City of Cincinnati donated funds to restore it to its original beauty and it was partly finished. She and Benton would have to talk about a date for the wedding. As a matter of fact, they had a lot to talk about.

Mercy thought of Travis and how she was going to tell him. She would tell him tomorrow, after she told Madison. Boy, she missed her mother so much right now. She was feeling very alone in the house. Mercy wished her mother could see her ring. She just kept looking at it. She couldn't believe how beautiful it was.

Benton didn't get home until late the next morning. He had a great night of sex that lasted all night. He knew that this woman was falling in love with him and she kept asking him if he told his girlfriend about them yet. His mistress, as most mistresses do, had dreams of marrying Benton herself. She knew he had money and knew she would be secure for life. She was tired of living pay check to pay check. She wanted a mansion, and most of all, she wanted Benton. She could usually get any man she wanted. She was beautiful, and she knew how to please a man.

Benton got home and went in the back door where the kitchen was. His mother was sitting at the counter drinking coffee. She looked like she had been up all-night crying. Her eyes were red and swollen and she was holding an ice pack on her forehead. Benton hoped she wasn't in the mood to talk about Mercy. He said, "Hi Mom", as he poured himself a hot cup of coffee. She didn't say anything to him at first. Benton sat down at the counter across from her. She looked up and said, "How could you have embarrassed me in front of our family and friends that way? You know there is no way I'm going to let you marry that low class, uneducated girl." Benton's face was turning red with anger, but he replied, "Mom, I know you are upset, but please, let's not be throwing out insults. You know I love Mercy." His mother knew that Benton had taken Mercy to the yacht the night before. The captain had called her later and told her that Benton and Mercy did not stay long and wanted to know if he should have disposed of the food and lock it up. Because of that, Benton's mother figured that they did not exactly make love all night. She said, "Benton you will only love Mercy until she gives in to you, you just like the challenge and once you have had her, you will be done with her just like all the other girlfriends you have had." Benton only briefly wondered how his mother knew they had not had sex, but really didn't care. Benton answered, "Mercy is different somehow. I love her and we are going to get married mother, whether you like it or not but I am hoping that you will give us your blessing and help with the wedding plans." His mother replied, "Well, just for the record, I think you are making a big mistake, BIG, and I will never give you my blessing. Why couldn't you have chosen one of my friend's daughter?" Benton looked her in the eye and said, "I want Mercy, and I'm going to have her for my wife, so you might as well accept it mother, you can't change my mind." She replied, "Well, maybe I can't change your mind, but I can certainly cut you off from your trust fund." This made Benton angry, his face turned red and she could see a vein popping out on his forehead. He said, "Mother, do what you want to me, but you won't change the outcome, so please try and get use to the idea of having Mercy as your daughter-in-law." His mother didn't say anything then, but he could see the wheels turning in her head. She said, "I know the exorbitant price that you paid for that ring. I just called our family jeweler and he told me, we are good friends. He told me you paid twenty-five thousand for it, which is just ridiculous. A girl like that who doesn't have any money can't appreciate the value of things. You should have gone to the local store and picked her out a hundred-dollar ring instead. She wouldn't have known the difference. Oh well, the two of you can live on what that cost when you run out of money and can't pay your mortgage." Benton said, "I'm really tired, I'm going to bed now."

Benton went upstairs and went to bed. He was exhausted after such a long night and then having to face his mother this morning. He lay there and couldn't go to sleep. He was tossing and turning and couldn't get his mind to shut off. Would he still want Mercy after he has had her a few times? He thought he still would, he thought he loved her. Should he have given her such an expensive ring? Maybe not, she would have been happy with a lot less. He had two pills of some kind that his mistress gave him to relax. He got up and got a glass of water and took them both. He was soon snoring.

Mercy had called Benton a couple of times during that afternoon, but a maid kept telling her he wasn't available. Maybe he was out running errands or something. She called her best friend Madison. She hadn't talked to her in a couple of months, they were both so busy. Madison still lived at home. She asked Madison if she could come over and see her and Madison said, "Sure, I'm not doing anything else."

When Mercy got to Madison's and walked in the door, she grabbed Madison's hands and started jumping up and down and yelling. Madison made her stop long enough to tell her what the celebration was about. Mercy showed her the engagement ring. Man, it was huge! Madison started jumping up and down and hugging Mercy. Madison couldn't believe that Benton had finally ask Mercy to marry him. She was so jealous that she could hardly stand it. Mercy was also marrying into money, which made Madison more jealous. Looks like Mercy got the whole pie and she didn't even get a slice. It was hard for Madison to pretend she was excited for her. The whole time Mercy was there, all she talked about was Benton and her wedding. Mercy ask Madison if she would be her Maid of Honor and of course, Madison agreed, they were best friends, after all. Mercy stayed and visited with her friend for another couple of hours and then she said she had to go. They both promised each other that they would keep in touch and get together more often.

Mercy's dad had pretty much let her have his car since he retired. Mercy does all the shopping and he pretty much doesn't do anything. Mercy has tried to take him out to different places, but he won't have it.

She walked up to Travis's house to tell him about her engagement and to show off her engagement ring but more importantly, she wanted to make sure that he heard the news from her. Travis was sitting on the front porch, as usual, playing his guitar. A big smile came on his face when he saw Mercy get out of the car. Travis loved her so much and she looked especially good today, she had a glow about her. Mercy ran up on the porch and gave Travis a big hug. They sat down, and Mercy said, "I just wanted to let you know that Benton and I are engaged." She showed him the ring. Travis tried not to look surprised or jealous when he said, "Oh Mercy, that's so nice that you're finally going to get married but to bad it's to the wrong man." He made a smirk and she gently punched him on the arm. They joked around for a few minutes and then Travis looked at her and said, "Mercy do you love Benton?" She hesitated for a moment, which spoke volumes to Travis. Mercy said, "Yes, I do Travis." Seeing the look on Travis's face, she said, "I love you also Travis, but in a different way. You know that. You know I'll always love you first." As she said those words, she wondered if it really wasn't more than that. Could she love Travis after all? Well, maybe, but she was in love with Benton, or so she thought, for the last four years. She was a little afraid of marriage because she had heard how everyone says people change after they get married and it ends in divorce. Also, looking at her parents' marriage, she didn't want to end up like them either. She told herself that she wasn't getting cold feet, just feeling the jitters of every young person that's headed for the alter.

Travis turned around to face her on the porch. He had turned into such a handsome man, it almost took her breath away. She was noticing things about him that she had never noticed before, his strong jaw line, his broad shoulders. He had turned into quite a man. He was almost 6'4", whereas Benton was only 5'9", just four inches taller than she. Travis cupped her soft cheeks in his hands and held her face gently. He said, "Mercy please, I just have to tell you this. We have been friends since we were little kids so please give me the courtesy to tell you what I feel I need to tell you. Mercy relaxed in his hands and she could smell the wonderful fragrance of his aftershave on his neck. The fragrance was calming somehow. He had always used the same kind. Mercy replied, "I already know what you are going to say Travis, and it won't change my mind but go ahead." Travis was determined anyway. He had rehearsed this speech for months but now couldn't remember a single thing, so he would just speak from his heart. Travis didn't talk, it was more like a soft whisper coming from his full lips. "Mercy" he breathed, "I know I have said these things before but please be patient and listen to me. I love you. I have loved you since we were little I think. I don't think there has ever been a time that I can remember that I didn't love you. You are so beautiful, and kind hearted. We are so much alike, raised pretty much the same. I can't imagine my life without you in it. I need you, you are the very air I breath. Travis stood up and bent down on one knee. Mercy gasped with shock. "Mercy, if you marry me, I will love and honor you forever." Mercy just stared at him, lingering a little too long. Travis stood up and said, "I know you are already engaged, but I wanted you to know how I feel and I wanted you to know that the proposal is always good should you change your mind." Mercy had tears in her eyes. Benton had never expressed his feelings like that to her, just a "me to" when she said she loved him. Finally, she told Travis, "Thank you so much Travis for loving me and I will keep your feelings in mind if I decide not to marry Benton but there is a slim chance that that will happen, I love him, I love you both. That is the first time Mercy every told Travis that she loved him in this way and it felt so good! Even if she just meant it as a friend, he loved the sound of it. He kissed her cheek and she hugged him and then headed for home.

Mercy knew that Travis would be upset, and she

thought that she was mentally prepared for it, but she wasn't. Travis touch some deep feelings within her today, she didn't want to think about what that could mean. She loved Benton.

CHAPTER 14

Mercy worked hard at the hospital and made a few new "work" friends. They would go out after work sometimes, for breakfast. Mercy also went out with her friend Madison, but not as much anymore. Madison seemed distant for some reason and she said it was nothing, she was just busy working at nights in the coffee shop.

Mercy loved her job at the hospital. With her and Benton in the medical field, they could talk about their careers and they knew what each other were saying. They also talked about Benton's new friend, Sydney. Benton seemed to like him a lot and he said that Sydney was so smart and that he really helped him with some of his harder classes.

It was Friday and Benton was coming home tonight for spring break. Benton would be out of med school at the end of May and then he would be starting his internship in Sydney's hometown of Chicago, at Chicago General. Sydney also played guitar and was trying to teach Benton. Benton told Mercy that you didn't get to pick where you did your internship. Mercy was disappointed that he wasn't going to be closer to home. He would be a five-hour drive away. Mercy couldn't wait to see him. She talked to him at least twice a week on the phone. They had plans to make for their wedding and this week would work on the details.

When Benton arrived home that Friday, he invited Mercy over for dinner. He was hoping that his mother would soften up and start to accept Mercy a little bit more. Surprisingly, when he told his mother that he had invited her, she just said, "Okay, that's fine." If this is what he really wanted, even though he was her only child, she knew she would have to get use to the idea. Benton was elated and told Mercy how his mother had reacted, so she would feel more comfortable coming to his house.

Mercy arrived around seven. Benton's mother asked if she could please park her car around the back. She really didn't want any of her neighbors to see that raggedy old car in her driveway. Mercy, of course, did as she asks. They sat down to a delicious dinner. Benton's mother and father sat at the head of the table. Benton's mother said, "I had the cook fix all of your favorite dishes for your homecoming tonight." Benton replied, "I know my stomach is about to burst. Thank you so much mother. She replied, "Your welcome." Benton's father told him how proud of him he was. They had never had a doctor in the family before, and people will have to get used to calling him Dr. They all had easy conversation and included Mercy whenever they could. The couldn't have been more gracious to her.

After dinner and a wonderful dessert, they were all sitting around the table talking about how good dinner was and how they had all eaten too much. Benton's father suggested that he and Benton retire to the library for a brandy and to catch up. Benton wasn't sure if he should leave Mercy to the mercy of his mother or not. When Benton looked at Mercy, she said, "It's okay." After Benton and his father were well away from earshot, Benton's mother said, "Mercy, have you and Benton made any wedding plans yet?" Mercy replied, "No, we were planning on talking about it this weekend. We are trying to set a date soon and will try to announce it to everyone. We want to get married in November, around Thanksgiving time. Benton will have a few days off from his internship then and he will be settled into an apartment. It is so expensive to live in Chicago, that Benton said he wanted to get an apartment with his friend Sydney. We will only be living there until he gets finished with his internship in two years. I plan on working at Chicago General, while he is doing his internship. When Benton is finished with his internship, we plan on moving back here to our hometown in Cincinnati. Benton's mother couldn't wrap her mind around why Benton wanted to share an apartment with someone when he can well afford his own apartment. Besides, she thought, "Why would Benton want a roommate when he will be newly married?" Benton's mother said that if it was okay with Mercy, she would like for them to have a big wedding and invite all her wealthy friends and family. Mercy told her, "I would be happy if you would help us plan the wedding, but we have decided to have a small wedding, with less than one hundred people. Benton's mother was disappointed again. She wanted to give her son the best wedding ever had in Cincinnati. She wanted the big Catholic church wedding with hundreds of people, the whole nine yards. She had never thought for a minute that Mercy wouldn't want that. Every girl wanted a big wedding. She replied, "Well, I would still like to help in any way I can." Mercy said, that she and Benton would like that very much. Benton and his father returned from the library and Benton announced his plans for the year.

PART II

CHAPTER 15

Benton and Sydney got a nice apartment within walking distance of Chicago General. It was a deluxe, three bedrooms with a large terrace and parking space. It cost them two thousand, five hundred per month but they could afford it. Benton had unlimited funds from his trust fund from his Grandpa on his mother's side and his parents sent him money every month or anytime he asked for it. The gave him whatever he needed without question because they were so proud of him becoming a doctor and would do anything to see that happen.

Benton and Sydney's internship at the hospital called for long hours at the hospital plus more studying to do. Benton wanted to go out to a new club that was the talk of the young and hip of the hospital staff. Benton said, "C'mon Sydney, let's go out, we never get out of this apartment." Sydney replied, "Benton, I'm so tired and we have studying to do." Benton was a little agitated and said, "Well, I'm going with or without you. I am sick to death of looking at these walls, working and studying all the time. We never have any fun anymore." Sydney looked at him tiredly and said, "Okay, just for a little while, then we have to come back and hit the books." Benton promised that they would go for just a little while.

They went to the club and there was a long line to get in. The club had two bouncers posted on either side of the door and a velvet rope leading up to it. Benton and Sydney were both very good-looking guys and got in with no problem. The place was packed with people. They finally made it to the bar and ordered a drink. There were scantily clothed women everywhere. It was like a banquet for Benton. He couldn't take his eyes off them. He thought he was so far away from home and what Mercy didn't know, wouldn't hurt her. He tried to pick up a few different women, but his usual tactics didn't work. He'd tried the same lines he's used on the girls back home. The women here were so much more street wise and savvy then his home town. He would have to be a little bit more persuasive. He bought drinks for quite a few women that night but none of them seemed really interested. Sydney didn't see anyone he was interested in either, so they decided to get back to the apartment. Sydney could be kind of bossy, but Benton usually let him have his way because he had never really had a close guy friend before. That was also okay, he and Sydney got along great.

Of course, Benton knew that Sydney was gay, but it didn't bother him. Sydney like cooking, cleaning and taking care of Benton. Sydney didn't have any steady boyfriends and didn't want one right now. He and Benton could talk about anything and they just enjoyed each other's company. Sydney secretly had a crush on Benton be he would never tell him and take a chance on messing up what they had together.

Benton thought, before going to sleep that night that

he would have to call his mistress to come up next weekend and spend the night. He would have to buy her a car to come up because she drove an old clunker. He knew he could get a local call girl, even an expensive one but his mistress knew what he liked and how he liked it. He dares not try to satisfy his deviant sexual appetite on a local girl because they usually had a bodyguard nearby. The only problem with his mistress is that she thought that they were going to get married someday. She thought that he would break off his engagement to Mercy for her. She was getting restless about it and wondering when Benton was going to tell Mercy about them. Benton could keep putting her off by buying her what she wanted. He tried to tell her many times that she was his mistress, not his girlfriend but he also kept telling her that he loved her, which came so easy when it wasn't true, which led her on.

Benton would also have to call Mercy tomorrow to plan for her to come up here and see him. Mercy was going to move up here with him when they got married, but until then, she would only visit, and she would sleep in the spare room. Benton's roommate, Sydney, thought this was weird. You just didn't hear of any girls being virgins anymore, especially ones that were engaged.

Mercy worked hard at the hospital in the ER. She had seen so much tragedy and situations since she started working here, it made he grow up in a hurry. She no longer felt like that timid, little girl inside. She felt she did her job well and could old her own with anyone. She dealt with catty women but didn't have to deal with bullying anymore and if she did, she was better prepared to handle it now that she was older. Her birthday was in a couple of weeks and she would be twenty-one. Benton said that he would come home and celebrate her birthday with her. When she had showed her beautiful engagement ring to the girls at work, they all thought it was stunning and they were so happy for her. Her friends were all in love with doctors that worked at the hospital. It was kind of hard to keep up with who was dating who. Mercy missed Benton so much, but she took extra shifts to keep herself busy and her mind off him. She liked his roommate Sydney. Sydney was easy to talk to and seemed genuinely nice. Mercy was glad that Benton had a good friend up there.

Mercy liked her life now. She had purchased a new car and a new used truck for her father, even though he still rarely left the house. His drinking had escalated since her mother's death and Mercy was always worrying about his health. She tried to see Benton on the weekends, but she didn't like leaving her father alone. She had asked Travis to check in on him when she went to Chicago and he always said it was a pleasure to do it for her. Travis was the best, he would do anything for her that she asked. She and Travis still saw each other now and then, and tried to go out to dinner occasionally, just to catch up on what each other was doing. Madison joined them when she could. Madison didn't have a steady guy and Mercy always kind of hoped that she and Travis would one day hook up. That would be awesome to have her two best friends get together.

Madison still worked at the coffee shop during the day and she bartended at a local bar at night. Tips must be good for her because she also bought a new car. She bought a little, red, Mustang convertible. Madison loved that car and she really babied it. She was always washing it.

Travis's father owned a local garage where they fixed transmissions on cars among other things. His father's business had grown the last couple of years. He caught the building next to the garage for more space and hired two new employees. Travis worked for his father. He liked working at the "shop", as he called it. He had learned so much about cars and other kinds of motorized vehicles. Travis could fix almost anything. His father depended on him to make sure that each job got finished on time. He harassed Travis some, but not too badly. His father loved having him there with him. He would introduce everyone that came into the shop to Travis as, "His Partner". His father also had the name of the shop changed to "Dison & Son Automotive". Travis was okay with that, but he kept telling his father all along that that he wouldn't be working there forever. He wanted to follow his dream in the music business. Travis could not only play the guitar, but he also sang very well. Travis had a beautiful, deep voice. Sometimes, after the shop closed for the day, he and a couple of his buddies would sit around the shop and jam together. Travis also played and sang at some of the local bars on the weekends. Travis was twenty-two years old a couple of weeks ago and he thought that he wasn't getting any younger, he was ready, ready to start trying to make it big in the music industry. Music and Mercy were his life.

Travis called Mercy one Saturday night, hoping that she wasn't in Chicago to see Benton. She was home. Her father hadn't been feeling well and so she thought she should stay home this weekend and take care of him. Travis asked her if she could go out for just a little while. They could go get pizza. Travis told her that he had something to talk to her about. Mercy said, "Okay, I think I can get out for just a little while. I will meet you at Garcia's Pizza at six this evening." Travis replied, "That would be great".

When Mercy arrived at the pizza parlor, Travis was already there and had gotten a booth for them. He stood when she approached the table, always a gentleman. He said, "Hi Mercy, you look as beautiful as ever." He gave her a kiss on the cheek. She replied, "Thank you, and might I say, you are looking especially handsome tonight." They both laughed at themselves, acting so proper when they were such close friends. Travis had on black jeans, white shirt, cowboy boots and cowboy hat on. He did look so handsome tonight. She really missed Benton, but she was remembering how Travis had held her so close to him on the top of a dark mountain one time. Travis hadn't changed a bit since then. You could always count on Travis to be in the same, easy mood. She mostly misses seeing his crooked, little grin every day. Mercy asked, "How have you been Travis? You look really well." Travis liked that, and he replied, "Thanks, I've been pretty good, just working at the shop every day with my father." Mercy asked, "How is that going? Are the two of you getting along okay?" Travis responded, "Fine, we have been working really hard, the business is growing every day. Cars are getting more and more gadgets on them so there is more to fix, which means more business for the shop." Travis looked a little troubled. Mercy knew Travis well enough to know that he would tell her what was on his mind when he was ready, she didn't push it. Travis said, "About six months ago, a man brought in a very trashed Harley and wanted to trade it for work on his car. My dad saw the value in the bike, even though it needed so much work. My dad gave me the bike. He knew that I loved the bike. His only stipulation was that I had to work on it only after business hours when the shop was closed. Well, I have been working on it for the last six months and now it is finally finished. I rode it over here and it purrs like a kitten. It is outside, would you like to go see it?" "Sure" Mercy said, she didn't think she had ever seen a Harley up close before. When they stepped outside, she was surprised that she hadn't seen it on her way in to the pizza parlor. It was beautiful, a lot of chrome and painted a candy apple red that faded to the back in flames. Mercy said, "Travis, it's the coolest thing that I have ever seen. I can't believe that you rebuilt this whole thing." Travis replied, "I'd take you for a spin, but I only have one helmet. She said, "That's okay, I'm a little afraid of them. I've never ridden a bike before." Travis said, "I just got my bike license a month ago. I'm still getting used to how she runs myself, but it's not too tough to ride one after you learn the basics." They went back inside to their booth. Mercy had a strong feeling that Travis didn't ask her here just to show off his bike. He wasn't a show off. Their pizza came, and they ate while talking about what was going on in their lives. Travis noted, "I see you are still engaged. Well, if your just engaged and not married, I still have a chance. All is not lost." Mercy looked at him teasingly, "I will keep you in mind, should I ever become unengaged." He smiled at her. Finally, he got around to telling Mercy why he was here. "Mercy, I've decided to leave the shop and take a trip down south." She asked, "Where are you going?" She was suddenly apprehensive, although she didn't know why. "I'm taking my guitar and I'm going to go to Nashville and see if I can get discovered as a country music star." Mercy asked excitedly,

"Really? Travis, I think that is great. You will never know if you could have made it until you try. I think you are good enough to make it big. You are going to be famous! My best friend is going to be famous!" Travis didn't think Mercy would be this excited for him and answered, "Hold on, that's a one in a million chance but my dad knows somebody, that knows somebody who owns a recording studio down there and I can at least do a recording and have something to show the Big Wigs down there. I know it is a really long shot but that has always been my dream and I'm going to go for it." Mercy asked excitedly, "When are you leaving Travis?" He said that he was leaving next weekend, after he tied up a few loose ends at the shop. Mercy asked, "Are you driving down? Is someone else going with you are you going alone?" He replied, "No, just me, all by my lonesome. Don't worry, I'm a big boy. I can handle myself. I'm going to pack my guitar and a few things and ride down on my Harley. It should take me about six hours to get there." Mercy asked, "Do you really think you should ride the Harley since you have only had a license such a short time?" He said, "I'll be fine, you don't have to worry about me." Mercy and Travis ate and talked with ease, just as they always have.

It was Sunday night and Benton had just gotten off the late shift at the hospital. He was dead tired, but he still had to carry a pager and be "on-call", just in case they needed him, which almost always happened. The weekends were always full of bar fights, stabbings or some type of injuries. He'd just walked in and sat down on the couch. Sydney was also home. Sydney ask him if he'd like a drink. Benton replied, "Okay, that'd be nice". Sydney was in the kitchen cooking something up. Sydney loved to cook and did every chance he got.

Benton was not happy that Mercy hadn't come up to see him this weekend. He didn't get to see her that often as it was. She said her father was sick, yeah right, she was probably hanging out with that guy Travis that she likes so much. She always said that they were just good friends, but now he was beginning to wonder because she talked about him all the time.

Benton's mother kept badgering him about how Mercy wasn't right for him, how he could do so much better, that he needed to worry about his career before marriage. Maybe his mother was right. Maybe she was getting to him. When he was finished with his internship, he wanted to go into surgery. He wanted to be a plastic surgeon, that's where all the money was, taking care of all those rich women. Maybe he was in too much of a hurry to get married he thought. He was even wondering if he even really loved Mercy or if he was just being defiant to his overbearing mother. He didn't know, maybe he felt this way because he was just so damn tired. Benton woke up on the couch. He must have dozed off for a while. It was nine in the evening and he didn't remember the last three hours. He must have really been out like a light. He got up and went into the kitchen. He found a note on the counter that read, "Went out for a while, there is food in the microwave". He wondered where Sydney went because he never went anywhere. Then he remembered, Sydney had started this new exercise class at the YMCA. Sydney didn't have a boyfriend that Benton knew of, at least he never talked about anyone. He said that he had been bullied all his life because of his small frame and now that he is grown, he wanted to work out and see if he could build up some muscles. Sydney's new thing was also eating right. There were all kinds of things in the frig. Most Benton couldn't even name. Benton opened the microwave and took out the plate that Sydney had left him. Benton didn't know what it was, maybe chicken and what he thought was bean sprouts. Benton threw it in the garbage can. He wasn't about to eat that. He would call for a pizza. Suddenly, he was very hungry. While he was waiting on his pizza, he called Mercy. She answered the phone on about the fifth ring. Benton said, "You sound like you are all out of breath." She replied, "I am, I was just getting out of the car when I heard the phone ringing and I know that my father never answers the phone. He says no one ever calls him so why answer it?" Benton suspiciously said, "Well, where have you been? I thought you had to stay home with your father." Mercy didn't like his tone of voice and said, "I met Travis at the pizza parlor, he wanted to talk." Benton was suddenly angry, "Oh, you have time to spend with Travis, but you can't come and see me? I thought your father was so sick that you couldn't go out." Now, Mercy was getting angry. She asked him "Benton, why do you sound so angry, are you in a bad mood?" He said, "No I just don't understand why you couldn't come up here to see me because your father is sick, but you have time to go out and have pizza with Travis." Mercy replied, "Benton, it wasn't planned. It was a last-minute thing. Travis had something important to tell me." Benton said in a hopeful voice, "I hope he told you he was getting married." She answered, "No, he isn't getting married. He told me his is going to go to Nashville to try and make it in the country music industry. Benton started laughing, "Yeah right, that's the stupidest thing I ever heard of. No one just goes to Nashville and gets discovered. Besides, I've heard him, and your home boy just isn't that good." Now it was Mercy's turn to be angry. She said, "Benton, a person has to follow their dreams. I'm proud of Travis and I think if anybody should be a star, it should be him." Benton didn't like the way Mercy was defending him so diligently. Benton felt like she cared more for Travis than she did for him and he was a little jealous, which surprised him. Benton suddenly said, "I don't like this conversation much, I'll call you in a couple of days." Mercy replied, "Please Benton, don't act like this, you know I love you." Benton replied, "I'm not so sure sometimes." Mercy knew that Benton needed constant reassurance from her of how she felt. She said, "I'll just talk to you later in the week. That's fine with me." She hung up the phone and she felt miserable. She didn't like it when she and Benton argued. They seem to be doing more and more of that lately. Benton had even accused her of being interested in one of the Doctors that she worked with just because she had talked about him a few times. She told Benton that it was normal to talk about people that you worked with day after day. Sometimes, she wasn't sure of how Benton felt about her, which was not good since they were engaged.

Benton called Mercy on the following Wednesday evening when he knew she would be up and getting ready for her night shift at work. He told her that he would finally get a night off on Friday night and wanted to know if she could come up late Friday afternoon and spend the night. Mercy didn't hear any of that same anger in his voice that he had last Sunday when they talked, so she said, "Yes, I can come up. My father is feeling better and I miss you. I can't wait to see you. We still have some wedding plans to make or at least set a date. I'll see you Friday afternoon." She thought that Benton sounded excited about seeing her and she was missing him.

CHAPTER 16

Sydney was off pretty much the same nights that Benton was. It so happened that he was off and not doing anything on Friday. He decided to cook a nice dinner on Friday since Mercy was coming up. He really liked Mercy. She was a sweet girl and she was very smart also. She could talk about anything. Sydney liked to talk to her about art. One of Sydney's favorite past times was going to the art museum. He was planning on going Friday, to give Benton and Mercy some alone time. Sydney thought that when he got out of school, he might take some art lessons.

Friday was here before Mercy knew it and she had a hundred things to do before she left for Chicago. She had to fix some food and leave it in separate containers for her father. Since her mother babied him, he had never cooked a day in his life. If she didn't cook him something, he just wouldn't eat, and he was already too thin.

Again, Benton thought maybe his mother was right, maybe Mercy wasn't right, but Benton was looking forward to seeing Mercy. He did genuinely miss her or maybe he was missing being back in Cincinnati where he grew up. He didn't know for sure but the one thing he did know was that he was happy when he was with Mercy. Mercy somehow made him feel like he was the only person in the world and her honesty with him made him feel like he could be a better person.

Benton and Sydney had a maid service that came in and cleaned once a week. They were coming today, Thursday. Benton always made sure that everything was nice and clean when Mercy came. He didn't want her to feel like it was just two dirty bachelors living here, just in case she changed her mind and wanted to move up here. He understood that she didn't want to leave her father, especially when he wasn't feeling well but he also had a sneaking suspicion that she didn't want to leave her precious friend Travis.

Sydney had made a nice dinner of steak, baked potatoes and vegetables. Even though Mercy didn't drink, Benton even made sure they had a nice bottle of red wine. Mercy arrived about five in the afternoon. She had her own key and so she just let herself into the foyer. Benton heard the door instantly and walked into the foyer. There she was, so beautiful. She hugged Benton hard and cupped his face in her hands and told him how much she missed and loved him. Benton said, "Me to" and hugged her back. They walked on inside, so Mercy could greet Sydney. Sydney said, "Mercy, you are looking more beautiful than ever." She replied, "Thank you Sydney." Benton said, "Mercy, could I get you a drink?" She replied, "A coke would be nice." Sydney chirped up, "Stay there Benton, I'll get it." When Sydney disappeared around the corner of the kitchen, they hugged again. Benton said, "It's so nice to have you here Mercy. I really wish you'd reconsider moving up here with me." She said, "Oh Benton, you know I can't do that. I've explained about my father." He replied, "I know, I know, I was just asking again for the hundredth time." They sat on the couch and talked and kissed and hugged. Sydney came out of the kitchen and happily announced that dinner was ready. Sydney was always in a good mood. They were seated at their lovely dining room table and Sydney had it set perfectly. Sydney knew a lot more about etiquette than either one of them did. He also had purchased Benton some fresh flowers for a center piece. They all had easy conversation throughout dinner. Mercy drank one glass of red wine. She didn't trust herself to drink, so she tried to never drink too much. Sydney announced that dessert was served. He had made a red velvet cake for dessert, Benton's favorite. Mercy and Benton looked at each other as if to say, "I'm too full to eat another bite." They did take a few bites since Sydney was so kind to make it for them. Sydney beamed throughout the whole dinner because they kept telling him what a wonderful dinner he had prepared. Sydney said, "Oh, you two go out on the terrace, I'll clean up. You two never have enough time together and you shouldn't spend it cleaning up.

They walked out on the terrace with their drink. The terrace gave the appearance of being outside, but it was enclosed with thick glass with thick, wooden beams running from the top and angling down. It was beautiful. Mercy didn't ask Benton what he paid in rent here but assumed "Mommy" was footing the bills. They had very easy conversation, just like it has always been between them. Sydney stuck his head out the door and said that he was leaving and would be gone until late tonight. He was going to his exercise class and then to his art lesson, that was just starting tonight. Sydney didn't make them feel like he was leaving just because of them, although he did feel a little twinge of jealously because he wouldn't be spending his rare night off with Benton. That was okay, he really liked Mercy. Many times, he thought Mercy was way too good a person for Benton.

Mercy and Benton stayed up late talking. They finally talked about setting a wedding date. They decided to wait until Benton had finished his residency. He was just too busy right now and with his schedule it was hard to plan anything. He told Mercy that even if they could set a date for the wedding, he would be going back to the hospital the next day, no time for a honeymoon. They both decided that they didn't want to start their marriage off this way. Benton was secretly happy about this since he was starting to have second thoughts about marriage. He wanted to put his plastic surgery career at the forefront.

Mercy and Benton sat on the couch making out until about one in the morning. When things really started to heat up, Mercy told Benton she was tired. She was going to call and check on her father and then she was going to go to bed. They heard the key in the door, Sydney was home. He said, "I hope I didn't interrupt anything?" Mercy replied, "No, we were just getting ready to go to bed. Did you have a nice evening?" Sydney said that he had but he was tired also and was going to retire. Mercy and Benton decided that they would get up early and go out to breakfast and then spend the day walking round downtown Chicago until Mercy had to leave, about five in the afternoon.

Mercy slept in the spare room, where she always slept when she was here. She kept the room full of her personal items just, so she wouldn't have to carry them back and forth and because it made her feel more at home here. Sydney had decorated the apartment and he was very good at it, especially with unlimited funds from Benton. Mercy really liked this room, it had a relaxing feel to it. It also had a half bath off this room, so she didn't have to leave to find the main bathroom in the middle of the night. She got ready for bed and climbed in the soft, king size bed. She thought it funny that this bed was so big, and she had grown up sleeping in her little roll-a-way bed. She also thought about Benton and how good it was to see him. She thought it would also be nice to share such a big bed with him. She knew that was impossible at this point. She knew what would happen if they slept together. She thought that Benton seemed a little different to her tonight. She couldn't quite put her finger on it except that maybe it felt like he was a little distant, or maybe his mind was on something besides her. She fell asleep thinking about their relationship, but she also had a fleeting thought about Travis and the fact that he would probably be gone to Nashville for a long time and she wouldn't see him.

It was about three in the morning and Benton still lay in his bed awake. He thought about Mercy in the next room. He thought about her laying in that big bed, probably wearing and old t-shirt and panties and how sexy she would look in them. He thought about sneaking into her bed and kissing her. He thought about how ridiculous this was that they couldn't sleep together. Her high and mighty morals getting on his nerves. "That's it" he decided, enough of this cat and mouse game. They were engaged after all. Didn't he buy her a $25,000 ring? Wasn't that proof enough that he would marry her? Maybe he wouldn't marry her, he just didn't know right now, she was making it hard for him lately. Being apart from her was making him rethink his relationship with her.

Benton was tired of hearing about "her momma" and how she was raised, or maybe he was a little jealous. His mother never paid that much attention to him when they were alone, just when someone was around that she wanted to impress. Well, what if it didn't work out between them? Benton decided that he wasn't going to let Mercy go without having her. He had already given her so much of his time, money and heart, at least more than to anyone else. She also should thank him for getting her out of that poor white trash neighborhood, and it was time for payment. Benton knew that he was drunk. He had drunk quite a bit tonight, but the way he was thinking now sounded quite logical to a drunk man in need.

He quietly opened Mercy's bedroom door and walked in. He was standing next to the bed watching her sleep soundly and snoring lightly, which he adored. The moonlight shining on her from the window next to the bed made her look beautiful and innocent. Maybe he should just leave, he thought for a second, then decided, no, she owed him. He climbed into bed next to her and put his arm around her. She turned over on her back, still asleep. He kissed her lightly on the lips. Mercy woke up and was startled and started to scream but quickly saw that it was Benton. She whispered, "Benton, what are you doing in here?" He quietly replied, "This is my apartment and I have the right to be anywhere I want in it." Mercy thought to tread lightly with him, she said, "Okay, do you need to talk to me about something, are you okay?" He said, "I just wanted another kiss goodnight." At that he kissed her, lightly and sweet at first but then hard and demanding. As he kissed her he was running his hand all over her body. He was pulling at her shirt, trying to get it off. Mercy broke her lips free and said, "Benton, stop! You don't want our first time to be like this, you are drunk." Benton didn't pay any attention to her, he already knew that she would protest. He kept up his assault of her body. He was sitting on top of her now and she could barely breathe. He held her hands above her head with one hand while he ripped off her panties with the other. Mercy was suddenly so scared of Benton. She knew he was really drunk but she knew she had to stop him. She wasn't nearly strong enough to stop him and she couldn't seem to talk him out of what he was determined to do. Mercy didn't know what else to do but scream. She knew the walls were practically sound proof but that's all she had between rape and freedom. She screamed to the top of her lungs. To prevent her from doing that again, Benton covered her lips with his mouth. How could she expect him not to want her after all this time? Suddenly, the door burst open and there stood Sydney with a baseball bat. He said, "I heard a scream. I thought there was an intruder. Sydney knew full well there was no intruder and had a good idea of what was going on. Sydney had tried to stay awake tonight, just for this reason. Sydney had a feeling something like this would happen tonight. He not only wanted to protect Mercy but also Benton, because he knew that Benton would regret doing this tomorrow. Benton jumped off the bed and walked up to Sydney, grabbing the bat, saying, "No Sydney, there is no intruder, just Mercy and I having a little fun, that's all. You can go back to your room now." In the meantime, Mercy had jumped up and ran for the bathroom and locked the door. Benton was suddenly exhausted. He looked at Sydney and said, "Everything's okay, really." Mercy came out of the bathroom with her clothes in her hands and announced to both that she was leaving, going home, with no explanation, but there was none needed. Benton said, "Wait Mercy, let's talk". She said, "No, not now."

Mercy was trying to put her clothes on while crying and walking to her car in the parking garage. She didn't know what had come over Benton. She knew that he had been drinking heavily, but he had never gone this far before. Whatever she knew about tonight, she knew that she would never be staying the night here again. She was so grateful to Sydney for coming into the room, he saved her. She would thank Sydney later for what he did. Benton is a big man and it took a lot of bravery to come in that room tonight, even with a bat. She had a five-hour drive home, so she had plenty of time to think about it. She should have locked the bedroom door. Mercy thought that she would go to Madison's tomorrow and talk to her about it. She wanted to talk to Travis, to get a man's perspective on what happened, but she knew that Travis would be angry about it and besides it was embarrassing to talk about these things to a man. She wished her Mother were still here for the hundredth time, her mother would tell her what to do.

Mercy called Madison the next day to see if she could come over and talk to her. Madison said that was fine, she was unpacking, and Mercy could help her. Madison had just bought a new house in Mt. Adams, on the east side of town. Mercy wondered how she could afford such a nice place on a bartender's salary. She must be making really good tips.

Mercy was worried about what else Madison was doing to afford such a place. Madison gave her the address and Mercy told her she would be there around one o'clock.

Mercy arrived at Madison's address. There was an iron gate at the entrance and an intercom button to push to let someone in. Mercy pushed the button and Madison opened the gate for her. Mercy drove up the long, winding driveway with beautiful oak trees lining each side. The driveway circled in front of the very large house. Madison was waiting on the front step when Mercy got out of her car. "Mercy!" Madison yelled, and she sounded excited to see her. Mercy said, "Wow, Madison, you live in a mansion. It's beautiful." Madison replied, "Wait until you see the inside. It has ten bedrooms with bathrooms, a pool and a tennis court out back." Mercy asked her, "Did you win the lottery or something without telling me or what?" Madison had a ready answer for her, "No, I had a rich uncle that left me a lot of money. I was his only niece and I was his favorite." Mercy thought, "She is an only child." Madison said, "I'm moving my parents in next week. They will have the east side of the house, so I will still have a lot of privacy." They walked into the grand house together. Mercy was so impressed. This house wasn't as big or as nice as Benton's parents, but it sure made an impression. Madison said, "Let's go into the living room, it's about the only room I have with furniture in it. I'll get you a drink." Madison left to get them a drink. Mercy walked around the room. It was sparsely decorated but done in good taste. Madison must have had a decorator to help her. Madison came back into the room and handed Mercy her drink. She said, "Let's sit down on the sofa." The sofa was white, so Mercy was trying to be very careful about spilling her drink on it. Mercy looked at Madison and said, "It's really a beautiful place. I'm a little jealous." Madison replied, "Don't be, I still have to work at the bar for a while to help furnish this place. I never thought in a million years that I would be living in such a grand place. Mercy, how have you been? Are you still working at the hospital in the ER? Are you still living at home, taking care of your father?" Mercy replied, "Wait, slow down Madison! I know we have a lot of catching up to do, it's been quite a while since we have seen each other." Madison said, "I'm usually working or sleeping but I'm hoping to quit working soon anyway, at least as a bartender." Mercy said, "Yes, I'm still working at the hospital and I still love being a nurse. Working as an ER nurse will make you grow up in a hurry. I've seen things that no normal person should ever have to see. I'm still living at home and taking care of my father. There isn't much to do for him, just cook and do his laundry. He quit working when Momma died, and he has been suffering from a broken heart ever since. All he does is sit in front of the television all day and hardly talk to anyone. I worry about him." While Mercy was talking, Madison noticed the huge engagement ring on her finger. Madison said, "Oh, I see that you and Benton are still engaged. Have you set a date yet?" Madison was seething with jealousy. She should be the one wearing that ring. Mercy said, "No silly, you would be the first one to know since you are going to be my maid of honor." Madison replied, "Well, what's on your mind Mercy. I know you didn't come here to talk small talk, is everything okay?" Mercy told her what had happened when she went to Chicago to see Benton. She said, "I just don't know what to do about it Madison. I know I have made him wait a long time and I've already decided that I'm not going back up there to spend the night anymore. I'll just go for the day." Madison replied, "No, don't go back up there for the night, the same thing might happen again." Really, Madison didn't want her going back up there at all. She said, "Mercy, maybe you should think more about this relationship with Benton. Maybe it's not going to work out after all. This relationship did start when you were sixteen and you never dated anyone except Benton. Maybe you should go out with some other guys before you make such a commitment." Mercy thought about it and said, "No, I love Benton and he loves me, there's no one else for me." Mercy wouldn't admit that she did think about Travis sometimes. They talked more but Mercy ended without getting any more insight about what happened than she already had. Maybe she would do nothing. Things had a way of just working out for the better. She would call Benton later tonight and talk to him about what had happened at the apartment. Again, Mercy told Madison what a nice place she had and offered to come and help her in the house anytime she wanted. Mercy also told Madison how beautiful she looked. Madison had gone from a gangly girl to a real knock out. Madison had her mother's Irish good looks. She was tall at six feet. She had a slim build but had curves in all the right places. She had gorgeous, thick chestnut hair and beautiful green eyes. Mercy was always envious of her best friends looks and wished she was a beautiful as Madison was. Madison had a lot of guys running after her in high school. She could get any guy she wanted. Bartending was a great job for Madison. She was a people person and with her looks, she made better tips than anyone. Madison let the guys at the bar think they had a chance with her. She teased and flirted and led them on, night after night but they still always came back for more.

When Mercy left, Madison was livid. She didn't know about Mercy's and Benton's engagement, and that ring. Oh my God, it was huge and must have cost Benton a fortune. What was he doing? He was supposed to be trying to slowly get rid of Mercy, not asking her to marry him. Benton had told Madison that he didn't want to break it off with Mercy completely until after he was finished with his residency because he didn't have time for all the drama that would bring right now, and he had to keep his eye on the bigger picture of becoming a plastic surgeon. Madison could understand that, but what she couldn't understand was why did he have to get engaged to Mercy.

Madison didn't feel any guilt about what she was doing. She and Mercy had known each other almost all their lives but Madison didn't consider Mercy to be her best friend of all time. Truth was, Madison was always jealous of Mercy. Mercy was beautiful in a different sort of way. Her features were a little plain, but she had such a sweetness about her that people naturally gravitated to and she was smart. Madison was just a "c" student. Madison thought that when Mercy graduated from nursing school that Mercy thought that she was better than her. Madison was just a bartender, but she would show Mercy who was the smartest in the end, when she was married to Benton. Madison wasn't sure if she loved Benton enough to marry him, or if she just wanted him because he was Mercy's. That would pay Mercy back for acting so high and mighty about graduating from college. Madison thought it was time for her to have another one of her little meetings with Benton's mother at the bar. Benton didn't know anything about these little meetings that she was having with his mother. She put a call into her right away. She also called Benton. He wasn't going to get away with this without a great explanation.

Madison waited at the bar for Benton's mother to show up. She was there within ten minutes. Benton's mother gave Madison two hundred and fifty thousand and told Madison she would receive another two hundred and fifty thousand when Benton and Mercy break up. That's how important it was to her and Benton, he just doesn't realize it yet. Benton needs to marry someone of his same social and economic status. This made Madison a little angry because she came from the same side of town as Mercy. How was she going to feel when she finds out that all she paid for is for Benton to get rid of one lower class girl, to marry another and then all her payout money will be for nothing. The worst thing that could happen, in Benton's mother's eyes, would be for Mercy to get pregnant. Madison had met Benton's roommate; Sydney and she was very confident that Sydney really had a love interest in Benton. He would help keep Benton and Mercy apart as much as possible. In the meantime, they all had to be as sweet to Mercy as could be so that she wasn't suspecting a thing. She was going to lose Benton and she wouldn't know what hit her. Benton's mother left the bar, after telling Madison that she would not be giving her any more money until the job was completed.

PART III

CHAPTER 17

It was Friday night. Travis was all packed and ready to go to Nashville. He wanted to leave late, when most of the traffic had died down. He hadn't made any reservations anywhere, he would just play it by ear. He was so excited to finally be able to follow his dream of becoming a huge country singing star. Mercy always told him how good he was, and he sure hoped that she was right. He would miss Mercy. She was his light when he was feeling a little down. She was always there for him and he loved her. He had a feeling that Mercy was not as in love with Benton as she thought she was and he was determined not to let Benton win her heart. He was going to pull out all the stops and do whatever it takes to get Mercy to love him as much as she loves that "pretty boy". Travis just hoped that he could do that before Mercy made the biggest mistake of her life by marrying Benton.

It was the next Friday night, Mercy's turn to work the weekend. She worked every third weekend. This was the weekend that Travis was going to Nashville. She had called him earlier and told him to have a safe trip and wished him much success and that she would see him when he returned home.

Travis was finally on his way, sitting atop his beautiful Harley that he had completely restored. The bike would be the envy of many men. He was driving down 275, a two-lane highway. There was s semi-truck in the right lane and Travis was behind him. Suddenly, the truck switched lanes to the left. At the same time, Travis was trying to get into the left lane to pass the truck. Travis didn't quite make it around the big truck. Maybe if he's had a little more experience riding a bike and knowing what gear to be in, the accident would have never happened. Travis hit the guard rail, to avoid hitting the truck. Travis's body connected to the rail and sent him flying forty feet in the air. When Travis hit the pavement, he was unconscious, but he was still alive.

An ambulance was there in no time. They assessed him for neck and back injuries and quickly got him to the nearest hospital, which happened to be the one that Mercy worked in. When they brought Travis into the emergency room and put him in a little section behind a curtain, there were many people in there doing something to or for Travis. In the emergency room, they cut his clothes off so they could put an IV in and to listen to his heart and lungs better. They were all standing around the gurney, Travis, becoming slightly more alert, saw faces he didn't know and couldn't understand what had happened to him.

When the doctors and nurses asked Travis a simple question, he didn't know the answer. Like his name, date and year. After assessing him, the doctors determined that Travis had a broken pelvis, a bruised kidney a lacerated liver and an obvious concussion. They were preparing Travis for surgery to fix his damaged liver and to reset his pelvis back into the correct position. They were concerned about him having a concussion but that was the least of their worries.

When they brought Travis into the emergency room and put him in a little section Travis was moaning loudly. One of the doctors said, "I will have the nurse get you some pain medicine just as soon as we evaluate your mental status and then you will be much, much, more comfortable. While walking through the emergency room, Mercy stopped dead in her tracks, she thought she heard Travis's voice down the hall but that would be impossible since Travis was on his way to Nashville, wouldn't it? She heard it again, he yelled, "Mercy!". She went to find him. He was in the second cubicle down. Mercy pulled the curtain back and there were about ten doctors and nurses surrounding him. The blood drained from Mercy's face and her knees felt weak. Someone scooted a chair underneath her. One of the nurses told her that they were getting ready to take him upstairs to surgery. Mercy thought Travis would be in Nashville by now and asked the nurse nearest to her, "What happened?" The nurse answered, "motorcycle accident involving a truck." Travis looked right into Mercy's eyes but didn't seem to recognize her, he just kept on yelling her name. One of her fellow nurses asked, "Do you know this guy?" Mercy replied, "Yes, he is one of my best friends. Is he going to be alright?" she said in a shaky voice. Her fellow nurse said, "I think so, but he has some pretty severe injuries, even a possible head injury. Right now, we are more concerned about him bleeding out from his liver because he has some very bad lacerations. Mercy couldn't think of what to say so she said, "He wears a helmet, that much I know. He's always safety conscious." That sounded dumb even to her own ears, then she asks, "Can I just squeeze up by his head for just a second while they are pushing him down to surgery?" The nurse replied, "Sure, go ahead. Do you know if he has any family we could call?" Mercy answered, "I'll call them, I know them." They were getting ready to roll Travis down to surgery. He had tubes, wires and blood everywhere. He looked confused, but he did not say anything else. Mercy looked in his eyes and the fact that she was there didn't even seem to register. Mercy said, "Travis, it's me, Mercy. You've had a bad accident, but you are going to be okay. Do you hear me Travis? You are going to be okay." She heard Travis mumble, I love you Mercy and she said, "Me to." She kissed him lightly on the forehead as they whisked him away to surgery. Oh my God Travis! Now Mercy could go into the little room behind the nurse's station and fall apart.

She thought she would die if anything happened to Travis and to not be able to see him looking back at her was the most awful feeling in the world. They had great doctors here, she just had to believe that he would be alright. She pulled herself together and called Travis's parents' house. Travis's Grandma answered the phone and Mercy asked to speak to Travis's Mother. When his mother got on the phone, she told her about Travis's accident and they said they would be at the hospital right away. Mercy couldn't believe this was happening, not to Travis, he was such a good person. Of course, she realized that had nothing to do with it. She knew that he was not experienced enough on the Harley yet. She started praying, asking God to please save her best friend.

Travis's surgery lasted nearly three hours and one hour in recovery and then he was taken up to ICU to be watched carefully. They had done a CAT scan after surgery on his head which showed that he had some fluid on his brain. The surgery staff assured Mercy that they would give her frequent updates as long as someone in Travis's family gave them permission to release information about him. They were very sweet people. Mercy could see why Travis was such a sweet guy. His Grandmother stayed home because she didn't get around that well and because she was already so upset. Travis's little brother stayed home with her.

Travis was in ICU and doing well. His liver laceration was sutured up and pins put in his pelvis. The Drs. Wanted to keep him sedated because of the pain he would be in when he woke up, but they couldn't do that because they needed to evaluate his brain injury. Travis slept all night. He didn't even open his eyes once. Mercy was so worried about him. Finally, in the early morning, she had to go home and get some rest and shower.

When Mercy got home, there was a message from Benton on the answering machine to call him when she got the chance. She put a call into him and he picked up on the fourth ring. She told him what was going on with Travis and how upset she was and that she was going back to the hospital as soon as she could. Benton sounded totally indifferent when he said, "Why? he's just a friend and his parents are there. Do you really think you should be hanging out with them at a time like this? "Benton sounded angry. Mercy replied, "Yes, they said they feel more comfortable when I am there because I work there and can give them more information. Besides, I'm so worried about him, especially his brain injury." Benton said, "Sounds like you care about him a little more than you were ever willing to admit." Now

Mercy was getting angry and replied, "Benton, don't be silly. I've known him practically all my life and we are best friends. Of course, I'm scared to death for him." Benton said, "Well, with all that going on, I guess you won't make it up here this weekend." She answered, "No, probably not. I'll stay here until I know for sure that Travis is out of the woods. Benton, about the last time I was up there...it was partly my fault and I share the blame. It's okay between us, right?" He said, "Right, don't worry about it, things like that are bound to happen sometimes, especially when we have been together so long now." It was kind of a snide remark coming from him, but Mercy didn't have time to think about that now. She told Benton, "I have to get some sleep and go back to the hospital." He said, "You don't have to rush me off the phone, just so you can run back over to see him" Mercy couldn't believe how jealous Benton was becoming, "Benton, I also have to work tonight, remember?" He replied, "Okay, sorry, I was just looking forward to seeing you this weekend, that's all." She answered, "Me to and I love you" and hung up the phone.

Mercy couldn't believe how difficult Benton was being when she needed him most. He knows how much she cares for Travis and how worried she is. It's always about him lately and what he wants and needs. Benton is a Momma's boy, which she knew from the beginning, but he is showing how spoiled he really is, more and more lately.

Mercy checked on her Father, sitting in front of the television of course, he was just the same, nothing new. She went on up to her room and fell into the big bed with the feather mattress, the one that two of her older sisters use to share. Now that she was the only one left at home, this is where she chose to sleep. She sunk down into the feathers and closed her eyes. Her mind was racing. She couldn't turn it off and relax. She had thought about some of the changes she had seen in Benton lately and how she didn't like them but justified all his words and actions because of doing his internship and how hard it was. She thought about Madison, how they use to be the best of friends for years and now they hardly ever see each other. She didn't know if she believed the story Madison told her about the rich uncle, but where else could she have gotten the money? She certainly wasn't a high-class call girl, working as a bartender where she did. She thought about Travis and the tears started coming and wouldn't stop. He only wanted to go after his dream and thought he was prepared. He was truly a good guy that did everything right but just couldn't seem to catch a break.

When Mercy saw Travis lying in that hospital bed, his skin pasty, his eyes not really focusing, it broke her heart. She knew then that she did love him. She loved him for a long time she thought, she just didn't realize it until now, until she almost lost him. She couldn't imagine her life without Travis, without her best friend, without her protector, without that one person that made her feel special above all others. When he gazed into her eyes, she could feel how much he loved her, and she was surprised that she hadn't realized it before. She thought about a life with Travis, going from town to town while he tried to get discovered. It would be an exciting life, but she wanted to be settled in her hometown. When she compared Travis to Benton, she thought that Benton was still the one she wanted. Mercy felt safe and secure in Travis's love for her, but in Benton's arms, she felt excitement and a sense of danger, she didn't know why. She would marry Benton as planned, he was the one she wanted but she would have to nurse Travis back to health first. Mercy felt she owed Travis for all the times that he was there for her, she wouldn't leave him now to go to Chicago to be with Benton. Benton would wait, she was sure of it.

Mercy heard the alarm going off, she just couldn't seem to wake up enough to turn it off. Finally, she did. She dragged herself out of bed and downstairs to the shower. She got ready for work, fixed her father something to eat and left it in the refrigerator for him and left for work early to see Travis.

When she approached Travis's bed in the ICU, she didn't see any movement. He had still not woken up. She went to the nurse's station to look at Travis's chart. The nurses afforded special privileges to each other. Mercy looked over the chart and didn't see anything she hadn't expected to see. The thing she was worried about now is Travis regaining consciousness, he should have by now. His brain had stopped swelling now, which was a good sign. He should be coming around soon. When he did finally wake up, he would be in a lot of pain from his liver surgery and the pin they put in his pelvis. They wouldn't give him anything for pain now because of his brain injury and the fact that he was in a coma, he didn't need it yet. He didn't know if he was even having any pain. He looked very peaceful like he was sleeping. Mercy held his hand and his hand moved slightly. Mercy knew that this movement wasn't Travis squeezing her hand but an automatic nervous system reaction. Mercy whispered, "Oh Travis, I's so sorry you wrecked your bike and are so badly hurt. I'm going to be here for you until you are one hundred percent well. Mercy bent down to his ear and said, "I love you Travis, I really do, I know that now." She raised up and she could have sworn that she saw a little smile on Travis's face. She shook him lightly and said, "Travis, wake up, it's me Mercy!" He did not wake up, he did not open his beautiful, blue eyes.

Travis's parents arrived, and Mercy told them that Travis was doing just fine and that his body had been through so much that he would wake up when he was ready, not to worry. They would spend the whole afternoon with him. Mercy stayed a while but then went on downstairs to work. Mercy would run upstairs from the ER every chance she got for the next week, even picking up extra shifts because she knew she would be there anyway.

Madison had called Benton last week, after hearing about Travis and wanted to know if she could come up and see him next weekend. Benton said that was fine because Mercy would be busy with Travis for a while. Benton didn't see what was so important about Travis that Mercy couldn't leave him for a weekend and he was still a little bit angry about it. After the way Mercy left him the last time she was here, Benton was more than ready for some female company. Benton would see if Sydney could go to his friend Rob's house this Saturday.

Madison wasn't Benton's only woman that he saw on the side, he also saw a woman here in Chicago that he met at a club, named Evelyn. Evelyn was a high-priced call girl that would be there whenever he wanted, and she was okay occasionally, but he preferred Madison. Madison was gorgeous, and she knew exactly what he liked.

Sydney was getting a little bit tired of these weekend

women that Benton would have over, but he couldn't really complain much since Benton paid the rent. Sydney still took care of Benton when he was home. Sydney had dated a couple of guys, one he met at the hospital named Rob. Sydney really liked Rob a lot and Rob wanted Sydney to leave Benton and move in with him. Rob told Sydney, "I don't see why you stay here with him, beside the apartment is really nice. You don't owe him anything and he's not even gay. You would never have a chance with him you know." Sydney really didn't have an excuse for wanting to stay with Benton. Benton could be a real pain in the ass sometimes, but he loved him for whatever reason. Sydney knew that they could never be a couple, but he still loved being around Benton and taking care of him. Sydney loved it when Benton would tell him that he has told him things that he would never tell another human being. It made Sydney feel special to him. He told Rob, he just wasn't ready to move out yet.

Sydney overheard Benton talking to Madison on the phone and he knew that she was coming over on Saturday. He and Madison didn't get along at all. Madison didn't understand why Benton was living with a gay guy and resented him being here instead of her. He would have to leave when she and Benton got engaged.

When Benton got off the phone with Madison, he turned to ask Sydney if he could be somewhere else on Saturday night when Sydney said, "I know, I heard. Yes, I'm sure I can go to Rob's on Saturday night. It's no big deal." Sydney thought this might be a good time to bring up his and Rob's relationship and said, "Benton, you know that Rob has been trying to get me to move in with him for a while now, what do you think?" Sydney was holding his breath as Benton said, "Well, of course, I love having you here Sydney but if you want to move in with Rob, go ahead. Do you love Rob or something?" Sydney said, "No, not really, I just like hanging out with him is all." Benton said, "Good, I like having you here and you are my best bud. Don't even think about moving if you're not one hundred percent." That made Sydney feel good and he replied, "Okay, but yeah, I can go to Rob's on Saturday night, no problem."

Sydney doesn't like to be around when Madison comes anyway. Madison not only resents him but is mean to him. She doesn't like anything about Sydney and only sees him as a butler for Benton. These feelings are mutual between her and Sydney. Sydney doesn't like what he hears in the bedroom when she is here. She and Benton have a very weird kind of relationship. Madison thinks that she is going to be with Benton one day, that he will marry her, and Sydney knows that he never will. Madison already knows too much about what kinds of things Benton likes, things that he wouldn't want a real wife to know. He loves Mercy anyway and Sydney doesn't know why Madison can't see that. Benton is just using Madison for his carnal pleasure. She still comes up here every time Benton ask her to, like she was his little sex slave or something. Sydney wondered if she even knew that Benton and Mercy were engaged? He knew that Madison and Mercy use to be best friends but hardly saw each other anymore, so he didn't know why Benton always wanted Madison and thought that he really didn't want to know either.

It was Saturday night and Madison would be here here

any minute. Benton had gotten out all their toys and things they like to play with that he secretly kept locked away in his bedroom. Benton thought, "This is going to be a fun night. Madison is just what I need." There was a light knock on the door and it was Madison. Benton let her in. Benton could immediately sense that Madison was in one of her moods when she was going to pressure him to get rid of Mercy. Benton had her favorite drink ready and ask, "How was your trip up here?" "Good, I guess you heard about Travis's accident?" He replied, "Yes, that's why Mercy didn't come up this weekend, she is too busy looking after him." Madison secretly liked that Benton was in pain over this. That pays him back for the pain he caused her sometimes. Madison pushed on, "You know, Mercy has always had a thing for Travis. They grew up together and even went to the prom together." This conversation was rubbing Benton the wrong way and he said, "Let's not talk about it tonight, okay?" Madison was impatient, "Well, we have to talk about Mercy sometime Benton, now is as good a time as any." Benton groaned, "There's really nothing to talk about now is there?" Madison was getting angry, "Well, why did you give Mercy an engagement ring, and expensive one at that, if you also care about me?" Benton knew Madison would bring up the engagement sooner or later and was dreading this conversation. Benton decided to go with the truth, besides what did he have to lose with Madison except a little fun in the bedroom? He said, "I ask Mercy to marry me, but we haven't set a date yet and now, to tell you the truth, I'm having second thoughts. I'm not sure that Mercy even loves me. I'm not sure I want this kind of drama while I'm trying to finish my residency." Madison said, "You know she's not right for you Benton, you know that I can make you much happier." Benton looked at her and smiled, "I know what you can do for me." Madison decided not to push it any further and asked, "Where's Sydney? Is he gone for the night?" "Yes" Benton said, "We are all by our lonesome." Madison replied, "Good, that little twerp gives me the creeps anyway." Benton pulled her toward the bedroom and locked the door.

CHAPTER 18

It was Friday morning and it had been a week since Travis's accident and he had still not woken up. Mercy was off tonight so she could go and spend most of the night with him. When he was stable, he had been moved from the ICU to a regular surgical floor. When Mercy walked into his room, it was eerily quiet. She pulled a chair up beside his bed and took his hand in hers. He looked so peaceful, just like he was at home, taking a nap. You'd never know he had been through so much in the past week. She laid her head down on his hand and for some reason, the tears started to flow. She cried for him and all that he had been through and the fear that he may never wake up again. Through the haze of her tears, she heard a whisper, "Mercy, Mercy". It was Travis, he was awake, even though his eyes weren't open, he said her name. Mercy said, "I'm here Travis, I'm right here." He whispered, his voice hoarse from nonuse and whispered, "Why are you crying?" She answered excitedly, "Oh Travis, I'm so glad that you are finally awake, why I was crying is not important, what's important is that you are awake and talking to me! "Where am I" he said. Mercy was so happy she shed even more tears but tears of joy this time. "You're in the hospital, you had a bad accident on your Harley. You have been asleep for the past week." He didn't look surprised but said, "My hip hurts." Mercy replied, "You had a broken pelvis, but they pinned it, it will get better soon." She had tears of joy running down her face as she said, "Travis, I know your just waking up, but I have something to tell you." He said, "What is it Mercy? I hope not any more bad news." She looked him in the eyes and said loud and clear, "I love you." She was shocked herself and didn't even know why she blurted that out, then she said, "I care about you a great deal and you worried all of us so much, especially your Grandma. I will have to go and call them to give them an update. Do you want me to ask the nurses for some pain medication for you?" He answered, "No, I'm just tired." He closed his eyes and he appeared to go back to sleep. Mercy was elated! This is the best news she could have hoped for today. She was sure that Travis was going to be okay now. She had been so worried she couldn't even eat or barely think about anything else. Mercy kissed Travis's cheek and told him to rest that she would be back in a little while. She stopped outside his door, closed her eyes and gave a special thanks to God for bringing Travis back to her. She went to the nurse's station to let them know that Travis had woken up. She then placed a call to Travis's family and gave them the good news. She was so elated. Travis was going to be okay!

Mercy continued to go to the hospital every day to check on Travis's progress. He was now able to use crutches without much pain in his hip from his pelvis injury. It's just a slow healing process. One night, while Mercy sat next to Travis's hospital bed, Travis said, "You know Mercy, since I have been lying here in this bed, I have had a revelation. I'm not so sure I want to be a famous country singer anymore. I think I want to work at the shop with my Dad and learn all about his business because someday it will be mine." Mercy asked, "Travis, why did you change your mind, you sing and play so well?" He said, "I've had a lot of time to think about what was most important to me in life and one of those things is spending time with his family, especially my father, in the garage. Travis had a lot to learn but his dad loved teaching him. Making it in Nashville is a one in a million shot and although I love music, I also love working on cars and bikes, so I have decided that is what I want to do with my life. I may try to go to Nashville later in my life but for now I am truly satisfied here. Mercy, I am so sorry for what happened with the wreck and how worried you were. My parents told me you hardly left my bedside and I want you to know that I appreciate that. I think I felt your presence here, even when I wasn't awake. Does that sound weird?" "No, not at all Travis. A lot of people report things like that when they are in a coma. I'm glad you felt my presence here beside you. I wanted you to know that I was here for you all the way. I never wanted you to feel like you were all alone." He answered sincerely, "Thank you Mercy. I love you to." Mercy just looked at him and didn't say anything to that last comment.

Mercy was going home to get some much-needed rest. She was off tonight and when she got up she would give Benton a call and see how he was doing without anyone to hang out with, he was probably lonely up there all by himself. She knew that Sydney liked to go out with his friend Rob on the weekend and knew that he probably wasn't there.

Mercy called Benton to give him the good news about

Travis. Benton said, "Well, it's about time he woke up and stop monopolizing all of my fiancé's time." For Mercy's sake, he threw in, "I'm glad that he has come around and is doing better." Mercy thanked him for that. She asked him what he was doing tonight, there in that big apartment all by himself. He answered, "Oh, just studying and catching up on my sleep, you know they work us such long hours." Mercy felt sorry for him and sorry that she didn't go up to see him this weekend. Mercy told him, "I'm going to try to make it up their next weekend Benton but I'm not making any promises. I'll have to see how Travis and my Dad are doing, but I really do miss you and want to see you." Benton said, "Me to." All the while, he had Madison pulling on his arm. He had put his finger to his lips to signal Madison to be quiet. That was the last thing he needed was for Mercy to find out that Madison was here. Mercy said, "Yes, I need to come up there soon. We have a lot to talk about and we need to set a date for our wedding and make some wedding plans." He answered, "Oh, we will for sure make some wedding plans when you come up Mercy." This made Madison angry and she started throwing things around the room, making noise on purpose. Mercy asked, "Is Sydney or someone there with you Benton?" "No, it's just the television is on. Maybe we can get together next weekend?" Mercy said, "I'll have to look at my work schedule. I'll talk to you soon Benton, love you." He replied, "me to".

When Benton got off the phone with Mercy, Madison was angry and said, "Benton, when are you going to drop her? You know that she isn't right for you. You two will never be able to live together without criticism from everyone around you. Break off the engagement and stay with me. We could make each other happy. I've bought a big, beautiful house on the east side of Cincinnati, in Mt. Adams and I'm sure you would love it. Benton didn't know where she got the money but didn't ask. He never dreamed in a million years that the money came from his mother. Benton looked at Madison and said, "Madison, you know I have told you one hundred times before, I am marrying Mercy and you are my mistress who gets paid very well to keep her mouth shut. I'm sorry if that hurts, but you have known this from the beginning. You have been making plans for the two of us all along, that I had no say in. It's true, we have a great time together and I consider you a friend, but that is as far as it goes. That is as far as it will ever go. I don't love you. I'm not even sure anymore that I love Mercy but as far as this conversation about you, Mercy and I are concerned, it is over, and I will not discuss my other relationships with you again. I will never leave Mercy for you, and you have known that from the very beginning. I like being with you, you satisfy me like no other woman ever has, and you get paid very well for it. If you can't handle this job, just let me know and we can end our relationship now. "Wow" was all Madison could say. Deep down she already knew all of this, but she was still hoping to lure him away from Mercy one day. She had forgotten what a hold Mercy had on him and she sure didn't know what that was. She looked at Benton and said, "Fine, I understand, discussion closed." Madison was a big girl and she would put her "big girl panties" on and go on and do the job she came to do in the first place.

The next morning, when Madison was getting ready to leave, she was feeling a little devious because of Benton's complete dismissal of her the night before, even though they had a great time later that night. In the bathroom that was connected to the guest room, she opened a small drawer in the sink vanity that was empty and left one of her earrings, one of which Mercy had given her, lay in the bottom of the drawer where it couldn't be missed. Benton didn't know who he was messing with, and it sure would make his Momma happy when Benton and Mercy broke up and then she could collect the rest of her money that was due, that she felt she had earned. She didn't care how she got the money, she was just tired of being poor and she would never go back to that lifestyle of being a bartender again, even if she had to screw the president. Benton's mother would have to pay her more money when all of this is over, to keep her silence, and she was sure she would.

Travis was doing a lot better the next week, even had been up and walking around with a walker. He was improving more and more every day. Mercy thought it would be safe to leave him now and she would call Benton and see if she could go up and see him this weekend.

She called him that afternoon. She said, "Benton, I's like to come up and see you this weekend, if that's okay." He was surprised and replied, "Sure, that would be great." To be nice, he asked, "How is your friend Travis.?" Mercy gave him an updated report. Benton told her, "We will go out somewhere special this weekend and maybe we can finally set a date to get married." Mercy replied, "That would be great Benton. I was getting a little worried that maybe you were getting cold feet or something." "No way, we have been together going on four years and I'm ready now. I'm ready to tie the knot to the most beautiful woman in the world." Benton could be so charming when he wanted to be. Mercy said, "Okay, I'll see you on Saturday then. I love you." "Me to" he said, as usual and then hung up the phone. Sydney was standing nearby and ask, "So you need me to disappear on Saturday night again?" Benton said, "No, Mercy is coming up. Don't worry, nothing will happen like it did the last time. I don't plan on drinking a drop on Saturday. We are going to set a date for the wedding." Sydney thought, "Good, about time." then he wouldn't have to see that witch Madison anymore. He couldn't stand being around her and she him"

Mercy was excited about seeing Benton. It had been a few weeks since she had been up to Chicago to see him and she really missed him. To assure herself that Benton wouldn't act up like he did the last time she was there, he had promised her that he would not drink a drop on Saturday or Sunday., the whole time that she was there. It was nine in the morning and time for her to shove off. She went into the living room to tell her father goodbye and to tell him that she left him food in the fridge. He said, "Thanks Mercy," and then went back to watching television. He was getting worse by the day. He had almost stopped showering, washing his hair or even taking care of himself in any way. Mercy thought that maybe she would have to check into putting him in a nursing home when she got back. She couldn't give him the care he needed. She didn't know if he would even put up a fight or not.

The drive up to Chicago for Mercy was uneventful and traffic wasn't bad at all. Benton seemed genuinely happy to see her. They seemed like the same old couple. Benton took Mercy to a very nice restaurant and then they went to one of the many art museums here, which they both enjoyed. They got back to the apartment late. Mercy loved it when

Benton didn't drink. He was so much more engaging in their conversations.

They sat on the couch. Mercy said, "I was thinking a fall wedding Benton, what do you think?" He replied, "I don't know, I was thinking more about June because in June, I can get off for two months. That would give us time for a proper honeymoon. Mercy said, "Where do you want to go on our honeymoon?" He replied, "I already have the place picked out, it's a surprise. All you have to bring is your swimsuit and flip flops." "OH, that sounds exciting Benton but let's get back to this wedding date. June is not very far away, only four months, not a very long time to plan a wedding." Benton said, "Ask my Mother for help, she would love it and if anyone could get it done, she could." Mercy said, "You know, I think your right. I'll ask her and maybe that will even make our relationship a little better." Benton excitedly said, "Okay, how about June 20? That's my birthday and should be easy for me to remember in coming years." Benton said with a grin. Mercy said that was fine with her, that she had two weeks of vacation time coming and she would go ahead and put in for it now. Now, both kind of felt like things were getting a little more solid. They both decided they were tired and going to bed.

Mercy slept in the guest bedroom without any incidents from Benton. Benton stayed in his own room all night. Sydney must have come home last night, she heard him messing around in the kitchen, making something wonderful, like he always does.

Mercy took a shower and open the vanity drawer to get her hairbrush that she kept there. She immediately saw something sparkling. She picked it up and knew what it was immediately. She was so hoping that it wasn't Madison's and that Benton had a good explanation of what it was doing here. Mercy knew that she had to turn it over in her hand and look for Madison's initials, even though she really did not want to. It took her a few minutes and then she turned the piece over. There was Madison's initials as big as you please. Oh my God, what is going on here anyway? Mercy marched out to breakfast table where Benton was sitting and asked him what Madison's earring was doing in the vanity of the bathroom. He looked dumbfounded for a second and knew that he had to think very fast, he said, "Oh, I forgot to tell you, Madison and one of her boyfriends stopped by on their way to a show up here, she said that you would want her to stop and check on me. I remember her complaining how her earrings were too heavy, I guess she pulled one off and the cleaning lady just put it in the drawer. Mercy was a little skeptical but realized that his explanation was plausible. She said, "Okay Benton." Mercy told Benton how she had bought the earring for Madison as a house warming gift because she couldn't think of anything else to buy her since she has everything. Benton said, "What do you mean, she has everything?" Mercy said, "Well she lives in a ten-bedroom house in Mt. Adams on the east side of Cincinnati. She said that a rich uncle had left her a lot of money." Benton's mind was racing, he knew that he didn't pay Madison that well to live in a place like that. He would have to find out if she had other important clients that paid her that well. The more men she was with, the more chance he had of getting found out by Mercy and he didn't like it one bit. Sydney had prepared a late lunch for all of them. Mercy thanked Sydney a million times.

PART IV

CHAPTER 19

Before Mercy left Benton's apartment, she talked to him about her plans to put her father in a reputable nursing home, where she thought he would be more comfortable. Benton thought it was a good idea. Mercy said she would discuss it with her siblings before she made the final decision but ultimately the decision was hers since she was the main caregiver. The rest of her siblings just kind of disappeared into their own lives.

Mercy left a couple hours later to return home. She thought about the earring again for just a fleeting second and then she put it out of her head. When she saw Madison again, she would ask her why she never mentioned seeing Benton up in Chicago. It probably just slipped her mind. Mercy also couldn't wait to get back home and see how Travis was doing. She was so happy at his progress so far.

A couple weeks later, Mercy went to see Travis. He was doing well and not using the walker now. He was walking on his own. The Doctors were going to let him go home on Monday. Mercy was thrilled with this news. When she saw Travis standing up with his cowboy hat on and how handsome he was, it made her heart flutter in her chest. She didn't know why he made her feel that way, but she did know that she had feelings for him and if anything, ever happened to him she just wouldn't be able to stand it. She told Travis that she would be at his house on Monday evening to check on his progress. Travis said, "There's nothing like having my own personal nurse to take care of me."

It was Sunday and Mercy thought that she would just take a ride to Madison's, so she could find out about the earring and give it back to her. She didn't think anything was going on with her and Benton, she just though it strange that she hadn't mentioned it when she was there a couple of weeks ago.

Madison let her in the gate and was waiting for her at the front door when she arrived. Madison said, "What a pleasant surprise! It's good to see you again Mercy, so soon." Mercy replied, "I know, it's good to see you again also. How is the house unpacking going?" "Fine, why don't you come and sit down in the parlor and I'll get us something to drink?" When Madison returned, Mercy tentatively said, "Madison, I have something for you." Madison asked, "What is it Mercy?" Mercy held out the earring to her friend. Madison just had a fleeting moment of surprise on her face and then she said, "Oh, thanks so much Mercy, where did you find it? I've been looking all over for it." Mercy said, "I found it at Benton's apartment in the guest bedroom bathroom drawer." Madison said, "Oh, I probably lost it there when Daniel, a fellow co-worker of mine went up to Chicago to see a show and we stopped by to see Benton because we were running a little bit too early. We only stayed a few minutes." Madison had to think fast on her feet and she was always good at that. In her business, you had to do that a lot. Madison could see by Mercy's face that she believed her, but what would Benton say?

Madison knew that she would be receiving a phone call from Benton soon. Of course, he will think that she had left the earring there on purpose and no amount of lying about it will make him happy, so she will just let him get it out of his system. No sooner had that thought left her mind when the phone rang it was Benton. She could tell by the caller ID. She answered it and Benton said, "What the hell are you trying to pull by leaving an earring in the drawer in the bathroom that Mercy uses when she is here?" Madison interrupted quickly. She didn't want him to know that Mercy was here. Madison said, "Now isn't a good time, I'll call you later." And she hung up the phone. Mercy thought that was a strange conversation. Madison said she would go to the kitchen and get them another drink. While she was gone, Mercy picked up the phone and looked at the caller ID and saw that it was Benton's apartment. Why is he calling Madison? Why wouldn't Madison talk to him because she was here? Strange things are going on around here. Mercy didn't know but she was sure going to keep her eyes and ears open from now on. Madison came back into the room and handed Mercy her drink. Madison assumed that she may have looked at the caller ID, so before she got a chance to say anything, Madison said, "That was Benton on the phone. I'm not supposed to tell you, but he is planning a little engagement party for the two of you. I think it was supposed to be a surprise, but I didn't want you wondering why Benton was calling here. Mercy said, "Oh, now I have made you go and spoil it, that's okay, I never did like surprises anyway. We have set a date for the wedding.

It's going to be on Saturday, June 20th. I know it's very soon and weddings take a long time to plan but we are having a very small, unassuming wedding, which doesn't make Benton's Mother happy in the least, but she will have to deal with it. Madison's eyes got big and she didn't hear anything after June 20th. How could he set a wedding date?

Madison thought that Benton was going to break it off with Mercy in June when his first year of residency was over. He said he was waiting until then because he didn't want the drama right now. He got engaged and now he is going to marry Mercy, just like he planned all along. He never had any intention of breaking up with her and being with me, she thought. Man, how stupid could a girl be? He was only using her for her deviant sexual appetite, which Madison would have to admit to herself, that she enjoyed also. Using her because Miss High & Mighty here, wouldn't let him near her cat until they were married. What a goody two shoes she was. Madison admitted to herself that she kind of knew all along that Benton was using her, but she really liked him a lot. Why couldn't Mercy just go off and marry Travis and leave the rest of them alone?

Mercy looked at her. Mercy said, "Hello, earth to Madison, are you here?" Madison snapped out of her monologue to herself and said, "Oh, I'm so sorry, I was thinking about Travis and how well you said he was doing. It's awfully nice that you are going to keep him at your house to take care of him Mercy. Mercy answered, "What, I never said that." Madison replied, "Well, I just thought that was a no brainer since you are a nurse and all. Travis couldn't have any better care, and I think you owe him. Mercy didn't like the attitude that came over Madison suddenly. Why was Madison making her feel like she owed Travis just for driving her around a few times? Well, she guessed she did owe him and besides, he was her best friend. Why shouldn't she take care of him until he is up on his feet and finished with physical therapy. Mercy said, "Madison, I hadn't thought about that, but that is a great idea. I will take care of Travis at my house until he is finished with his physical therapy. I guess I do owe him that much and besides, I'd love to do it. It gets kind of lonely around the old house with Dad gone. Madison asked, "Where is your Father?" Mercy answered, "He's in a nursing home about five miles away. I see him almost every week. He really needed more intimate care than I could give him, and he also needed to socialize rather than sit in front of that damn television all day anyway, I think he really likes it there. I'm in that old house all by myself so it will be nice to have Travis there to keep me company.

Madison smiled inwardly. How perfect could that be? It will keep her away from Benton on the weekends. Benton will be angry with her for taking Travis in and Benton's Mother will be pleased. She amazes herself sometimes, the things she comes up with. Madison said, "You should call Benton later and tell him. He will be pleased that you are such a good Samaritan, a caring person, even if he doesn't like Travis that much." Mercy made a face and answered, "Right, he won't like it a bit, but he is a big boy. I think he can handle it."

When Mercy left Madison's, she decided to stop and run the idea past Travis to see what he thought about her taking care of him at least until he was finished with his physical therapy. She stopped at the hospital and went up to his room. His parents were there visiting. His parents had had him late in life and they were both getting up there in age. Mercy told them she would come back later, and they said no, they were just leaving, just walking out the door and how nice it was to see her. When they left, Mercy asked Travis how he was feeling. He said, "Oh, I feel okay. I just feel bad that when I get home, I will be a burden on my aging parents. They aren't getting any younger you know." Mercy said, "That's kind of what I came here to talk to you about. How would you like to come to my house and I will take care of you until you are finished with your PT?" Travis replied, "Although I like the idea of you taking care of me, I really don't want to be an imposition on you either. Besides, you have your Father to take care of. She'd forgotten to tell Travis. "Nope, Dad is in a nursing home. It's a much better situation for him right now. So, I'm in that old house all by my lonesome. I'd love to have you come and be with me and keep me company while you are getting well." Travis searched her face to see if she really meant it. "I thought you were moving to Chicago?" Mercy replied, "I was, but now I still need to be here in case my Dad needs me. Travis, please think about it, it wouldn't be any trouble in the least." He said, "I don't want to cause any problems between you and Benton, but I do think my parents would be grateful. Okay, I will stay at your house, but you have to promise me one thing." "What is it?" she replied. "You have to promise me that if I become too much of a pain the ass, that you will kick me back home." "Okay, I promise." She visited a little while longer and then headed home. She was off tonight so she decided the house needed a good cleaning before Travis came to stay. She also had to call Benton and let him know what was going on. Maybe he would be understanding, or at least not too angry about it.

She got home and got settled and decided that now would be a good time to call Benton. He would probably be home from the hospital by now. She dialed his number. Sydney answered the phone and said, "Hi Mercy, how are you? I heard that you and Benton have set a date. I'm so happy for you." She responded, "Thank you Sydney, is Benton home?" He said, "Yes, he is out on the terrace. I'll take him the phone." Mercy thanked him.

The next thing Mercy heard was Benton's voice, "Hello Mercy, what a pleasant surprise. I was just thinking about you." "I was just thinking about you also Benton. I have something to tell you and now please, please don't get angry and try to be understanding okay?" Benton hated when Mercy talked like this. It was usually something that would really piss him off." She continued, "I am going to move Travis in here with me, so I can take care of him and he is finished with his PT. What do you think?" Benton replied sarcastically, "Do I have a choice? It sounds like you two have already made up your mind without me, as usual." She said, "Benton, please don't be angry. You know that I think of Travis as a brother and besides his parents are too old to take proper care of him and I owe him for things that happened in my past during my high school days." There was anger in Benton's voice. "This isn't high school, and you don't owe him anything." Mercy was feeling a little angry towards Benton for making a mountain out of a mole hill. "Well, maybe not, but I feel like I do, and it would only be for a very short while. Please be okay with it. I don't want to fight while we are trying to get our wedding together. It's too much stress for me." Benton gave in to Mercy, like he usually does, "Okay, I'll try to cope with it. Just don't do anything too personal for him and kick him out as soon as he is ready, okay?" Mercy agreed with a smile in her voice. Benton would do almost anything to see her smile and make her happy. He couldn't believe that he ever let his Mother inside his head and make him have a second thought about her. He will never do that again. He is in love and always has been in love with Mercy. She is the only woman for him.

Mercy went and picked Travis up from the hospital on Monday and took him home to her house. She got him all fixed up in her Dad's easy chair and waited on him hand and foot. He would sleep in her parent's old bedroom downstairs, so he didn't have to climb steps.

Mercy was enjoying playing house with Travis. She found out that she really did like to cook, and she didn't mind cleaning and laundry that much at all. She and Travis got a routine going with his exercises and meals. They ate their meals together except when Mercy was working. When she had to go to work, she made sure he had everything he would need within arm's reach and he could always call his Mother down the street if need be. She felt it was safe to leave him alone.

In the mornings when she helped him with his bath and at night when she helped him into his pajama's, she couldn't help but notice his tanned, broad shoulders and muscular arms. Travis was very well built. He caught her looking at him sometimes, but he pretended not to notice. He secretly liked that she liked looking at him. He almost never wanted to go back home. He liked it here with Mercy. Mercy couldn't deny there was a lot of sexual tension in the air. She was also amazed at how much easier it was with Travis. Conversation was easy, and he was so interesting to talk to. He knew a little bit about everything. One thing she did learn during these weeks of Travis's convalescence is that she could sing well. Travis played his guitar at night and she would sit and sing with him. It brought them a special kind of closeness. Travis was finally through with his PT and had improved so much in the last four weeks. He could walk well on his own without much pain at all. Travis was ready to go home. Out of all the things he asks about his accident, he never ask about the Harley and what had become of the last remnants of it. Mercy guessed he figured out it was not salvageable. Travis didn't know if he would ever want to get back on a bike again. Travis, however, did not give up on his dream of becoming a Country Western star.

Benton called Mercy's house every day for the last five days. He wanted to know if Travis had gone home yet. Benton knew from talking to Mercy that Travis was well enough. Tonight, when he called, he got the news that he had been hoping for. Travis was going home tomorrow. Benton was glad about that. The less time Travis spent with his fiancé, the better.

The next day, Mercy helped Travis pack his things and helped him get ready to move back down the street with his parents. It was going to be a sad goodbye for them both. They had gotten so used to living with each other. After diner Travis was ready to leave. He was sitting at the kitchen table, just having finished dessert when he looked at Mercy and said, "Mercy come over here for a second." Mercy answered, "I'm right here Travis." Mercy thought that Travis has a strange look in his eyes. He said, "No, come over here to my side of the table." Mercy got up and went around to his side of the kitchen table. Travis reached for her waist and sat her on his lap. She didn't protest, except to say, "Travis, I'll hurt your hip." "No, it doesn't hurt, and you don't weight more than a wet hen." Mercy always liked his analogies. Travis put his arm around her waist and gazed into her eyes. He said, "Mercy, I don't know how I will ever repay you for taking such good care of me these last four weeks. You went above and beyond, and I just want you to know how much I appreciate that." She said, "I know you do Travis, and I also know that you would do the same for me if the situation had been reversed." He whispered, "Not only did you take care of me, but you also lifted my spirit and that makes me love you more. You do know how much I love you, don't you Mercy?" She whispered back, "Yes, I think I do Travis." He said, "You know when I was just waking up in the hospital and you said you loved me, did you mean it?" Mercy didn't quite know how to respond to this question and knew that she had to tread lightly here. She didn't want to give Travis any false hope, but she couldn't lie to him either. Mercy said, "Yes, I meant it. You know I have always loved you Travis." Travis said in his very soft, sexy voice, "Mercy would you please kiss me goodbye?" She looked at him sadly, "No, not goodbye Travis, we will see each other all the time." "No, he said, "Will you kiss me goodbye now because we will never have this moment together again." He bent towards her and she was powerless to stop him. He brushed her soft lips ever so lightly with his, then he let her go. He stood up and walked out of the room to get his things. Mercy knew it had to be this way, but he left her wanting so much more. When Benton kissed her, did he leave her wanting more?

She couldn't really remember that feeling after being kissed by Benton.

Benton called that night to see if Travis really did go home and Mercy assured him that he did. She tried not to sound sad about it, but she couldn't help herself. It didn't go unnoticed by Benton. Benton suggested that she come up to Chicago next weekend, he really wanted and needed to see her. He missed her so much. She said there was no way that she could take off the next weekend because she had used up most of her personal time taking care of Travis, but she could probably come up the weekend after that. He said, "Okay" but he wasn't happy about it.

CHAPTER 20

Benton was surprised at how much he did miss Mercy. He still wasn't quite sure if he should be getting married to Mercy or not, or to anyone right now for that matter but he did believe that he loved Mercy. His Mother was pushing him on details of the wedding and he and Mercy had pretty much decided to elope. Mercy didn't have enough family members to come to a wedding to make it worthwhile to spend the money and, she didn't like being the center of attention. Benton didn't really care one way or another. Benton would just as soon go to Las Vegas and get married. He knew that if he took this step with Mercy that he would be giving up all his extracurricular activities with other women and with Madison. Madison was pushing him to get rid of Mercy. Madison kept telling him that Mercy wasn't right for him and how they had nothing in common. Benton felt like too many people were pushing him to do different things and he just didn't need that right now when he was trying to finish his residency.

Benton didn't have to worry about Sydney being home on the weekends anymore he pretty much stayed at Rob's all the time now. Sometimes he saw Sydney during the week as one of them were coming and going. Sydney really liked

Rob but didn't want to make a full commitment to move in with him yet.

Sydney had seen Benton a couple of times this past week and Benton did mention that Madison was coming over on Saturday night. It seemed to Sydney that Madison was coming over more and more lately and Mercy was coming less and less. Sydney had heard about Mercy taking care of a sick friend and Benton couldn't even be faithful to her for that short a time. Sydney didn't see what Benton saw in Madison. A million girls could do what Madison does for him. Sydney was tired of all of Benton's games and Mercy was a great girl. She didn't deserve someone like Benton. She deserved someone so much better. Sydney knew that it was wrong, but he called Mercy and told her that she had better come up here on Saturday because Benton really needed her right now and if there was any way that she could get off work Saturday night even, that she should come up. Sydney told Mercy that Benton had been really depressed lately because he hadn't seen her in a while. Mercy told Sydney that she would see what she could to. Sydney knew full well what Mercy would find when she got to the apartment. Sydney didn't care about Benton anymore. Rob helped him see that Benton was just a user and made Sydney realize that he didn't need Benton, so Sydney didn't even care if Benton ever spoke to him again. Mercy would find out the truth about Benton. Mercy told Sydney that she could come but wouldn't be there until about nine at night. She said not to tell Benton, she wanted to surprise him. Sydney knew who the surprised one would be.

The weekend got here fast, and it was Saturday already. Madison was due here at any minute and Benton had ordered Chinese takeout for the both. When Madison sat down to dinner with him, he poured both a nice glass of wine. Madison asked if Sydney would be home tonight and Benton told her probably not. He hadn't seen Syd in a few days. Madison said, "Good I hate that little twerp." Benton said, "Come on now, let's not be cruel, he's a good guy."

When Mercy got to Benton's apartment, she opened the door with her key. She walked in and there was hardly any light on, so she figured that Benton must be asleep. She heard noises coming from Benton's bedroom and she stopped outside the door. She heard a woman's voice that sounded vaguely familiar. When she opened the door, Benton and Madison were sitting next to each other, fully clothed on the bed, talking. Benton jumped up and said, "Mercy, what a nice surprise!" He was so happy, he hugged her. She was stiff in his arms. All Madison could think of to say is, "Hello, Mercy." Madison thought, "Good thing she wasn't here a half hour from now or she would really be surprised." Mercy said, "Madison, what are you doing here? What is going on?" Benton said, "Mercy please, it's not what you think. There wasn't anything going on." Madison hated to see Benton grovel that way. It was unmanly. Madison just happened to be in town and stopped by thinking that you were up here this weekend." Mercy said, "Well, what were you two doing in the bedroom?" Benton hurriedly answered, "I was showing her my collection of movie memorabilia that was in my closet." Mercy felt kind of stupid and said, "Oh, okay, Madison what are you doing up here, so far away from home?" Madison said, "I'm trying to decorate that big old house of mine and I came up here to go through some of the art galleries. Believe me, Benton is perfectly innocent of any wrong doing. Mercy was starting to believe them when Sydney walked in the door. Sydney said, "Oh Mercy, I see you have finally caught the two of them together." Mercy looked at the both of them and said, "Madison, you are supposed to be my best girlfriend. How could you do such a thing to me? Benton, I have been faithful to you since day one and this is what I get in return?" Mercy snatched off her engagement ring and threw it at Benton's head, then she walked over to where Madison was sitting and punched her right in the nose. Madison screamed in pain. Mercy turned on her heel and walked out with tears streaming down her face. Madison didn't feel too badly about it. Maybe now she and Benton could have a real relationship and she could also collect her other $250,000.00 from his Mother because surely Mercy and Benton wouldn't get back together after this night. Benton ran after Mercy and tried to grab her by the shoulders. Mercy threw him off and yelled, "Just leave me alone Benton!" Benton let Mercy go. He thought that it would be better to try and talk to her when she had calmed down a little bit. He said, "okay Mercy, I'll leave you alone, but don't try to drive home right now in the dark while you are so upset." She yelled, "Oh, now you are worried about me. Isn't that cute?" Mercy got in her car and left the parking garage with Benton standing there with his mouth open. For once, he didn't know what to say.

Benton went back to his apartment and confronted Sydney. He said, "Sydney, did you set me up tonight? Did you call Mercy and tell her to come up?" Sydney replied, "Yes, as a matter of fact, I certainly did. It wasn't right what you were doing to poor Mercy. Galivanting around with whores and doing God only knows what with them, not to mention with Madison, Mercy's best friend. Mercy is trying to save herself for you and has been faithful to you for the last four years. Benton, you don't deserve a girl like Mercy." Benton punched Sydney in the face and hurt his own hand in the process. Benton told Sydney, "I've let you live here for the past year, rent free, and now this is how you repay our friendship. Get your shit and get out." Sydney got up off the floor, holding his bloody cheek and said, "You wouldn't have noticed, because you are so into yourself, that I already moved out weeks ago." Sydney left the apartment for good, and not feeling bad in the least about what he had done. He just felt bad for Mercy.

Benton looked at Madison and said, "I suppose you knew about this tonight also?" She answered, "Of course not, do you think I like getting punched in the nose? I didn't know anything about Mercy coming up here." Madison never liked Sydney but was secretly thanking him for his unknowing help in getting rid of Mercy for her. Now, she can get the rest of the money Benton's Mother owes her and she can finally have Benton also. Benton's Mother doesn't know about the second part. His Mother believes that once Benton and Mercy are broken up, that she will go her separate way, which she and Madison had never talked about. Madison never had any intention of leaving Benton.

Benton walked over to the liquor cabinet to pour himself a drink. He didn't mind that Sydney was gone. Sydney was getting on his nerves anyway and his OCD was getting much worse. Every time Benton even sat a glass down, Sydney was snatching it up to wash it. He was driving him crazy.

Benton felt bad for Madison and thought that her nose

was broken. Madison was so beautiful, she would have to go to the hospital to have it fixed. It was really starting to swell. Benton didn't mind that Madison saw Mercy walk in on them except now she would be bugging him about them getting engaged.

Benton felt bad for Mercy but was really, glad that she hadn't walked in a half hour later or she would have seen a lot of things she didn't want to see, like him and Madison dressed in leather with whips and chains. Benton knows that she would have never forgiven him for that. Instead, it was bad enough, being caught in a bedroom with one of her best friends or ex-best friends. The only thing that made Benton happy in the least on this night was the fact that Mercy was willing to fight for him because she is not a violent person in the least.

Mercy was on the highway, both hands gripping the wheel, tears streaming down her face. She still wasn't quite sure what she had walked in on tonight. Benton said he was innocent, Madison said she'd stopped by. Sydney wanted them to get caught together so she "would know what was going on." Well, she still didn't know what was going on in that place. Benton seemed very repentant and his excuse was plausible. Was she making excuses for him because she loved him? What was Madison doing there? Mercy didn't really believe her story of just stopping by, looking for decorations and art for her new home. Mercy knew that Madison just wouldn't go through that much trouble for furnishings. What were they talking about when she was listening through the door? Did it concern her? Mercy had a million questions running through her head. Mercy wanted to call and talk to Travis about it, but she wouldn't because that would give him more fuel to hate Benton. She didn't have anyone to talk to or anyone to turn to. Boy, how she really wished her Mother were here, she would tell her what to do. Her aunt had also passed away recently so she just didn't have anyone except …her Father? He was still in the nursing home. Mercy had never talked to him about such things before and didn't know if she could start now, but he was all she had so she would give him a try. She decided to get up early in the morning and go to the nursing home to visit her Father.

CHAPTER 21

Mercy cried all night and was missing the beautiful ring on her left hand. She just didn't know if this could ever be fixed or not. She got up early the next morning, got in the shower and stopped at the Dunkin Donut store to pick up a special treat for her Dd. Dunkin Donuts, donut holes were his favorite. She played over and over in her mind how to start this conversation, but she kept coming back to "just blurting it out."

She walked up the front steps of the nursing home. There were white wicker rockers sitting all along the long veranda with a few people sitting in them, slowly rocking back and forth. She went inside and registered at the nurse's desk. She asked one of the nurses how her Father had been doing. They said he was doing extremely well. He had finally started opening up to other people. He has made a couple of buddies that he likes playing cards with and even a couple of female friends he plays canasta with. He also loves the food here and has been gaining weight and looks great. "Wow", Mercy said. She couldn't believe it, but she was so happy that her Dad was in a place that he loved and was enjoying his retirement years with his new friends.

Mercy went to his apartment. All residents here had a

three-room apartment, which consisted of a kitchenette, bedroom and living/dining room, and the furnishings were very nice. This facility took anyone of the residents who wanted to go, to the grocery store and pharmacy once a week on their bus.

Mercy walked in and her Father was sitting on the couch, eating a sandwich. He looked up at her and she couldn't believe it was the same man. He was bright eyed, clean shaven and had indeed put on some weight. Mercy said with a smile in her voice, "Dad, is that you?" He replied, "Of course it is silly, come and sit down with me." Mercy sat down, and her Father hugged her tentatively. He wasn't quite sure if that was okay with her or not. He said, "It's so good to see you. You have been my only visitor here. The rest of the kids don't come, and I don't blame them much. I know I wasn't exactly a very good Father to all of you." Mercy didn't comment on that. She just said, "Dad, are you still drinking?" His face was beaming when he replied, "I haven't had a drink since I've been here, for six months. They have meetings right here at the facility and I have a sponsor here. I've also made a few friends that have also quit drinking. We give each other support." Mercy could hardly believe her ears and she replied, "Dad, that is so wonderful. I'm so excited for you!" He told her, "I tried to quit drinking many times before but the stress of raising seven kids and keeping food on the table, I just couldn't do it then." Mercy nodded, "You have now and that is the important thing." He looked her in the eye and he said, "Mercy, I know I haven't ever told you, but I just want you to know how proud I am of you. You've grown up to be a beautiful woman and I'm so proud you are a nurse. I tell everyone here that you are a nurse and help save people's lives." Mercy seemed a little surprised and replied, "Thank you Dad for saying that. It means so much to me." He said, "You know Mercy, no one in my family ever even graduated high school. Me and your Mother only went to the eighth grade. We had to quit school back then to work and help support our families. Times are different now, and well, I just wanted you to know how proud I am of you." Mercy got tears in her eyes. She never thought in a million years that she would ever hear her Father say anything like that. He said, "How is the old house, still standing?" She replied, "Yes, still there. I still live in it." He said, "That old house holds a lot of memories for me and your Mom. I guess I had to move out of there to ever move forward with my life. I loved your Momma so much, she was a really good woman." With all the stress Mercy had been under and the mention of her Mother, she started to cry. Mercy said, "I miss Momma so much and I don't have anyone to talk to about things." Her Father replied, "I ain't as smart as your Momma was, but if I could help in any way, I'll surely try. What is it Mercy, what has gotten you so upset?" Mercy replied, "I don't know if you can help me or not but here goes." Mercy told him about Benton and what he has put her through throughout their relationship and how his parents didn't like her. She told him about the engagement and how she had thrown the ring back at him, but she also told him how much she loved him. Mercy then told her Father about Travis. Her Father said, "Yes, I remember Travis. The good-looking kid down the street." She said, "Yes, that's him." She told her Father about her whole relationship with Travis, how they had been lifelong friends and helped each other through hard times in their lives. Mercy then told him about Madison, how she thought they were also lifelong friends but now they really weren't, and she would miss that relationship. Mercy's Father listened to every word, which was kind of strange for Mercy. He said, "Wow girl, you do have a lot on your mind. I never was one for up and telling someone what to do about their business. Let me think on it for a day. Come back tomorrow and I'll tell you what I think. I don't want to tell you anything wrong or your Momma will come right down here and whip my ass." Mercy laughed at that and said, "Okay Dad, I'll come back and see you tomorrow then. Is there anything I can bring you?" He replied, "Maybe a little cornbread, they don't know how to cook any kind of soul food in this place. They make sweet corn muffins that ain't worth the cornmeal."

Mercy was in a much better mood when she left the nursing home assisted living area. She just couldn't believe the change that had come over her Father. She had never seen him look so good or even talk to her for that matter. She would have to stop at the store to get what she needed to make him some cornbread. She had watched her Momma make it so many times, she was sure she could make it just like her, or at least close.

When she got home from the store and put her bags on the table, she was suddenly exhausted. She was mentally and physically exhausted. She would have to work extra shifts this coming week to pay back this time she was taking off. This weekend sure didn't go like she had planned it. She thought it was funny how your whole world could turn upside down in one day's time. She made a cup of tea and sat down at the table. She guessed she had been daydreaming for a while or asleep standing up. She wasn't quite sure which when she heard a knock at the back door. She went over to the back door and parted the faded, yellow curtains and there stood Travis, as handsome as ever. She didn't know if she really wanted to see him right now. She was just so confused about everything in her life. She let him in. "Hey Travis, didn't I just see you yesterday?" she said in a teasing voice. He said, "As a matter of fact you did." She said, "What brings you here tonight. Did you miss me already?" She didn't know why she was flirting with him as if she didn't have enough on her mind. He answered, "Of course I did, but I have something to tell you. You know that old church down on the corner that you love so much? The one that you used to go and sit in the bell tower every day?" She was surprised and said, "How did you know?" He said, "I was in love with you even then and I watched you all the time. I knew what you were doing." She looked a little embarrassed and it brought back sweet memories. She said, "Yes, what about the old church?" Travis replied, "I was trying to think of something I could get you or something I could do for you to repay you for taking such good care of me and I knew that you wouldn't let anyone pay you outright." She said, "right, continue". He told her that he had a great idea. He called some of his buddies that also played music and they decided that they were going to get a bunch of groups together and get sponsors and have a fund-raising event on the church parking lot to help raise money to restore it. The city said it didn't have enough money in the budget to restore it completely but if we could raise half, it would find the other half of the money to restore it. Mercy got tears in her eyes, she said, "Travis, that is the nicest, kindest thing that anyone has ever done for me. You don't know how much I would love that. My family and I went to that church when we were little." He said, "I know. So, did I. It will be your gift from me but also a gift back to our community" Mercy replied, "Travis, I would be glad to help, just tell me what you need me to do. I can sell raffles, recruit vendors and food service, we can do this Travis!" She had forgotten about her bad mood for the second time today.

Her telephone rang. Benton's number came up and she didn't answer it. Travis said, "Are you and Benton fighting again?" She replied, "Not really, I don't know, I don't want to talk about it right now. I do however, want to tell you about the visit I had with my Father. It was just so unbelievable, and she preceded to tell him. "Travis said, "Oh Mercy that's wonderful. I'm so glad for you and your Dad." Travis walked over and hugged her and kissed her lightly on the cheek and said, "I have to go, lots of work to do to get that old church in shape. We are hoping to meet a September first deadline and its already April, not much time." He was so excited, she couldn't help but smile as he left. She decided not to call Benton back until tomorrow, at least until she talked to her Dad. She was so excited about restoring the old church, she got busy and started cooking for her Dad. She made him some fried chicken and gravy to go along with the cornbread.

It was about noon the next day when Mercy got to the nursing home. She had hoped that she got there before her father had eaten lunch. She did, he was in his living room talking to one of his buddies. Her Father said, "Oh, there she is, my beautiful daughter." To his friend. Her Father made the introductions and his friend politely excused himself. Mercy said, "Dad, I brought you the cornbread you ask for and as an added extra bonus, I made you some fried chicken. It probably doesn't taste anything like Momma's, but I think you will like it." He grabbed up a chicken leg and took a bite, he got a smile on his face as he said, "It taste every bit as good as your Momma's. You never told me you could cook girl." Mercy smiled back and said, "Just one of my many talents." She sat with him while he enjoyed his lunch, of which, he ate almost all.

Mercy said, "Dad, did you think about what I told you yesterday. I still don't know what to do about Benton or even Travis for that matter. They both love me but now I'm not sure which one I love the most. He said, "yes, I gave it a lot of thought last night and for what it's worth and since you did ask, I'll tell you what I think. Benton sounds like a man that is driven in his career, a man that wants it all and doesn't care how he gets there. I believe that he does love you, but you are a challenge to him, a challenge to a man that can have almost any woman he wants, except you. Usually those types of relationships don't last after he gets what he wants. He will always be looking for something more. Don't believe for one second that he and your friend Madison didn't have something going on behind your back. He could probably lie his way out of anything." "Wow, was Mercy's response, you did think a lot about this. Don't you think you are being kind of harsh?" He answered, "You protect him and make excuses for him because you love him. This isn't the first time that you have caught him with another woman and it won't be your last. On the other hand, if you can put up with his indiscretions, I'm sure he would take very good care of you and probably be a great father." Mercy said, "Okay, what do you think about Travis?" He replied, "Travis is a good guy. He is honorable, and he is the kind of man that will keep his word about anything. He would love only you and be good to you for the rest of your life and he also would be a great father, but he can't give you the financial security that Benton can. With Travis, you will always be following behind him while he chases his dream." "Wow, Dad, I didn't know you had so much insight about relationships. How come we have never talked like this before?" He replied, "I watch a lot of television and we never talked like this before because I always had my lips on a bottle. I am a changed man now. I spent most of my adult life just trying to stay sober enough to get through a shift at work. That's why your Momma wouldn't let me talk to you kids much and I sure wasn't allowed to lay a finger on any of you. Your Momma took care of all the discipline and money in the house. I don't even know why she put up with me all those years. I guess she just loved me. You can't help what love does so whoever and whenever you choose to get married, I'm sure he will be the right one for you." Mercy hugged him and said, "Thanks Dad." She said, "On a lighter note, let me tell you about the old church down the street." Mercy told her Father about all their big plans to bring the old church back to life and he seemed very happy about it.

When Mercy got home, there were three more messages from Benton. She thought about some of the things that her Father had said and decided to call Benton back. He said, "Mercy, I'm so glad that you finally called me back! We must talk about this. What I told you about Madison stopping by was the absolute truth. I haven't seen any other women since we have been together. Sydney told you that I was seeing

Madison because he was jealous of you. Sydney always had it in the back of his mind that he and I would be together one day and when that didn't happen, he was jealous of you and just wanted to hurt the both of us. That's just the kind of person he was. He called Madison and told her to stop and see me when she was in town, he knew she was coming up here this weekend and then he called and told you the same thing. I'm so sorry Mercy, please forgive me. Madison will tell you herself that this is how it went down. Mercy was trying to digest all this new information and she was starting to feel bad about punching Madison in the nose. She asked, "Is Madison's nose alright?" Benton replied, "You broke it, but the hospital straightened it back out. It will be okay. I paid the hospital bill." Mercy said, "Thank you Benton but you didn't have to do that. I will have to personally go over to Madison's and talk to her and apologize for breaking her nose." Mercy was baiting Benton to see if he would protest her going to Madison's, he didn't. Benton said, "I am flattered though, that such a nonviolent person such as yourself would fight for me." Mercy responded, "I wasn't fighting for you, I was delivering what I thought Madison deserved. I will give her time to cool off and then I will go and see her. I wouldn't blame her if she didn't let me in." Benton replied sheepishly, "You aren't angry with me anymore then? Will you put your engagement right back on?" Mercy said she would think about it. She wanted to make him sweat a little for what he had put her through. She said, "The two of you were sitting on the bed with the door closed, that was pretty incriminating." He replied, "Mercy, I told you why. I had some old art work stuffed behind the door that Madison wanted to see."

Madison was standing in her hallway, looking in a mirror at her nose and thought, "That bitch, why did she have to go and break my nose? It will never be the same." She heard a knock on her front door. Madison was expecting Benton's Mother. She opened the door and let Benton's Mother in. She had a big smile on her face as she said, "So, the happy couple are all broken up, and she gave back the ring?" Madison answered, "More like she threw it at him. She broke my nose in the process." Benton's Mother said, "I have brought you a check for the other $250,000.00 that I owe you for breaking up the happy couple. I couldn't have done it without you, but I don't expect to ever see or hear from you again, is that understood Madison?" "Of course,", Madison said but she already had her own plans for Benton and his Mother, and his Mother didn't need to know about those plans just yet. Benton's Mother handed her the check and left.

CHAPTER 22

For the next week, Mercy was thinking about what Benton had told her and maybe he was telling her the truth. She just wished that she trusted that, but her gut feeling was that he was lying to her. She was off today, and it was nice out, so she thought today would be as good a time as any to pay Madison a visit. Surely, she wasn't too upset over her broken nose still. She may not even be home, but Mercy was in the mood to confront her about what had happened at Benton's apartment.

Mercy knocked on the front door and was surprised when Madison opened it so quickly. Madison said, "What are you doing here?" Mercy replied, "I've come to apologize to you for breaking your nose. I'm not a violent person and don't know what got into me and I just wanted to tell you how sorry that I am." Madison reluctantly said, "Apology accepted, won't you come in?" Madison thought it better to be nice to Mercy to stay on Benton's good side. They walked into the front parlor and Madison said she would go and get them something to drink. When Madison left, Mercy was standing next to her roll top desk and noticed the check sitting on top. The figure caught her attention immediately and then she saw who it was from. Mercy picked up Madison's bank book and saw entries made for large amounts of money from not only Benton's Mother but also from Benton. Right at that moment, Madison walked back into the room and caught her looking at her bank book. Madison thought, "How stupid could she be to leave that laying out where anyone, especially Mercy could see it." They locked eyes and Mercy got a cold shiver down her spine. Mercy said, "What is Benton's Mother paying you for?" Madison didn't have any more lies in her now so she decided to go with the truth, she didn't care, she had her money. "Benton's Mother was paying me to break the two of you up." Mercy said, "How long have you been sleeping with Benton?" Madison said, "Almost a year now. Someone must take care of him and since you wouldn't. It was too easy." Mercy almost punched Madison in her broken nose again but managed to keep her cool. She wouldn't get any information from Madison by showing hostility. Mercy said, "If you were already sleeping with Benton, what was he paying you for?" "Aww" thought Madison, the half a million-dollar question. Madison replied, "To sleep with him at his beck and call and to do thing to him that nice girls like you wouldn't." Mercy said, "I've heard enough." She turned on her heel and walked out.

Mercy got in her car and drove away. She was stunned, she didn't even know what to think. The man that she loved for so long and was engaged to marry was sleeping with her ex-best friend and his Mother was paying her to do it. Mercy knew that Benton's Mother could never stay out of their relationship. His Mother was out to get her from the beginning and just pretending to go along with what she and Benton Wanted. Mercy's heart was broken once again.

Benton had broken it one too many times. Why couldn't he just wait for her? Why did love have to be so complicated? Mercy just went home and went to bed, covering up her head and keeping the rest of the world out.

Madison immediately called Benton and told him what had happened, omitting of course, the part about Mercy finding his Mother's check, even Benton didn't know about that. Benton was so mad, she couldn't believe it. He said, "What did Mercy say?" Madison replied, "Nothing, she just walked out."

Benton hung up the phone from Madison and tried to call Mercy. Man, Madison had really gone and messed things up this time. Mercy had even seen in her bank book where Benton had paid Madison for sex and purchased her nice things. Now Mercy would know how Madison could afford such a nice place to live. Benton had decided to tell Mercy the truth also. He would tell her that they have been together for so long and a man has needs and he just couldn't help himself. He knew this explanation wouldn't win any points with Mercy, but he would have to go for the pity side of the coin. He tried to call mercy several times and she wouldn't answer the phone, so he kept trying.

The next day, Benton kept trying to call Mercy again and finally in the afternoon, she picked up the phone. He said, "Mercy" and that was all he got out of his mouth when she said, "We are done, don't ever call me or try to see me again, it's over, now and forever." Then she hung up the phone. She didn't want to hear any of his lame excuses. She went back to bed and pulled the cover back up over her head.

After a week went by without Travis seeing Mercy, and

J.C. Tolliver

she not answering her phone, he decided to go by her house. He went to the back door. He didn't see any lights on, but her car was parked out on the street. He banged on the door. When he didn't get an answer, he got very worried and decided to break in the back door. He opened it with a credit card. He searched downstairs for her first and then he went upstairs. He called her name the whole time, in case she was home, so he wouldn't scare her. He yelled up the stairs, "Mercy are you home!" No answer, Travis walked into her bedroom and there she was lying in bed with the cover over her head. He knew she was okay because she was moving her feet. He said, "Mercy, are you okay?" She said, "I'm fine Travis, please leave." He replied, "How long have you been in this bed?" She said, "For the last week except when I had to go into work." He was puzzled and said, "Why?" and that started Mercy crying all over again. She told him, "I really don't want to talk about it." Travis put his arms around her and said, "Okay, you don't have to talk about it if you don't want to." She just sobbed great big tears until she didn't have any left. In a nutshell, she told Travis what had happened. "Benton's Mother was paying Madison to break me and Benton up and Benton was paying Madison for sex. Of course, I broke up with him. We were together for four years and I just can't believe this is happening. I loved Benton and he broke my heart. I'll never trust another man." Travis just held her and let her go on. She felt a little better now. Travis asked, "Mercy why don't you come downstairs and I'll fix you some hot tea and then you will feel better?" Reluctantly, she said, "Okay". Even though Travis was happy they broke up, could kill Benton right now for breaking Mercy's heart.

He had never seen Mercy look so miserable and he didn't like it at all.

They went down to the kitchen and Travis fixed Mercy some tea and toast. She looked like she hadn't eaten in a few days. Travis looked at her in the daylight, she was pale, and her face was drawn. Mercy told Travis, "I was saving myself for my husband, for Benton. The only gift I had to give him, and he just couldn't wait. Not only couldn't he wait but he had sex with my best friend and paid her for it. It's just unbelievable to me Travis that he could lie to me for so long and he had the nerve to practically rape me the last time I stayed with him. I thought that he was my prince charming, he was the man that I dreamed about spending my life with. How could I have been so naive? His Mother is another story! Benton's Mother paid Madison quite well to seduce Benton and break he and I up. She just hated me while all the while she was being nice to my face. She even offered to help plan our wedding. I never told Benton, but at the beginning of our relationship, his Mother offered me money to stay away from him. Now, in hindsight, I should have taken the money." Travis just listened and didn't say anything, just let her keep talking and crying and getting it all out. Travis said, "Have you talked to Benton since your discovery?" She replied, "Yes, I told him never to call me or come around me ever again and then I hung up the phone. He hasn't called back since then. Travis was sitting next to Mercy in the kitchen. He pulled her over on his lap. She was as light as a feather. He held her for a long time. He said, "You know Mercy, not all men are bad or perverts like Benton. I'm not like him and I never will be. I have never lied to you and I never will. You know that I am here for you whenever you need me." Mercy replied, "Yes, I know that Travis, I think, I thought that Benton was a good man, now I just don't know what to trust anymore. I gave that man the last four years of my life, now for nothing. I believe that you are a good and honorable man Travis and you have never lied to me. Thank you for taking care of me and letting me cry on your shoulder." He replied, "That's okay, I have big shoulders." Travis decided that now was a good time to change the subject.

"Mercy, we have set a date for our fund raiser for the church. It's Saturday, May 25th. We could still really use your help if you think you will be up to it." Mercy replied, "Of course I'm up to it. I have cried enough over the loss of my relationship with Benton and friendship with Madison. Neither of them deserves my tears. I am a strong woman and I will get through this just like I've gotten through many difficulties in my life. The church project will just be the distraction I need. What do you need me to do Travis?" He said, "I'm so glad that you are fighting for yourself, that's my Mercy. You could have the flyers printed up and distributed. I will tell you what they should say and list the bands that will be playing. After those are done, we need to go around to the different businesses in the area and try to get donations or some things we could use for a raffle. Local businesses near the church will help because having the church back open will increase their sales. I found out that we can use the large parking lot next to the church to set up the bands and any booths that we have. My friends are contacting other groups that they know to come out and play. I also have a list of vendors from the summer town festival, that we need to call the and see if they would be interested in setting up at the Church that day. We also need people going from door to door, close to the church to collect donations. There is just a lot to do to raise that kind of money." Mercy said, "How much money do we need to raise?" Travis replied, "At least $200,000. I know it's a real long shot, but with careful planning, we might just pull it off. I think the whole neighborhood is getting excited about the old church. It's been such an eye sore for a while now and everyone wants to return it to its former glory." Mercy said, "Wow, that is a lot of money and there is so much work to do. I told you I would help in any way that I can. It will keep me busy while I'm trying to get over everything that just happened." Travis said, "I should be going, there is a lot of work to do. But before I go, Mercy, are you feeling alright? She replied, "Yes, why do you ask?" He said, "You look a little pale and like you don't feel well. Have you been eating?" She said, "Travis, I am fine. Please go and do what you must do today. Travis, how are you feeling? Are you Okay?" "Yes, I'm fine." Mercy was in a lot better mood when Travis left. He was such a good man. Mercy decided that the church project would be good for her. It would keep her mind busy and off Benton. She was finished having a pity party. Travis was right she is a strong woman, just like her Momma was, but he was also right, she didn't feel well physically. She felt run-down and exhausted. She guessed it was from being through so much drama lately and not eating well.

Mercy wanted to make one last phone call to Benton. She wanted to tell him what his Mother had done because it wasn't fair that his Mother got off scot free in all this mess. She wanted Benton to see how conniving she was. She was always perfect in Benton's eyes. It was 9:00 p m, he should be home now, she dialed his number. He answered, "Hello" She said, "It's Mercy."

Benton replied, "Mercy, how are you? Can I come and see you this weekend? Can we talk about what happened? I love you Mercy, and I miss you terribly." Mercy thought to herself, "Now you can say you love me, but you couldn't before?" Mercy replied, "No, Benton, you can't come over. I meant it when I said I didn't ever want to see or talk to you again. There's just one little thing that I forgot to tell you that I found out at Madison' house. You may already know but your Mother paid Madison $500,000 to make sure that she broke us up; all the while, being nice to my face. Your Mother also offered me $25,000 just to leave you, early on in our relationship. Apparently, no one will ever be god enough for her son. Now, I am finished, now I will never talk to you, Madison or your Mother ever again." He said, "But Mercy, as she was hanging up the phone. When Mercy hung up the phone, Benton just held it and stared at it. Was Mercy telling the truth about his Mother? Was Madison collecting money from his Mother to seduce him and brake him and Mercy up? His Mother would never do something like that, or could she? Would she? Benton thought, "Yes, she would do that. She thinks that money will handle anything, and usually she is right." Benton knew that she did it out of love for him and his career. He really wished she would stop meddling in his life. He is a grown man and almost a Doctor. She needs to let him handle his own affairs. He was going home this weekend and he would confront her about the money and he may even try to see Mercy. He knows that she still loves him despite what happened.

Benton went to his Mother's late on Saturday and she had some of his favorite foods on the table for him. She loved to see him really enjoy his meals. Benton sat down at the table, but he did not eat. Instead, he just fumbled with his napkin. His Mother was sitting at the head of the table. Benton Said, "Mother, I have something to ask you and please tell me the truth". "Of course, Darling, whatever you want." Benton replied, "Did you give Madison a large sum of money to break Mercy and I up?" His Mother looked him in the eye and answered, "Yes, I did. Mercy is not the woman for you and I just couldn't stand by and let you make one of the biggest mistakes of your life." Benton said, "Oh, so you are the judge on who is good enough, or not, for me to date? How much did you pay her Mother?" "I paid, 500,000 total." Benton replied, "I can't believe that you paid her that much! All the while, I was paying her also to be there for me when I wanted. Looks like we both made a big mistake Mother." Benton nodded to his Father then. His Father had not said a word since they all sat down to dinner. Benton got up and left the house to go back home. Benton's Father looked at his wife like he just couldn't believe she would do such a thing and so much money!

Benton decided since he drove this far, he might as well stop and see if Mercy was home and if she would talk to him. He parked his car out front, right behind hers. He hoped she would at least answer the door. He went around to the back door, just like everyone did and knocked. Mercy already knew he was there. She had seen him pull up out front. She couldn't believe that after all he had put her through, that her heart still started pounding when she saw him. She didn't know if she loved him or not, she didn't think so.

How do you love someone who is always hurting you? She barely opened the door. "What do you want Benton?" He replied, "Can't I come in and talk to you?" She thought for a minute. She really shouldn't even listen to any more of his lies but was curious as to what he had to say, so she said, "Okay Benton, you can come in, but just for a few minutes, I'm very tired." She let him in. She sat down at the kitchen table, but she did not ask him to sit. She said, "Say what you came to say and then please, leave me alone." He said, "Mercy, I know what I did was wrong on so many levels but please believe me when I say that I don't love Madison. It was just sex and nothing more. If we had loved each other, would I have had to pay her? She was the only one Mercy, I swear, please believe me. I needed that release and you saw what happened the last night you stayed in the apartment. I practically raped you. I tried to wait Mercy, I swear I did, with school and moving and everything else, the pressure was too great. I needed that release. Mercy, I am so sorry. I wasn't aware of anything my Mother did, so I can't apologize for her, but I know what I did wasn't right Mercy and I do love you so much. Please say you will at least think about giving me another chance, please Mercy, we have a long history together. You are the only woman for me." Mercy sat still and listened to all of it. Benton had said everything she had predicted. She said, "Okay, stop Benton. You've said what you wanted to say, now please leave and don't ever try to see me again." Benton said, "Please Mercy, won't you even think about coming back to me?" At that, Travis showed up at the back door, it was open. Benton looked at Travis and then he looked at Mercy. Benton said, "Mercy, I have to go back home tonight. I'm on-call at the hospital, please give us a second chance." Travis said, "Benton, I think you already got your answer. She asked you to leave and never come back." Benton looked at Travis and said, "You're the reason Mercy won't forgive me and come back to me. You have always tried to take Mercy from me because you love her. You have always wanted her." Mercy stood up and said, "That's enough from the both of you. I'd like for both of you to leave now. I'm tired and I want to go to bed." Mercy walked to the hallway and turned around to face them both. She said, "I'm going to bed. Lock the door on your way out." Both Benton and Travis looked at each other to see who would be the first one to leave. Benton started out the door when Travis baited him by saying. "Benton, you have done enough damage to Mercy. She doesn't deserve to be treated like that. You couldn't possibly love her. Let your Mommy find you someone who will put up with your lies. I love her like a real man should and I will take care of her." Benton turned around and went to punch Travis, but Travis was waiting for it and did exactly what Travis thought he would do. Travis ducked, and Benton fell right on the floor. Travis walked out while Benton was still on the floor. Benton picked himself up and locked the door on the way out.

On the drive back to Chicago, Benton thought, "Okay, let the cowboy have her. She wasn't good enough for him anyway. She will be sorry when I am a famous plastic surgeon. I could get any woman I want. To hell with her.

Mercy didn't know what went on downstairs last night, but she figured with the two of them together, it wasn't good. She hoped that Travis didn't get hurt but she would bet he didn't. She thought about the things that Benton had said. She didn't think there would ever be a way for them to reconcile their differences. There were things that happened, lies told, things that couldn't be taken back, things that could never be forgiven. Benton was her first love and that was special plus she had given him the last four years of her life. They did have history together. It's always been Mercy and Benton, but she knew that things would never be the same between them. She wouldn't go back to him, not now, probably never. She was still heartbroken every day and would be for a long time. She hadn't seen Madison since the day she last visited her. Good luck to the them both, Benton and Madison, they deserve each other.

CHAPTER 23

Any time Travis got to spend with Mercy was the best time of his life. He hadn't dated anyone since before his motorcycle accident, he just couldn't because he loved Mercy so much and no one else could fill her shoes. Travis, and Mercy were seeing each other a couple of times a week, planning for the church event. Travis would come over to Mercy's and bring pizza and they worked well together. Mercy made phone calls for local sponsors, they were stocking up on donations to be raffled off. and more donations for a silent auction. They had several local area bands playing music. They had recruited food vendors. They had set up an area in the church parking lot with picnic tables where people could eat and watch the bands. They had filled all the spots they had for craft vendors. They were glad to have such a large parking area because they had so many things going on. Mercy posted flyers everywhere, especially in her neighborhood, that's where most of the people lived that remembered going to the old church. Mercy and Travis didn't have any idea how much money they would raise or how close they would get to their goal of $250,000, but they were willing to keep on fund raising until the money was there. They were both committed to this project and wouldn't give up until it was completed. Mercy's Father even helped by stuffing envelopes for them. Everyone involved were in good spirits. They knew It was for a good cause.

The more Travis and Mercy worked together, the closer they became. They could finish each other's sentences. They thought the same way and had the same views on life. Mercy felt that this was because they were raised so much alike. It sent a thrill through Mercy every time she accidently brushed Travis's arm or leg or even when he gave her that sweet, crooked grin. Travis had no lasting effects from his accident and was more handsome than ever.

In the evenings, when they had been working on their project all day, they would just sit and veg in front of the television. On one night, they were watching a romantic movie. Travis scooted over closer to Mercy on the couch and put his arm around her. Mercy thought that this felt nice and so she let him keep it there. Travis always did look her in the eye when he talked to her and she loved his brown, bedroom eyes. Mercy could feel Travis looking at her now, she turned her head toward him. Travis said, "Mercy, you are such a beautiful woman." Mercy replied, "Travis, you always say that." He replied, "It's true, that's why I say it. I never get tired of looking at you." Travis decided that now the moment was right to kiss her. He'd been waiting for a moment such as this. Her full lips looked so soft and moist, he stared at them. Mercy knew that he was getting ready to kiss her, and she wanted him to kiss her. Travis bent his head to hers and brushed her lips lightly with his own. He didn't know if she would respond to him, but she did, so that gave him the courage to kiss her a little harder. Travis gave Mercy the most incredible kiss she had ever had. She couldn't help but compare. Benton never kissed her like that. She felt warm all over. His lips were soft and sweet on hers. When they kissed, it was like they had been kissing forever, like he was the one she had always been waiting on, the man for her. She had been falling in love with Travis for some time now and she knew that. She also felt that Travis loved her. Travis was awakening feelings in her that she hadn't felt in a long time. Travis looked at her face while he was kissing her. She had her eyes closed and her whole face just seemed to glow. Travis was kind and passionate but finally Mercy said, "Stop Travis." Travis stopped but said, "Why?" She answered, "Because I may not be able to control myself and take advantage of you. Besides, I'm not feeling very well, and I think I am just tired and need to go to bed." "I could go to bed with you." He teased.

The next day Mercy went to her Doctors office. She had not been feeling well lately and when she got up this morning, she felt terrible. She felt like she was getting a bad flu or something. Her head was pounding, she was running a fever, she has diarrhea and couldn't eat for fear of vomiting. She had never remembered getting so sick so fast before. When she got to her Drs. Office, she checked her over and ran a couple of test, a flu test and one for mono. Both tests came back positive. Her Dr. told her she should take some ibuprofen for her aches and fever. He gave her some medication for her vomiting and diarrhea and said that her flue should be cleared up in about a week. The mono however, could last for up to two years. She had hard lumps on the back of her neck.

When Mercy got home that day. Her back and shoulders were aching so badly, she took some ibuprofen with a little water and then all she wanted to do was go to bed. Before she went to bed, she called her boss at work and told her that it may be a few days before she could work again. She went to bed and she didn't remember anything until the next morning, when she woke up to the phone ringing. She didn't have a phone upstairs, it was down in the kitchen. She made it to the bathroom and that was as far as she could go, she felt like she was burning up but had left her medication in the kitchen where she had taken it the night before. She made it back to bed and fell back into a deep sleep.

That afternoon, Travis went over to Mercy's house, after not being able to reach her on the phone, he began to get worried about her. He pounded on the back door and looked in the window. He could see Mercy's purse on the kitchen table, so he knew she was home. When she didn't answer the door after a few minutes, he became worried and broke the glass in the door and reached in and undid the lock. When he went inside, he didn't hear anything at all. He yelled, "Mercy, where are you!" no answer. He looked around the first floor and then went upstairs to Mercy's bedroom. He quietly opened her bedroom door. The room was dark, and the curtains closed. He whispered so that he didn't scare her, "Mercy, are you awake?" No answer, he turned on the light next to the bed. He couldn't believe what he saw, and it scared him. He had never seen Mercy like this. Her hair was matted, her face was drawn and a kind of gray color. Her hair and nightgown reeked of vomit and sweat. He shook her, and she barely opened her eyes. She whispered, "Travis, what are you doing here?" He answered, "I came to see why I couldn't get you on the phone and here you are." Her throat was so sore and dry, she could barely talk.

She whispered, "Drink". Travis rushed to the kitchen and brought her a glass of ice water. He held her head while she took some small sips. Travis said, "Mercy, I am taking you to the hospital, you are very sick. You are burning up." When she could get the words out, she answered, "No Travis, I've been to the Dr. I have the flu and mono at the same time. I have been so sick, that I couldn't even take care of myself. All I want to do is sleep." He asked, "How long have you been in this bed?" She answered, since day before yesterday." He said, "You need to go to the hospital or you need to let me take care of you." She didn't have any strength left and barely answered, "Okay Travis, please take care of me if you want." She watched as Travis moved about. He found her medication for fever and held her head up while she swallowed them. Next, he found clean sheets for her bed and a clean gown for her. He went down to the kitchen and found a large bowl, filled it with very warm water, grabbed some bar soap, shampoo, spray in conditioner, washcloth and a couple of towels and took them to Mercy's room. She just lay there and stared at him. He told her that he was going to get her cleaned up and change her sheets. The way Mercy felt right now, she didn't care who saw her naked. She could be standing out on the street naked for all she cared. Travis pulled the blankets and sheet down and carefully removed her nightgown. He already knew how beautiful she was but hadn't realized how thin she had become lately. He rolled her over and put a towel beneath her to keep the mattress dry. He started at the top of her head and gently worked he way down to her toes, washing every inch of her. He covered her with a clean sheet and then put a towel under her head. He held her tiny head in his hand while he gently

233

washed her long hair in a shallow pan. He poured water over her hair to rinse it. He dried her hair the best he could with a towel and then put some spray-in conditioner on it so that it wouldn't get so tangled.

When she was all dry, he put a clean nightgown on her that he had found in her drawer. Then by rolling her from side to side, he changed the sheets on the bed and covered her with a clean blanket that he had found on a bed downstairs. Mercy's fever was a little better, and she had to admit that Travis did a great job of cleaning her up. She didn't know Travis was such a good caretaker. She guessed he knew how to do things from helping his Grandmother who lived with him and his parents. She felt clean, warm and cozy. She just wanted to sleep. Travis said, "Oh no you don't. Mercy, you can't go back to sleep yet. You need to get some food and fluids in you." She answered, "No, I feel nauseous and I will just throw it back up again!" He said, "I saw a medication bottle in the kitchen with medicine in it for nausea. I going to go and get you one and then I am going to make you some soup." She was too sick to argue with him.

Travis stayed by Mercy's side for the next four days until her fever broke, continuing to take care of her. He would sleep in the chair, but if Mercy even moved a little bit, he was wide awake. He sat next to her bed anticipating everything she could possibly want or need. He even helped her out of bed to the bathroom and waited until she had sat down. She was so weak, Travis was afraid that she would fall. She would call him when she was finished, and he would put her back to bed. Sometimes, she was so weak just from getting up that he would carry her back and put her to bed.

By the fourth day, her fever from the flu and finally stayed down. Travis made sure that she ate something, even if only a couple of bites, three times a day and he was constantly pushing fluids on her. She was finally starting to feel better. She sat up in bed on the fourth morning and told Travis, "Travis, thank you so much for taking such good care of me. I don't know what would have happened to me had you not come over to check on me. Who would have thought my cowboy was such a good nurse, better than me even!" She even giggled a little. Travis loved her so much and couldn't stand the thought of anything happening to her. He answered, "Mercy, you know that I would do anything for you. It was a piece of cake. I am just glad that I came over the other day also or you could have even been dead by now. You had such a high fever, and you were so weak, you couldn't even get out of that bed. Besides, I love taking care of you. I especially love changing your clothes and gave her a devilish grin. She thought for a moment and said, "You changed my clothes? You saw me naked?" He shook his head yes, "Of course I did, who do you think kept you all clean and cozy the last few days? I was the only one here. Besides, I won't tell anyone I saw you naked if you don't. And by the way Mercy, you have a beautiful body. You should just walk around naked all the time and never wear clothes." He was trying to make light of the situation and didn't want her to feel embarrassed, and of course, she knew that. She gave him a devilish grin then and said, "Well, I just might never wear clothes again!" He answered, "Fine by me, now lay down and get some more rest, you aren't out of the woods yet. You are still very weak and need to eat more." She said, "You are making me fat." Travis said, "Mercy, you are so thin now, it would take years to fatten you up. I could pick you up with one hand if I wanted to."

A couple of days later, when Mercy was up and about and able to care for herself, she sent Travis home. She didn't want him to get sick and he looked exhausted and she knew that he was even though he denied it.

When Travis left, Mercy was sitting at the kitchen table, sipping hot tea. She thought about what an amazing man Travis was and how much she really did love him. She could not imagine Benton even wanting to be around her when she was sick, much less take care of her the whole time. She knew how much Travis loved her. When he would sleep in the chair next to her bed, she would wake up and just watch him sleep. She thought about how far their relationship had come. She finally realized what Travis had known all along, that they were meant to be together.

She didn't realize just how much she loved him until now. She thought she was in love with Benton all those years but now, looking back, she thought she was just infatuated with Benton and proud of the fact that she, the poor girl, got the coolest guy in school.

Finally, the day of the fund raiser was here! Travis, Mercy, her Father and countless other people helped make this event possible. They all hoped that they could reach their goal and restore the old church.

Benton stopped by to see his mother and asked her to go to the church fund raiser with him. He also asked her for $25,000. His Mother said, "Benton, I'm not coming down to some festival in a bad part of town, carrying $25,000, just to give to you. I would probably get mugged or something." Benton said, "Okay, just bring me a cashier's check for that amount and then no one will see you with money." She answered, "For what Benton?" He said he wanted to bid on something down there at an auction. She replied, "What could someone be auctioning off down in that part of town to help him win Mercy back. "Oh, and Mother, please dress down, I don't want you sticking out like a sore thumb" She didn't really understand what Benton was talking about, but she would go down there and see and take him the funds he had ask for. After all, he was her only baby boy and she would do anything for him. Benton was smart and if he needed $25,000, she would give it to him.

Benton walked around the festival and he had seen Mercy and Travis together several times. They were looking at each other like they were in love, but Benton didn't see a ring on Mercy's finger, so he still had a chance to get her back. Benton watched Travis and Mercy on stage, along with a lot of other people. Mercy did have an angel's voice. Benton was jealous of Travis's guitar playing ability.

Benton was keeping an eye out for his Mother. He spotted her as she was walking towards him, she wasn't smiling she hated it down here in Northside. She said, "Where is the auction?" Benton answered, "Over here. It will be starting in a little bit. "Madison had also heard about the festival and auction and decided to go down and besides she liked walking past her old home. It reminded her of how far she had some. Madison spotted Benton and his Mother standing together with their heads together whispering Madison walked right up to them and said, "Well, fancy meeting the two of you here in this part of town. Benton and his mother both said at the same time, "Where're here for the auction Madison." She answered, "So am I." They all went into a pole barn that had been set up to look over the auction items. Mercy and Travis had spotted the three of them but said nothing to each other. Benton was very interested in an electric guitar that had been signed by one of the members of the band "The Who". It had been donated by one of Travis's old band members.

The auction had started and there were a lot of people there bidding. They were making a lot of money. Half way through the auction, a beautiful antique baby bed and dresser came up for auction. Madison won the bid of $2,000. Benton and his Mother just looked at her like she had lost her mind. She looked at them and said, "Well, I have to furnish that big old house, don't I?" Soon after, the guitar came up for auction. The opining bid was $1,000 and soon jumped to 5,000. Benton wanted that guitar, he raised his bidders card and yelled $25,000. Everyone turned and looked at him like he was crazy. The auctioneer didn't want any money from that family, but the money is money and it's for the church. Mercy knew why he was down here and didn't give him any credit for his bid and didn't thank him. Benton paid for his purchase and was holding it in his hand when Madison said, "You could learn to play that thing and then you could teach your son how to play." As Madison said this, she raised her shirt and rubbed her baby bump. Benton's mouth fell open and his Mother fainted on the concrete floor. Someone yelled, "Get some water!" Benton yelled, "No way that is mine!" Mercy wasn't standing very far from that group and she heard the whole exchange. The only thing Mercy thought was that she felt sorry for that baby. Going to have two parents like Benton and Madison, and a Grandmother that is even worse. Someone had revived

Benton's Mother. Before she could clear her head and say anything, Benton grabbed her by the arm and pulled her all the way back to her car. All the while, not letting go of his newly purchased guitar.

Madison was good at extortion, but money wasn't the only thing she wanted. She wanted Benton and she meant to have him. Like Benton, Madison was used to getting pretty much what she wanted. She would have him, and they would have their little boy.

When Benton's Mother was seated in her car, she looked at Benton through the window and angrily said, "Benton, is that your baby?' He replied, "It could be Mother, I don't know. I'd have to have a paternity test. I'm not the only one Madison sleeps with" His Mother just moaned and said, "Oh God, what did I do to deserve this?" She drove away. Benton thought, "That's my Mom, always thinking about herself and how she looked to others."

Madison was right on Benton's heels. When his Mother drove off, Madison said, "Benton, I'm sorry I had to tell you about the baby in this way, but you wouldn't exactly return my phone calls. "Benton answered, "Well, I've been a little busy trying to get my fiancé back, thanks to you." That made Madison angry, she answered in a loud voice, "Benton I'm talking about our little boy, not your ex-fiancé and it's clear that she is never letting you back into her life, besides, looks like she already had eyes for that hunk of a cowboy." Benton looked at her closely, "How many months pregnant are you?" Madison replied, "Three months, I don't really know the sex yet, but I will next month when I get an ultrasound." Benton said, "Well, you will never convince me it's mine until there is a paternity test done. Why are you doing this Madison, for money?" That hurt Madison, and especially since her hormones were all over the place, she started crying. Benton did not feel sorry for her. He turned and headed for his own ar. As he was getting ready to pull out, he saw Mercy and Travis over by one of the booths holding hands, "Isn't that cute" he thought.

A couple of days later, Benton's Mother called him "Benton, is that really your baby?" He answered, "I doubt it. I'm careful. I will get a paternity test and if it's mine, of course, I will be responsible for it, but I will never marry Madison. I don't love her, and she just wants money. I love Mercy. She is the only woman I have ever wanted." Benton's Mother was secretly glad to hear, "I'll never marry Madison." That would be worse than marrying Mercy.

Travis was on his way to Mercy's to give her the good news about how much money they made at their event. He knew she would be surprised. Although maybe not but she was surprised to get $25, 000 from Benton for the guitar. He obviously wasn't there to donate money but just to show Mercy he could be a good person. It doesn't matter to Travis because he knew that Mercy would never let Benton back into her life. He knew her, and he knew that once she was finished with someone, she was finished. He did not want to be on the receiving end of that.

Mercy was waiting for him when he arrived. She had fixed both breakfast. They had considered themselves "exclusive" for the last three weeks. Travis loved Mercy and she loved him, but she had not yet said it. She knew she loved Travis and she knew that she had loved him for a long time. It just took her some time to realize it herself. She thought she loved Benton, but she was in love with love, an infatuation. She opened the door for him and gave him a big, fat kiss. He said, "What was that for?" She answered, "Just because you are the greatest guy ever!" They both laughed. He sat down at the kitchen table and she got breakfast for them. He said, "Are you ready for the grand total of how much money we raised? We raised a little over $200,000, thanks to all our generous private donors. We didn't raise the $250,000 that we needed for the church but since the bank was paying half and we raised so much money, they decided to go ahead and pick up the cost! Mercy started jumping up and down, she was so excited. She said, "I can't wait to see it restored back to its former glory but most importantly, I can't wait to hear the bells ring."

PART V

CHAPTER 24

About four months later, on a Wednesday night, Travis stopped over Mercy's and ask her to go for a ride with him. Travis even blindfolded her. "To where?" she said, "Travis, isn't this a little bit childish, even for you?" He giggled like a little girl and said, "Yes, but just be patient, it will be worth it." He stopped the car a short distance away. He went around to her side of the car and helped her out since she couldn't see anything. They walked a few steps and he said, "Okay, I'm going to take the blindfold off now!" He stood behind her and untied it and let it fall to the ground. Mercy just stood there with a look of amazement on her face. Tears flooded her eyes and rolled down her cheeks. She whispered, "it's the most beautiful, little church I've ever seen. Even though the church was right down the street, she hadn't seen it because they had it covered up with big white sheets of plastic. The church was finished, completely restored except for the bell tower. They still had work to do on the tower. The church was painted white, the windows replaced the few stained-glass windows it had were repaired and new concrete walk and steps poured out front, along with a ramp and a hand rail for the handicap. It looked like she remembered it when she was a little girl and went to church with her

Mother, brothers and sisters. She asked Travis, "Can we go inside?" He said, "Yep, since I coordinated all of the work, I have a key." They walked slowly up the walk and the three steps to the front door. Mercy thought that she and some of the neighbors would plant some flowers along the walkway. She would get a neighborhood committee together to do some landscaping. It was their church.

Travis opened the double doors to the church and let Mercy go in first because he had already seen it. Her eyes took it all in. The beautifully shined walnut pews, the red carpet, the mahogany pulpit on the raised stage. There were three rows of chairs to the right of the stage for a choir to sing and on the left side of the stage sat the most beautiful baby grand piano Mercy had ever seen. Mercy looked at Travis with tears in her eyes and said, "it's more than I ever imagined it would be. I can't wait to show it to my Father and tell my brothers and sisters about it. Where did that beautiful piano come from? I know that we didn't purchase it." Travis responded. "It came from Madison with a note that said, "This is still my old neighborhood to." Mercy said, "Wow, that's unbelievable."

Mercy and Travis stood in the front of the church with the sun pouring in through the stained-glass windows. Travis was holding Mercy's hands in his. He got down on one knee and looked her in the eyes. She said, "Oh my goodness, Travis!" He said, "Mercy, I love you. I have loved you for longer than even I can remember. I know I don't have a lot to offer but everything I have is yours, including my heart and all my love. Would you please do me the honor of being my wife? I promise you, I will love and treasure you until I breathe my last breath. Please Mercy, will you marry me?" She looked at him and she was so filled with love for him, she was hoping that he would ask her to marry him soon. She answered, "Yes, Travis, I will marry you. I also promise to love and treasure you until I breathe my last breath." He put a beautiful ring on her finger. He stood up and they embraced each other and kissed passionately. Then, Mercy was so excited about their engagement, she started jumping up and down and yelling, "We're getting married!" Travis picked her up and started for the door. He said, "I guess you want to get married here, right? She answered, "How did you ever guess cowboy? Travis told her he wanted to get married right away. They set a date for February 14, 1977, Valentine's Day.

On the morning of her wedding, on Valentine's Day, Mercy wasn't nervous at all. She had her sisters at the house, helping her get ready for her wedding and they kept telling her not to be nervous and they didn't believe her when she told them that she really wasn't nervous at all. She loved Travis with all her heart and soul. It seemed like her love for Benton was a life time ago. There was a difference in how she loved Travis. She loved Benton with that all-consuming teenage love. Looking back, she thinks she was more infatuated with Benton and the idea of getting married and thought that Benton was her prince charming. She loved Travis in a way that she knew was real love. She knew that they would do anything for each other and be there for each other, no matter what. They could depend on each other. They were each other's soul mate and meant to be together for the rest of their lives. So, no, she wasn't nervous, she was excited about spending the rest of her life with Travis. She was so happy that she was able to keep her virginity, even though that was so hard sometimes. Now, she would be able to give that gift to her husband. This was the only gift that she could give him, and she knew that Travis knew how important that was to her. It was important to him in the way that he couldn't believe that she chose him to give it to. They were so in love and couldn't wait to start their lives together.

Mercy and her sisters were on their way to the little church down the street for the wedding. They were all giddy and laughing and making fun of Mercy about her wedding night and giving her advice. Mercy really thought about her Mother right now and what advice she would give her. She really missed her Mother so much and so wished that she could be here on this day with her. She knew she was so lucky to have her Father here and sober and able to walk her down the aisle. Mercy's sisters made sure that Travis was in the church, in the back room before Mercy came in. They didn't want him to see her before the wedding, bad luck they say. Mercy made it into the church without seeing Travis and went to the other small room on the other side of the church. Her sisters told her when everyone was seated and when it was time to come out of the side room.

Mercy came out of the room to see her Father standing there waiting on her. He looked so different but also so handsome in his tuxedo that he had rented. She looked in his eyes and saw tears there. She told him, "Come on Dad, don't cry or you will make me cry. This is a joyful day." Trying to make light of the moment, she said, "Be careful and don't step on my train. I love you Dad." He smiled and said he loved her to. They linked arms and her Father placed his right hand over top of hers to steady her. When the wedding march started, they started down the aisle. The little church was filled with friends and family. She smiled at all of them, thankful that they were here. She looked up ahead and saw Travis standing at the altar. My, he was a handsome man and she loved him so much. How could she be so lucky? Suddenly, when she got closer, she and Travis locked eyes and it was like there was no one else in the church but them. They only had eyes for each other. Travis thought that he had never seen a more beautiful woman in his life and he thought about how lucky he was that his dreams finally came true and Mercy was marrying him. His faced beamed with love for her and Mercy also saw a couple of tears in his eyes. When she looked at him, she had never felt move loved and adored by anyone and she knew at that instant that nothing could ever tear them apart.

They had a small reception at her house and then she and Travis were going to honeymoon on a beach in the Florida Keys. Their flight left later this evening. Her wedding day couldn't have been any more magnificent.

They flew to Florida that evening and made their way to a fancy hotel wedding suite. They would be here for five days. When they were walking toward their room, they were both exhausted from such a long day but neither one of them would say so. When they got to their room, Travis carried Mercy over the threshold. There was champagne, and roses lay on the beautiful, white comforter. They both seem to get their second wind after seeing their room and both were excited to sleep together and love each other. Mercy was nervous when it came time to go to bed. She wasn't sure what to do but her sisters told her not to worry, that it would come naturally. Travis moved very slow and patiently, all the while, telling her how beautiful she was and how much he loved her. No one saw or heard from them until they flew back on the sixth day.

Mercy had heard through the grapevine that Benton did, in fact, marry Madison, much to his Mother's chagrin and they had a little boy. Benton decided to get married for appearance sake since he was going to be an important plastic surgeon. Having a gorgeous wife by his side couldn't hurt. He had never thought about being a Father before, but he really wanted to try to be a good one. He still thinks about Mercy occasionally. Madison had told him that she heard that Mercy and Travis got married from her parents who live nearby. Benton knew all along that Mercy was in love with that cowboy. He resented the fact that Mercy turned down all the material things that he could have given her, and he thought she would be sorry for that one day.

He also realized, after he and Mercy had broken up, that his Mother was right, once again. He and Mercy would have never made it together. They really did come from two different sides of the track. Mercy would have never fit in his world and he in hers. Madison only fit in his life so nicely because she was so much like him. He didn't think he was really in love with Mercy, it was the excitement of the chase. It was the excitement of not being able to get what he wanted from her. He thought that he could have whatever, whenever he wanted. Mercy made it a hard lesson to learn. He tries not to think about Mercy too much because he still has a special place in his heart for her that will always be. You always remember your first teenage love.

CHAPTER 25

Twelve months from their wedding night, Mercy and Travis were in the delivery room. Travis was yelling "Push! Push!" into Mercy's right ear. Mercy gave him a look that said, "Shut UP!". She pushed as hard as she could and out came little Cayce, a beautiful little girl.

Cayce was the light of her and Travis's life. Mercy sat on her front porch rocking Cayce. Cayce had just started walking and she finally tired out. When Cayce was tired, she just wanted to sit on Mercy's lap and she loved for Mercy to sing to her. Mercy sang Cayce to sleep. It was eight at night, time for Cayce to go to bed anyway. Mercy just loved to sit and hold her while she was sleeping. Mercy thought of her Mother and wondered if her Mother liked to sit and rock her when she was a baby.

Mercy still worked part time as a nurse and loved her job. She felt like their lives were wonderful but not quite complete. She thought there was something missing. After thinking so hard about it, she realized what it was.

When Travis came home from visiting with his parents that night, Mercy said, "Travis, we have to talk about something." He sat down on a kitchen chair and said, "Okay, Mercy, what's up?" She said, "I've been thinking a lot about something and there is something I want to do. You have a two-week vacation coming up and I have three-week vacation, so like to go somewhere." He answered, "Where would you like to go? You know we can afford anything too extravagant." She said, "I know, but this is important. While Cayce is still little and can travel well, I'd like for us to go to Nashville. I know it has always been your dream and you have always put it on the back burner. I thought we could take a road trip down there. Maybe you, we, could get discovered by the music business. Travis, you are so talented. It just seems a shame to let that talent go to waste. Just give it some time and think about it, please?" He had a surprised his face and said, "Wow, I haven't thought about that in a couple years. Okay, I will think about it. You know I am getting older and they are probably looking for younger talent these days." She answered, "Travis, you are only two years older than the last time you wanted to go. Besides, in country music, age isn't really an issue. Just sleep on it and tell me what you think, okay?" Travis told Mercy he would think about it.

Travis thought about going to Nashville all the next day. In his mind he was thinking, "I have responsibilities now. I have a wife and a daughter to take care of, I can't just pick up and go like before. On the other hand, if I don't go, I will always wonder "what if?" He went back and forth like this all day until he was on his way home from work the next day. Driving home, he made his decision and would tell Mercy when he got home. When Travis got home that evening, Mercy was at the sink cutting up vegetables for dinner and Cayce was sitting in her high chair eating oyster crackers. He walked in the back door, Mercy turned and said, "Hi Babe." He said, "Hello, most beautiful woman in the world. Guess what?"

She answered, "What?" She didn't know why he was grinning ear to ear, but she liked it. He grabbed her by the waist and started jumping up and down. He yelled, "We're going to Nashville!" Mercy laughed and jumped up and down with him. She said, "Travis, you made the right decision, you will see. When do you want to go?" He answered, "I can take my vacation in three weeks. We will go then. If we stay longer, we will settle there for a while. Since I work for my Father, I will always have a job to come back to." She said, "If need be, I can take a long leave of absence from work. Three weeks! Okay, we will have to tell my Father but I'm sure he will be as excited as we are that we are going."

CHAPTER 26

Three weeks later, on a Saturday, Travis, Mercy and Cayce were getting ready to leave for Nashville. Travis still had his old truck but Mercy had purchased a new car a few months ago. The car was decorated with balloons, streamers and well wishes for their trip. The whole family was standing next to Mercy's, car, giving them good luck wishes and telling them "goodbye and be careful." Mercy had tears in her eyes when she told her father goodbye. Mercy told her Father, "If it looks like Travis and I are going to be in Nashville for any length of time, I will come and get you. I'm sure we can find a place for you also. I love you Dad." Everyone waved as the car started down the street. Mercy was looking back at her family, then she looked at Travis and said in a bright voice, "Let's go Cowboy!" He loved it when she called him that.

After about an hour into the trip, Cayce had fallen asleep and Mercy put her head back on the headrest and closed her eyes. She and Travis knew that they may have an especially hard time in Nashville, not just trying to make it in the music business but also finding work and supporting a family. Mercy thought about all that had happened since her sixteenth birthday and realized things had worked out just as they were supposed to. She loved her life with Travis, she loved being a nurse, she loved that she and her Father had a relationship. Growing up can be so hard and so many things can feel devastating at the time, but she believed in God and she believed that everything that had happened in her life was God's plan for her.

She opened her eyes and turned to look at Travis. Travis said, "Hello sleepy head." When they locked eyes, they felt their overwhelming love for each other and they were excited about this new adventure in their lives. They held hands in the car and road in silent contentment while looking at the road ahead.

THE END

ACKNOWLEDGMENTS

My husband Wayne, for his endless love and patience. He spent many nights alone while I spent many nights writing Mercy on my computer. He encourages me to keep writing books for others to enjoy. His kindness and love always carries me through to the end of everything I do. He is the love of my life. I always appreciate his support, honesty, and candor.

My publishing company, Authorhouse, for their help and guidance.

Most of all, a big "Thank You" to all my fans, and hopefully a lot of new fans for Mercy.

ABOUT THE AUTHOR

Ms. Tolliver grew up in Cincinnati during the 1960's and 70's. Mercy is her third novel. and she is very excited to bring this novel to young women. Ms. Tolliver has four grown daughters of her own. Ms. Tolliver is a wife, mother, sister, grandmother, nurse, artist and novelist. Despite her hectic life, she has always made time to develop her many creative talents. She hopes that you enjoy this story of a girl named Mercy.

Printed in the United States
By Bookmasters